TANZI'S
ICE

C.I. DENNIS

For Sara

JANUARY

TUESDAY

My mother is one of the few people I will allow to call me Vinny. My name is Vince. I don't know why I'm so touchy about it, but whenever someone says "Hey, Vinny," I feel like saying "Yes, asshole?" And that's on a good day.

Today was not going to be a good day—I could already tell, at five AM. Not only had the phone woken me up but my mother had started the conversation by calling me Vincent. She only calls me Vincent when somebody has died, or worse.

"Who died, Mom?"

"Did I wake you?" Her voice sounded weak, like she'd been up all night.

"No," I lied.

"I did wake you, I'm sorry. I haven't slept."

"You can call me whenever you need to. Don't worry about it."

"How's your weather?"

"Mom—" I said, not sure why she was stalling. "It's cold. Not Vermont cold, Florida cold. It was in the forties last night."

"It's twenty below up here," she said. "The cars won't start."

"Is your heat working OK?"

"Vincent," she began, "it was your father."

It took a moment to register. Jimmy Tanzi was dead. She began to cry on the other end of the phone line, and I cursed the distance between us. I had skipped my annual pilgrimage to Vermont over Thanksgiving; it was now the middle of January, and I hadn't seen her in over a year.

"Who told you?"

"Sheila," she said.

"I thought they didn't speak to each other anymore."

"She was with him at the hospital. She went out to eat, and when she came back, he was gone."

"His liver?"

"They wouldn't give him a transplant."

"He would have just ruined another perfectly good liver," I said.

"Don't speak ill of the dead, Vinny," she said.

"I can't think of anything good to say," I said.

"The wake is on Friday."

"Are you going?"

"You know, we never got a divorce. I'm still his wife."

"I know," I said. "And it drove Sheila crazy."

"I'm going," she said. "I want you to go with me. Your brother and sister won't go."

"Did you ask them?"

"They won't go," she said. "I don't even know how to reach your sister. But the point is I want you to come home. I need you here."

"Mom," I said, "you know I'll do whatever you want, but I really don't want to go to his funeral."

"You can skip the funeral," she said. "We're just doing the wake. We'll bury him in May when the ground thaws, and do the service then. But I want you here when the police come by."

"What do you mean?"

"His liver didn't kill him," she said. "He was suffocated, in his hospital bed. The police want to ask me questions. I told them I wanted you here first."

"Oh shit."

"Vinny."

"I didn't mean to say that out loud," I said. "I'll get a flight out today. Tell the police we'll talk to them tomorrow."

"OK," she said.

I have a trunk in the back of a closet with my Vermont clothes. A down parka, heavy socks, long johns, turtleneck shirts, hats and gloves—I could wear all of it at once and I'd still freeze my ass off. When it's twenty below outside it hurts to even draw a breath. I packed the clothes in a duffel bag with my toilet gear, a lockable, hard-sided case for my Glock 30 automatic and a couple of clips. I doubted I'd need it, but I felt better with it than without. This was not a pleasure trip; someone had just snuffed out my father's wretched life. The cops would have their hands full with that one—I could only think of a few dozen of us who might have had a motive.

*

I called Barbara from the road, about halfway between my home in Vero Beach and the airport in West Palm. Tuesdays were her sleep-in days, when her first class didn't start until ten. I knew better than to call too early—she could be a real porcupine until she had a few cups of coffee.

"Did I wake you?"

"It's OK," she said, "I had to get up to answer the phone anyway."

I laughed. "You're in a good mood."

"I don't know why," she said. "I was up until three studying this goddamn biochemistry."

"You are going to be such a wonderful nurse," I said. "So genteel and compassionate."

"Yeah, a real Clara fucking Barton," she said.

"Wow, you are revved up for eight in the morning."

"Too much coffee," she said. "So far in two weeks of nursing school I've learned that the whole medical industry runs on caffeine."

"And insurance reimbursement," I added.

"Where are you?"

"On the way to the airport," I said. "I'm going to Vermont."

"Why?"

"My father passed away."

"Oh Vince, I'm so sorry."

"Don't be. I'm just going for my mother."

"You didn't get along with him."

"It was worse than that," I said.

"Will you be back for Friday date night?"

"The wake's on Friday," I said. "Sorry."

"That's OK. I'll just hit the bars and see who's available."

"There's an anesthesiologists convention out at Dodgertown, you could try them."

"On second thought, I think I'll rent a chick flick and eat a whole box of Oreos."

"I'll be sorry to miss that," I said.

"Call me from Vermont," she said. "Do they have cell towers up there?"

"Sort of," I said. "They make them look like pine trees."

"Take care of yourself."

*

There was an hour to kill at the gate before the flight left. In my work I do a lot of sitting, waiting, and people-watching, and I am good at making the time pass quickly. I read the *Miami Herald*, chatted with an inquisitive little boy about Buzz Lightyear, checked out the tanned college girls (who were self-consciously looking around in their big sunglasses, hoping everyone was checking them out), watched an Asian family eat a three-course meal on the plastic seats, swapped small talk with a retired electrician, and even helped untangle two older women who had gotten their wheelchairs enmeshed. How could anyone be bored at an airport?

I had a middle seat, which I was lucky to get, and the bereavement fare made it affordable, if not comfortable. One of the college girls was already in the window seat next to me, texting. A very large male human being lowered himself into the aisle seat on the other side of me, and the flight attendant got him a seat belt extension. I'm six-two and substantially built, and the airline had allotted us just enough legroom for the average kindergartener. Maybe if the college girl sat on my lap we could all fit. I decided I would let her suggest that, not me.

My cellphone buzzed. The last thing I wanted to do is to talk on the phone with two strangers within close earshot, but I looked at the caller ID. It said "VT ST POLICE TROOP A". I pushed the answer button.

"Vince Tanzi," I said.

"Vince, this is John Pallmeister."

"John Pallmeister? The caller ID said State Police."

"I left the Barre P.D. a long time ago. I'm an investigator out of the Middlesex barracks."

John Pallmeister and I had started with the Barre, Vermont, police at the same time, thirty years back. I'd lasted one year, and then realized that if I was going to be a cop, I'd rather do it somewhere warm. I spent twenty-five years as a deputy with the Indian River Sheriff's Department in Florida before I retired, or rather was asked to retire, and became a private investigator. I miss being a cop, but I don't miss all the rules.

"What can I do for you, John? I'm on a plane that's about to take off."

"I'll make it fast," he said. "Just wondering when I can see you and your mother. She said tomorrow, but we want to get on this now."

"What's the hurry?" I said. "She'll have an alibi. She's seventy-four years old for God's sake. She hardly leaves the house."

"When do you get in?"

"I change in New York and get to Burlington at five."

"I'll pick you up at the airport."

"John, no offense but I'm going to get a rental. I'll call you tomorrow, and we'll set something up."

"How much do you know about your father's death?"

"Not much. My mother said he was in for a liver problem, but he was suffocated. I assume that's what you're trying to figure out."

"And the life insurance?"

"There wouldn't be any insurance," I said. "My father lived from barstool to barstool. His girlfriend used to support him, but she dumped him years ago."

"He left a million-dollar life policy to Mrs. Francine Tanzi," he said. "Your mother. Somebody in Canada paid the premiums. We don't know who it was yet."

"That makes no sense," I said.

"I'll see you at the airport," he said, and hung up.

*

I had a window seat on the leg from JFK to Burlington, and the terrain below us went from brown to white as we tracked north, above the Connecticut River. I know the landmarks from the air and spotted Lake Morey, frozen solid, nestled among the foothills of the Green Mountains. My father had taken me ice fishing there when I was nine years old. He caught a few perch that day, and I caught frostbite on my earlobes and the tip of my nose, which stayed pink for a week. He kept a bottle of peach schnapps in the glove compartment of his truck, and he drank half of it on the way home.

John Pallmeister was waiting for me at the baggage carousel. His face had widened some but otherwise he had the physique of a twenty-year-old, which was the age he'd been when I'd last seen him. His hair was grey stubble, shaved close under the trooper hat. He wore the single gold bar of lieutenant, a higher rank than I'd ever achieved in the sheriff's department. I saw his cruiser idling outside with a cloud of vapor coming from the exhaust.

"I hope you have some warm clothes," he said, shaking my hand.

"Got a parka in the bag," I said. "I left my golf clubs home, though."

"You won't need them," he said. "It's warmed up, but it's still ten below."

"You have to be crazy to live here."

"It's not so bad," he said. "Except for when all you Florida people come up in the summer."

My duffel came and we went outside. Even with my parka on the cold hit me like I'd just stepped onto a planet with no oxygen. It hurt to inhale. I hustled the bag into the trunk and jumped into the warmth of the front seat of the cruiser.

"Did you eat on the plane?" he asked.

"It must be a while since you flew anywhere," I said. "They don't do that anymore."

"Let's get a burger," he said. He drove us to Al's French Frys, an eatery on the commercial strip near the airport. Al's had been there pretty much forever and the fries were the best in the state. John left the cruiser running while we went inside to order, which was probably against police protocol but there was an unwritten rule in Vermont that when it was this cold you could leave your car running and anyone who dared mess with it would be sent straight to Hell.

We got back into the car and I ate my burger, trying my best not to drip ketchup on government property. "We don't suspect your mother," he said, balancing his drink as he drove. "There wasn't anyone who looked like her on the security tapes."

"Are there cameras in the rooms?"

"No, just the lobby and the entrances. It happened Sunday night. Plenty of people came and went, but no older women."

"How do you know he was suffocated?"

"There were signs of a struggle. The IV needle was pulled out. Things were knocked on the floor. Whoever did it used a pillow, and your father ripped a hole in it with his teeth. He was pretty tough for an old guy."

"Any DNA evidence?"

"Maybe some skin under his fingernails. The coroner found something, it could just be dirt. We're looking at it."

"So why do you want to talk with my mother?"

"Wouldn't you?" he said. Of course I would. A million dollars in insurance was a lot, especially in Vermont. Follow the money.

"Fair enough," I said.

"You were in Florida on Sunday, right?"

"You're joking, right?"

"Actually, I'm not joking." He took his eyes away from the road and looked straight at me. "I remember the last time I saw your father in the hospital. It was thirty years ago, shortly before you quit the force and moved south. Your dad had a broken rib, a broken jaw, a concussion, two black eyes, and some teeth missing. I went back and dug out the report."

"Did you dig out the report on my mother too? After he beat the shit out of her?"

"She refused to testify against him. You know that."

"Yeah, right. The cops never found the guy who did it."

"And we never found the guy who beat up your father, almost to death, later that same night."

"That was long time ago, John."

"People hold grudges all their lives," he said.

"You going to read me my rights?"

"Relax, Vince," he said. "Your father wasn't a popular guy. You're just one on a long list."

*

We were on Interstate 89, headed southeast toward Barre. It was already dark, but I could make out the silhouette of Camel's Hump looming over us, profiled by the early evening stars. We rode the next half hour in silence, all the way to my mother's house, a modest '50s ranch in the hill neighborhood east of Main Street. Lieutenant Pallmeister parked the cruiser in the driveway and got my bag from the trunk.

"Thanks for the ride," I said. "I'll call you in the morning."

"Hold on a minute," he said. "You said I could talk to her to-night."

"I said nothing of the kind. Unless you have a subpoena, you're not invited in."

Pallmeister frowned, but he wasn't going to waste time arguing in the frigid cold. He got into his cruiser and backed out, the tires making a rubbery, crunching sound against the ice-covered surface of the road. He and I may have been rookie cops together a long time ago, but that didn't mean anything now, and my tendency was not to get too cozy with the police until I had a better idea of what was going on.

*

My mother is almost my height, but she weighs half of what I do and I could feel her bones as we hugged.

"Long time, Vinny," she said. "You smell like French fries."

"I stopped at Al's," I said. "You smell like garlic, and I mean that in the nicest possible way."

She laughed. "I made you *spaghetti aglio e olio*. If you're not hungry—"

"I'm suddenly hungry again, Mom. Go right ahead."

"Pour yourself some wine." My mom doesn't drink, and as fussy as she is about food, she has no idea when it comes to wine. I twisted the screw cap off a three-liter bottle of Carlo Rossi Paisano and prepared to regret it in the morning.

"Was that a police car you arrived in?"

"State cop," I said. "A guy I used to be on the Barre force with."

"Is he the one who wants to talk to me?"

"Yes."

"It's about the money, right? He had insurance. They don't think I killed him, do they?"

"Whoever killed him was strong," I said. "He put up a fight."

"Your father was built like an ox," she said. She was right. He was a head shorter than my mother, but was incredibly strong from moving around granite slabs at the memorial factory.

"You remember the time you took me to the Tunbridge Fair, and I got stepped on by that ox?" She and I had been taken to the hospital by ambulance that cool September night. I was fourteen years old. My older brother and sister had refused to go to the fair; they were afraid my dad would get drunk, and they were right. He'd spent the whole time in the beer tent, unaware that I'd been hurt, and he eventually passed out in our car.

"I thought you'd have a limp for life."

"It's still sore sometimes," I said. "That thing must have weighed three thousand pounds."

"The insurance company called me yesterday. The police found the policy when they looked through your father's apartment. The insurance man was very nice. He said how sorry he was."

I took a sip of the wretched wine and looked around her kitchen. Very little had changed since I'd moved to Vero, thirty years ago. The same chintz curtains, knotty pine wood paneling, yellow Formica, and an avocado-colored fridge that hummed a little louder every time I returned home.

"They probably want to keep the money. Did he offer you an annuity?"

"He said they could provide an income for me for life."

"That means they want to sell you an annuity. You don't have to do it, you can just take the money. We'll go to the bank tomorrow and see what they have."

"When do you want to talk to the police?" she said.

"I'll call them after breakfast," I said. "Did you know anything about the insurance?"

"No. I don't see your father much," she said. "I mean—I didn't see him. I have to get used to him being gone."

"You must be relieved."

"Yes and no," she said. "He and I loved each other, once. You kids don't understand that."

"Mom, I'm fifty years old. I'm not a kid. I understand what you're saying."

"He did have some money," she said. She was turned away from me, standing at the stove. I could barely hear her over the rattling of the exhaust fan. "Now and then I'd get an envelope, in my mailbox. Hundred dollar bills, held together with a paper clip. No note, no return address."

"How did you know it was from him?"

"He wrote a name on the envelope. Something he used to call me when we were first married."

I left that alone. Her face had reddened, and it wasn't from the heat of the boiling water on the stovetop.

"I thought he lived on his Social Security."

"He had a part-time job, driving," she said. "He came to the door once, a few years ago, to get his birth certificate. He had to apply for a passport, back when Canada stopped letting you in without one. He was dressed in a suit and tie and was driving a big white Cadillac limousine-kind-of-thing with dark windows."

"Limo driver? You're kidding."

"He was sober. He looked nice."

"Do you know what company he drove for?"

"He drove for a family in Stowe. They're only up here for part of the year. The man's name is Brooks Burleigh."

Brooks Burleigh not only had a house in Stowe, he had one in Florida, New York, London, Colorado, and god knows where else. He also owned a huge piece of northern Vermont. The Burleighs were originally loggers and were shrewd land traders. They'd accumulated a quarter-million acres of Vermont forestland, and they owned millions more north of the border in Quebec. Brooks Burleigh was the oldest son and ran the company. I'd met him once at a soirée in John's Island, a pricey enclave in Vero Beach, but even though he was a fellow Vermonter, we were from different worlds. In his world they used Carlo Rossi Paisano to clean the bugs off the brightwork on their Range Rovers.

"I saw him at a party once," I said. "I was doing security. He was drunk and loud from the time he got there. Maybe he and Dad were drinking buddies."

"Your father stopped drinking," she said. "He met Mr. Burleigh at one of those meetings. Neither of them drank anymore."

"How do you know this?"

She took the pot off the stove and poured the pasta into a colander in the sink. The steam rose and froze in delicate, crazy patterns of rime against the surface of the window above. "He took me to dinner," she said. "He only drank water, and a lot of coffee."

"When was this?"

"This past October. It was our anniversary."

I was so shocked I accidentally took a big gulp of the cheap wine. It actually tasted OK. "Mom—"

"Like I said, you kids don't understand," she interrupted.

"He almost killed you that night. Thirty years ago."

"He wanted to be a married couple again," she said. "He wanted to move back in. He said he would take care of me."

"Did Sheila know about this?"

"I had to promise not to tell. He said he wasn't ready yet, he had some things to finish, and that I couldn't tell anyone."

"You were going to let him move back in?"

"I hadn't decided," she said. "Maybe. But it's no use now."

She put the pasta back in the empty pot and added the *aglio e olio* sauce. The whole room filled with the steamy aroma as she mixed it and served me a plate.

"Do Carla and Junie know anything about this?"

"I don't know where Carla is," she said. "She doesn't keep in touch."

"And Junie?"

"He's in jail," she said. "Up in South Burlington. He was arrested the same night your father passed away."

"For what?"

"He beat up somebody, in a bar," she said. I wasn't surprised. James Tanzi, Junior, or "Junie" to us, had my dad's temper and then some. He was in jail as often as he was out. "I drove up to see him, after I called you this morning. I didn't have enough money to bail him out. But I will now."

"I can take care of it," I said. "You haven't seen that money yet."

"Vinny—"

"What, Mom?"

"He was wearing a hospital outfit. I forget what you call them."

"Scrubs? He was dressed in hospital scrubs, in jail?"

"Yes," she said.

"Oh shit," I said, and this time she didn't protest.

*

I took the lower bunk in the bedroom I'd shared with my brother. It was mine; Junie was two years older than me and had permanently claimed the top bunk as his own. The bed springs sagged under my weight, and the effects of the wine and a long day of traveling were starting to make me sag also. I opened a book that I'd started on the plane, but the words blurred and after a while I turned out the light and lay there, listening to the pinging of the baseboard heater. I wasn't drunk—just tired, although my mind was still turning over the bits of information I'd gleaned during the day. Some people count sheep—I count clues.

Unfortunately, I'd already gathered a few clues that were pointing me in a very unpleasant direction. Junie could have entered or left Central Vermont Hospital in scrubs and not made an impression on anyone who reviewed the security tapes. The cops apparently hadn't connected the guy they'd booked for a bar fight, dressed in scrubs, with the old man who was suffocated hours earlier. Junie was in jail in Burlington and the hospital was in Barre, thirty miles south, in a different jurisdiction. They might never make the connection.

They might not, but I did. I didn't like my father. I never spoke to him or visited him, and I would never forgive him for the way he had mistreated my mother while they were together. But for all my faults I don't kill people, unless they're about to kill me first. I'm just not wired that way.

My brother was not like me. He could have taken out the miserable bastard.

He'd already tried once.

WEDNESDAY

I checked the weather on my phone out of morbid curiosity. It was twenty-one degrees below zero, at seven in the morning. Not a record low, and not all that unusual for Vermont in January when it could go into a deep freeze for weeks and then suddenly jump back above the freezing point, during what the locals called January Thaw. If you live in this state you find yourself constantly talking about the weather, which is so unpredictable as to be bipolar, and you skeptically listen to the hopelessly inaccurate television forecasters who are tolerated, affectionately, as one might tolerate a doddering older relative.

My mother was up already cooking sausage biscuits, which are my downfall along with everything else she makes.

"Did you sleep OK?" she asked, as I lumbered, unshaven, into the kitchen.

"Fine," I said. "I'm getting a little big for that bed though."

She gave a nervous laugh. "Vinny, what are they going to ask me?"

"We'll find out, Mom," I said. She slid a plate of the biscuits in front of me, and I could feel my arteries clogging in anticipation. "They said they want to know about the insurance policy. They don't think you did anything to Dad. You have an alibi, right?"

"You mean can I prove I wasn't there when he died?"

"Yes."

"I went to bed early that night. Mrs. Tomaselli came over to visit, but she left before it got dark. I made some food and watched the six o'clock news and then went to bed."

"I don't think it's going to be an issue," I said. "They want to know about the money. They'll ask you about that."

"What should I tell them?"

"You can just answer their questions. And it's OK to tell them that you and he had talked about getting back together. That would give them a reason for him to leave you the money."

"OK," she said, but she was clearly nervous.

"If they ask anything you shouldn't answer, I'll tell you," I said. "It's going to be fine, Mom."

"I don't even know if the car will start," she said.

"They can come here," I said. "And Mom—I wouldn't say anything about Junie right now, OK? I'm thinking of going up to see him."

"Are you going to bail him out?"

I thought about that. "Probably," I said. "I'll add it to his bill."

*

Lieutenant John Pallmeister and a shorter, bulldog-faced guy in a black overcoat stamped their boots on the rug in the small vestibule that led into my mother's kitchen.

"Vince," Pallmeister said, extending his hand without a smile. "This is Robert Patton, Border Patrol."

I shook both their hands, still gloved and ice cold. "This is my mother, Francine."

"I have some sausage biscuits left over," she said.

"Thank you Mrs. Tanzi but we'll get out of your hair just as quickly as possible," the shorter one said. He appeared to be in charge. They took off their hats and coats, passed out business cards, and sat down at the kitchen table. My mother filled two mugs of coffee and set them down in front of the cops.

"What brings the Border Patrol into this?" I asked.

"The policy was bought here, but it was funded from Canada," Patton said. "The premiums were more than thirty thousand dollars a year. Did Mr. Tanzi have access to that kind of money?"

"Doubtful," I said.

"Mrs. Tanzi?" he said, directing the question to her.

"He had a little money," she said. "But—oh dear, this is so confusing."

"How much?"

"He would give me some cash now and then," she said. "A few hundred dollars. He had a job, for the last few years."

"You guys can't find out who paid the premiums?" I said.

"Somebody knew what they were doing," John Pallmeister said. Patton looked sideways at him and frowned. Apparently, the State Police were along for the ride on this one.

"Are you guys actually looking for the killer? Or is something else going on here?"

"We have a lot of work to do," Patton said. "John's group is covering the basic police work. They'll be looking at the hospital records, checking out leads and so on. You were a cop, you know what I mean. My group is looking at the money aspect. That's routine, when we have a cross-border transfer like this."

"Is she going to get a check from the insurance company?"

"It would be a good idea to just wait on that," Patton said. "We have an investigation going, and the payment won't happen until it's closed. Mrs. Tanzi, you shouldn't make any financial moves based on the anticipation of this money."

"What does that mean?" my mother asked.

"It means you might not get the money, Mom," I said. "Not if it's part of some kind of illegal activity."

Neither of the cops spoke. My mother got up to refill their cups. "I don't really need any money," she said.

"Did you know anything about it?" Patton asked her. "The life insurance?"

"No," she said. "It was a shock. Jimmy and I—" she trailed off, holding the coffee pot.

"You can tell them, Mom."

"We were going to get back together," she said, blushing slightly.

"There are some things for you in his apartment," Pallmeister said. "Letters he wrote but apparently didn't send you. You can go in the apartment now if you like, we're done with that part of our investigation." He took a key from his pocket and put it on the table.

"Oh," she said.

"How well do you know Brooks Burleigh?" Patton asked me. I noticed he had a lopsided eye, and his nose was crooked. Somewhere along the line he'd taken some punches.

"Not at all," I said. "I did see him once at a party in Florida where I was working. Maybe five years ago. He was drunk."

"He's been sober for three years," Patton said. "So was your father. You have any family in Quebec?"

"No," I said. "Why do you ask?"

"Just wondering," Patton said.

"Come on," I said. "You want us to answer your questions, you need to answer ours."

"This is a police investigation," he said.

"Fine," I said. "You can leave then."

"Vinny—" my mother began.

"It's OK, we're done," Patton said. He and Pallmeister stood up and put on their coats. "Tanzi, come outside for a second," he said to me. It was a command, not a request. I donned my flimsy parka and stepped out into the frigid morning. We stood outside the vestibule, our combined breath rising in a cloud of steam toward the weak sun.

"Let's be clear," he said. "You may be a P.I., but this is a federal investigation. Stay out of it."

"Yes, let's be clear," I said. "I don't work for you. So have a nice day." As in, fuck off.

"You have no idea of the money and man-hours that are into this," he said.

"Not yet."

"Look. I know your background. You're good at what you do. But I need you to lay off. Please."

"Are you going to try to find out who killed Jimmy Tanzi?"

"We think it was a pro," he said.

"You do? Why?"

He shook his head. "I've already said too much."

Lieutenant Pallmeister started his cruiser, and Robert Patton eased into the passenger seat. He turned to me before he shut the door. "Any reason your father would cross the border into Quebec? Like, seventeen times in the past year?"

"He liked poutine," I said. Poutine is Quebecois soul food; a big pile of French fries, cheese curd, and brown gravy. It's a one-way ticket to a quadruple bypass.

Patton, the bulldog-face, actually cracked a faint smile. "We'll be in touch," he said.

*

My mother's ancient Subaru Outback started on the first try, although the belts squealed in protest until they warmed with the rotation of the pulleys. In Vermont you have your choice of driving a pickup truck or a Subaru. Everything else is going to get you dismissed as a clueless flatlander. Along with your choice of Outback or pickup, you can also choose the obligatory bumper stickers: Bernie '12 (Vermont's Socialist senator), VPR, Goddess Within, Free Tibet, Got Milk, or My

Other Car Is a Bicycle. That's for the Subaru. For the pickup there's your favorite NASCAR driver's number, Calvin peeing on a Ford, Chevy, Toyota, or Dodge (whichever one you're not driving), Gut Deer?, Ditch the Bitch Let's Go Muddin', I Brake For Moose, and of course, I Heart the Red Sox, or more to the point, Yankees Suck. There's some cross-pollination, but you don't want to mix up the stereotypes too much, like putting a goddess sticker alongside a Gut Deer sticker, or you'll confuse people.

I scraped the ice from both the outside and the inside of the windshield and drove down the hill to the center of Barre. The outskirts of the town are dominated by huge sheds that house the stonecutting operations. My father cut gravestones, or "memorials" as they call them in the business, for forty years until his back couldn't take it any longer and his Social Security check had to take over the bar bill. His father had worked there too, and there was a family plot in the Hope Cemetery that featured my grandfather Basilio's stunning carving of a trout jumping from a granite brook. The stonecutters had come over from Italy beginning in the nineteenth century, and there was an unofficial competition even among the poorest of them as to who could make the most beautiful gravestone for their own family. The Hope Cemetery is actually a tourist attraction in the warm weather.

I started up the long hill to the interstate, and my cell rang. It was Barbara. "Do you miss me yet?"

"Remember that Dan Hicks' song?" I asked. "How Can I Miss You If You Won't Go Away?"

"Dan Hicks, he was like Tommy Dorsey, right?"

"I don't know why I hang out with you young babes," I said.

"Because you're a cradle-robbing pervert," she said, and we laughed. "I passed my biochem quiz."

"Awesome."

"I think I can do this," she said.

"I know you can. You are going to be a wicked good nurse."

"Wicked?"

"That's Vermont-speak. It's starting to come back."

"I really do miss you."

"We weren't even going to see each other until Friday," I said. "You're supposed to be studying."

"I need a study break. Maybe I should get on a plane."

"If you were up here in this weather you'd get right back on the plane and go home," I said. "It's insanely cold."

"I could warm you up."

"Don't get all horny on me," I said. "Not fair."

"Where are you?"

"On the way to see my brother," I said. "He's in jail. I guess I'm going to bail him out."

"What did he do?"

"Bar fight," I said. "He does that."

"Is everything OK?"

"It's turning out to be more complicated than I thought," I said. "I don't know when I'll be back."

"You haven't run into your old high school girlfriend or anything?"

"No, not that. It's my father. He was murdered."

"Oh my God."

"It's all right. I'm just going to look into it a little."

"Be careful," she said.

"It shouldn't take long," I said. "I have to make sure to leave enough time to look up all those old girlfriends."

"I'm not jealous," she said. "But just so you're aware, if you screw around on me, I'll kill you."

"Duly noted," I said. She and I had only known each other for a few months, but the emotional cement was already starting to set, and I was ready for that. I think.

*

I called John Pallmeister a few miles before the South Burlington turnoff. He answered on the first ring. "Pallmeister."

"Tanzi."

"Mr. Tanzi. You didn't make any friends on the Border Patrol today."

"What was that all about? Don't tell me it's the insurance policy."

"It's not. But that's all I can say."

"Was my father involved in something?"

"Like I said—"

"Yeah, right, you can't talk," I interrupted. "Dude—you and I go back a long time."

"I see," he said. "When it's something you want, suddenly we're old pals."

"This is my father we're talking about, John."

"You told me you didn't give a rat's ass about your father."

"Christ," I said. "The cold must be getting to everybody. You need to move to Florida where people are actually fucking civil to each other."

"Tanzi—"

"Forget I asked," I said. "One question and I'll let you go. What time did he die?"

"Between six and six thirty. They fed him just before six, and his friend, I forget the name—"

"Sheila."

"That's right. She found him a half hour later. The other bed in the room was empty, and nobody heard anything. Like Patton said, it looked like a pro job."

"Why would anyone order a hit on an old man?"

"I intend to find that out," he said.

"I'd like to help," I said.

"Patton wants you to steer clear. He'll be watching you to make sure you do."

"I don't know if I can agree to that."

"You don't have a choice," he said. "By the way, I have a question for you. Where are your brother and sister? I need to interview them. I can't find either one."

"I'm going to see my brother today. I'll have him call you."

"Where's Carla?"

"That's kind of like where's Waldo. You remember her, right?"

"She and I were in the same class in high school. Sort of a free spirit."

"Sort of a flake," I said. "She moves around a lot. I have no idea where she is."

"OK," he said. "Vince, a word to the wise. Don't piss off Robert Patton. He thinks he's on a mission. You know the type."

"Which is exactly the type I like to piss off," I said.

"They can lock you up for no reason," he said.

"I'm good with locks."

"I remember," he said, and we hung up.

*

Visitors to the Chittenden County Regional Correctional Facility are not encouraged to wear guns, so I left my Glock in the car. I don't even know why I carry it while I'm in Vermont. I'm not on a case, there's little chance of meeting some perp I put away who just got out, and bullets don't go zinging by randomly as they do in some of my old beats in Florida. It's a cop habit, and probably a bad one, but it makes me feel secure, just like some guys like to carry a fat wad of hundreds, or some women like to maintain the entire Estée Lauder line of makeup in their purse. I signed in, and a chubby, humorless guy in a bright floral tie showed me to the Foxtrot Room where I waited for Junie.

They had exchanged his hospital scrubs for prison scrubs that were several sizes too large, and he looked lost in them. I hadn't seen James Junior in a couple of years, but he didn't look any better or worse than the last time. His face was sallow, and I wondered if he had strayed back into his smack habit.

"Fancy meeting you here," he said, as he sat down across the table from me. He didn't smile, and neither did I. Junie and I mostly kept our distance—we had chosen different paths and they seldom intersected.

"You heard about the old man," I said.

"Yeah."

"Where were you on Sunday?"

"Ask my lawyer," he said.

"You want to get bailed out of here or not?"

"I don't want to owe you anything."

"Did you go to the hospital?"

"I was home. Playing guitar in my apartment."

"In hospital scrubs?"

"I like wearing them, they're from when I worked at Fletcher Allen."

"And you wore them to a bar and then beat somebody up?"

"That's right," he said.

I noticed the scratches, going up his left arm. They were just starting to scab over. Pretty soon the police would know if the coroner had found anything other than dirt under my father's fingernails.

"The cops think it was a pro," I said. "A hit, like in the movies. But you still need an alibi."

"I can get someone to say I was home," he said.

"They have security cameras at the hospital."

"I know that," he said. His face darkened like our father's used to. "I'm not a total fucking idiot, Vin. Just because you're a cop doesn't mean you're any smarter than me."

"I'm not a cop anymore."

"Yeah, 'cause you fucked up."

"Maybe I should just let you rot here."

"Suit yourself," he said. "The food's good."

"The wake is on Friday. Mom wants us to go."

"I'd rather poke my eyes out."

"Are you playing out much?"

"Tonight and tomorrow at the Marriott. Guess I'll get a sub, unless you bail me out."

"Maybe I'll come hear you play," I said. "I'll be back in a few. I'm going to drop over to the court and pay your hotel bill."

"Thanks, man," he said. "But I'm still not going to the wake. And just so you know, I didn't kill him."

"But you were there that day? At the hospital?"

"I can't talk," he said.

"They don't record you here," I said.

"I know," he said. He gave me a look as if he was pleading. "Vin, you should stay out of this."

Jeezum crow, as they say up here. Everyone I met was telling me to get lost. That wasn't going to happen—telling me to mind my own business was like telling Junie not to play his guitar. Finding things out is what I do.

*

I stopped the car on the street in front of Junie's apartment. He had shivered all the way from the jail to his shabby, turn of the century walk-up on Pine Street, near where the city of Burlington meets Lake Champlain. The heat was on full blast in the Subaru, but the wind had come up and was blowing from the west, across the icy water. This part of the lake didn't usually freeze over until February, despite the extreme cold of January, the cruelest month.

We hadn't spoken much on the ride over. He turned to me before he got out.

"I can't pay you back, man."

"You won't have to unless you jump bail."

"I'm not going anywhere. But I hate this fucking weather."

"So don't I," I said.

"How long you here for?"

"Through the weekend. I'll probably go to the wake with Mom."

"Have fun," he said.

"You're supposed to call this cop," I said. I wrote down John Pallmeister's number on a Post-It.

"No way."

"Call him," I said. "I don't think they know about the scrubs or the scratches on your arm. With any luck they'll miss them. If you don't talk to Pallmeister, he'll come find you. You're better off if you can keep it to a phone call."

Junie shut the door of the Subaru and walked across the street to his building. I decided to make another stop while I was in town. Rodney Quesnel had an insurance agency on Cherry Street. He was a flinty old Vermonter, but he knew everything there was to know about the dry and stultifying world of life insurance, and I had some questions.

He had also been Carla's boyfriend, a long time ago, before she'd discovered girlfriends.

*

I parked in the public garage and braved the wind, which was now howling up Cherry Street from the lake towards Church Street. The temperature had warmed up some but was still below zero, and the morning shoppers dashed between storefronts, swaddled and quilted in Gore-Tex and goose down with the smallest possible opening for breathing and seeing. In the summertime this was a pedestrian paradise, and you could stroll along Church Street with your dish of Ben & Jerry's and listen to the street musicians. In mid-January, shopping was an extreme endurance event, limited to the hard core of addicted consumers who would still go out, even if they had to get there by dogsled.

Quesnel's office was warm, and I removed a few outer layers of clothing so that I could speak to the receptionist. "Is Rodney available? I don't have an appointment."

"And you are?" a skinny, raven-haired young woman asked.

"Vince Tanzi."

"Oh," she said. Apparently, she recognized my name. "I'll get him."

Rodney Quesnel was the son of a dairy farmer from the Lake Champlain islands. He still had the ruddy cheeks that farmers get from being outdoors in the Vermont climate. His hair was a wispy tangle of white strands, ineffectively combed over his shiny pink scalp. He stood about five feet tall; if he'd been any shorter he could have passed for an elf.

"How are you, Rod?"

"Good 'n' you? Come on back," he said, and led me into his office. It was a stately affair, like a men's club without the spittoons—all dark leather and mahogany with framed photographs of Rodney shaking the hands of dead Republicans.

"Thanks for seeing me," I said.

"Thirty years?"

"That's about right," I said. "Actually, I think Carla brought you home for Thanksgiving when you were dating."

"That makes it about twenty, then," he said. "I still wish she, you know…"

"Liked men?"

"Yeah," he said. "I keep thinking I was responsible."

"It doesn't work that way."

"I know," he said. "But it's not exactly a confidence builder."

"Forget about it, Rodney. You've moved on, right?"

"I'm still single," he said. "I see her on the street every now and then, and I blush myself pink."

I couldn't imagine Rodney being any pinker than he already was. "Have you seen her lately?"

"Not in a while. I heard she went out west, but then someone said she's living way up by the border in Swanton, house-sitting somebody's place on the lake."

"That sounds like Carla," I said.

"You here about your father's policy?"

"How did you know that?"

"We wrote it," he said. "The Feds are going to hold it up. We can't pay it out yet. Although your mother really ought to consider an annuity. I have some great—"

"Thanks, but no," I said, and his face fell. "She'll just take the payout, if there is one."

"You really ought to consider—"

"Rodney, no," I said. "No as in no."

"Man, you're a hard-ass."

"I heard the payments came from Canada? Is that legal?"

"Sure it is. The insuring company vets these things. They have big anti-money laundering departments. It was a trust, and it was set up right. I'm sure she'll be able to explain it, once the cops find her."

"Who are you talking about?"

"Carla," he said. "She was the trustee."

"What? Carla never had any money."

"She had enough to write the checks," he said.

"He had to pass a physical, right?"

"Oh yeah," he said. "For a million-dollar policy at his age he had to be perfect."

"What about the liver? He had cirrhosis."

"It wasn't diagnosed until after the policy was written."

"He drank himself silly every day. Didn't they ask about that?"

"He'd been on the wagon for a year. Apart from the liver, he was in excellent health. It was one of those things that just slipped through the underwriting. Basically, he beat the system."

"Did he say why he was doing this?"

Rodney ran his fingers through his thinning white hair. He looked uncomfortable.

"It's none of my business," he said. "I know you had problems with him, Vince. But in his last years he mellowed. He would even smile and tell jokes. He wanted to do something for your mother. He felt a lot of remorse about the things he'd done."

"It sounds like you two were friends."

"People open up to me sometimes," he said. "When they're talking about insurance—and dying—you'd be surprised what comes out."

"I still don't get where the money for the premiums was coming from," I said. "Certainly not from Carla."

"You know he was working for Brooks Burleigh, right?"

"That's what the police said."

"Money is all around Brooks Burleigh. It's like snow. It falls out of the sky."

"Do you know the guy?"

"I wish," he said. "That's a client I'd like to have. Even a tiny piece of his business would be more than the rest of my book."

"How would I find him?"

"You're in Vermont, Vince," he said. "He's in the phone book."

*

The Stowe exit is about midway down the interstate between Burlington and Barre. You get a spectacular view of the Green Mountains from I-89, which winds through river valleys and farmland, flanked by gentle hills on either side. The Greens have been sculpted and smoothed over time by weather and glacial ice, and from a distance they resemble women lying down.

Brooks Burleigh was in the phone book, but no one had answered. Perhaps they were in Gstaad or Thailand or wherever rich people jetted off to these days. The address was also in the book, and I typed it into my smartphone's GPS. All my P.I. gear was in Florida, and if this got complicated I might have to call someone to box it up and overnight it. Snooping without my tech toys was like knitting with my eyes closed, and this case (at least it felt like a case, even if I didn't have a client) was beginning to look like an Argyle sweater. I thought about calling Roberto, my 14-year-old Cuban American neighbor and computer whiz, but he would be in school, and I didn't want to bug him. I would just proceed the old-fashioned way for now; I was a pretty good investigator long before smartphones and the Internet, and there was a lot that you could accomplish just by knocking on doors and asking blunt questions.

The GPS pointed me up Edson Hill Road, high up a slope across the valley from Mount Mansfield, Vermont's highest peak and the location of the Stowe ski area. I pulled the car over for a moment to take in the spectacular view. The top of the mountain poked into a thin layer of clouds, and I could see the chairlifts running in the distance. Whoever was brave enough to ski in this weather would need some extra insulation and frequent breaks for hot cocoa—you could get frostbite in minutes if you left any skin exposed.

I was in a residential area, and this was definitely the right side of the tracks. Many of the houses weren't even visible from the road; they were surrounded by enough land to keep out the curious. After another mile the GPS told me I had arrived, and I stopped at a metal gate between two tall stone columns topped by security cameras. I was next to a speaker with a call button, and I lowered the window, letting in the frigid air. Before I could press the button, the gates opened.

Apparently I was being invited in.

The driveway was neatly plowed and sanded, and must have been half a mile long. I wondered if I was going to end up in Morrisville, the next village to the east. Finally, I came to a hilltop where the land flattened, and I found myself in the middle of a quintessential New England farm with barns, stables, snow-covered pasture and a classic Vermont farmhouse.

I parked the Subaru and walked across the packed snow to the farmhouse, which could have been out of a Currier and Ives print except for the security cameras, rooftop antennas, floodlights and wired windows. I wouldn't want to have to break into this place—I'm very experienced in that area, but this little spread was about as bucolic as Camp David. Somebody was rich, or paranoid, or both.

The door opened before I could knock. "Vince Tanzi?"

"Um…yes," I said. I was looking at a woman who belonged on the cover of a magazine. She was nearly as tall as me and had thick, black hair that was tied back and hung to her waist. She wore no makeup; she didn't need to—her dark eyes glowed, her perfect complexion beckoned. She wore sweats, but they looked expensive, and they didn't obscure her slender figure. I considered collapsing at her feet in hopes that she would take me as her love slave.

"You know the car?" I said.

"It comes up as registered to Francine Tanzi." Her voice was milky, with a slight Slavic accent. "I assumed it was you. I'm being rude. My name is Yuliana Burleigh. Please come in."

I crossed the threshold and entered a warm, brightly-lit hallway. The floors were polished Verde Antiqua marble, no doubt from the Barre sheds. I stripped off my coat and boots and felt the radiant heat coming from the floor, through my wool socks. Ms. Burleigh hung my coat on a hook and led me into a large living room.

"Please," she said, motioning me to a soft leather chair. She took a seat on a couch across from me. "Coffee?"

"No, thanks," I said. "You have a license plate reader?"

"Yes."

"So then you know someone in Homeland Security?"

She smiled disarmingly, and I once again considered extending my wrists for the handcuffs. This was without a doubt the most beautiful creature on the planet, with the possible exception of the manta ray exhibit at SeaWorld. My phone buzzed in my pocket, and I sneaked a look. Barbara. Holy shit, how do women know these things? I felt a pang of guilt as I turned it off without answering.

"Brooks knows everyone," she said. "I'm so sorry about your father."

I was going to say something negative about my father, but I stopped myself. "Thanks."

"Brooks really liked him, and so did I."

"You may not have known him that well," I said.

"He told us all about you," she said. "Everything. You were the one he felt the worst about. Brooks tried to get him to reach out to you, but he couldn't do it."

I felt my insides tighten. My father, reaching out to me? What the hell was that about?

"You are Mrs. Burleigh?"

"No, no, no," she said. "I'm his personal assistant. I just took the family name. Mine is unpronounceable."

"Try me."

"Tsegelnichenko," she said.

"You're right," I said.

"Brooks is away," she said. "But I know he'd love to meet you. He said he'd be back in time for the wake."

"Mr. Burleigh is going to my father's wake?"

"If that's all right," she said. Her accent was as sweet as the crusted sugar on a crème brûlée.

"Of course," I said.

"Will your siblings be there?"

Apparently this woman knew everything about the Tanzis. "Not likely," I said. "Junie is, um, not available, and I can't locate my sister."

"I have Carla's cell number," she said. Carla with a cellphone? Suddenly I was way off balance.

"Excuse me, but, how do you know so much about us?"

"Your father drove for Brooks. They became very close. They spent a lot of time together, in the car. Brooks travels to New York a lot, and he doesn't like to fly into Teterboro; he had a near-collision there one time. So Jimmy would drive him."

"Did Mr. Burleigh buy him the life insurance policy?"

"I don't handle his business arrangements," she said. A little switch clicked, and I stored that information. The policy was a business arrangement. She stood up. "Come into the kitchen. You look cold. I am going to make you a coffee."

I obeyed, and we entered a huge space that could have served as a church where Michelin three-star chefs went to worship. Expensive cooking gear hung from the beams, and the pink granite countertops held every imaginable high-end appliance. A vintage Aga stove dominated the stainless steel and cherry-wood landscape, and the welcome heat of the firebox radiated from its porcelain-clad surfaces. Yuliana chose a single cup cartridge from a drawer and inserted it into a Keurig.

"Dark roast, all right?"

"Perfect," I said. The coffeemaker made a slightly obscene sucking sound, and she handed me a warm cup. "Ms. Burleigh," I began.

"Yuliana," she corrected. She drew closer to me and reached her arm around my waist. I nearly dropped the coffee cup in surprise. She unsnapped the holster in the small of my back and withdrew my Glock 30. Jeezum crow, I'd completely forgotten I was wearing it.

"Sorry," I said. "I didn't—"

"The police like these," she said, as she held the gun. "I find them a little unstable."

"I used to be a cop," I said.

"Until they let you go, because you entered a house without a warrant," she said.

I had no idea how she knew that. I'd had to quietly negotiate my exit from the Indian River Sheriff's Department after twenty-five years, when I'd hastily broken into a perp's house to retrieve a murder weapon, and caused the whole case to subsequently unravel in court.

"Would you like to shoot?' she asked. "We have a range downstairs."

"Seriously?"

"Bring your coffee," she said, and she led me across the kitchen to a stairway.

*

I estimated that the farmhouse had about five thousand square feet above ground. There was almost that much in the cellar. It was part storage, part wine stash, part gym, and part bunker, with comfortable living areas and several side rooms with beds. Yuliana gave me a brief tour. One storeroom held enough food and water to last out a war, and another had what looked like a mini-arms depot for the Vermont National Guard. If the barbarians attacked, Brooks Burleigh would not only be ready, he'd win. She unlocked the door to a shooting range with four ultra-modern SRI stalls. Behind us were racks holding guns of every possible type, from black powder antiques to modern assault weapons including several AK-47s. If the fully-automatic feature wasn't disabled, these were highly illegal unless you had a very special permit.

"What would you like to try?" she asked. She took two sets of ear protectors from a bench and handed me one. I scanned the racks and hoped that the saliva from my mouth wouldn't make too obvious a pool on the floor. I'm not a gun-nut, but I appreciate good hardware, and everything was top of the line.

"Is that an FN SCAR?" I pointed to a beige-colored rifle with an evil-looking magazine. These were Special Ops weapons, and if they ever got onto the streets there would be no more crime, because everybody would be dead.

Yuliana took it down for me and replaced the empty magazine with a full one. The woman knew how to handle a firearm. She passed it to me and went to a control panel that automatically set up a cardboard target at the far end of the range. It wasn't a bull's-eye, or a deer head. It was a human silhouette.

I emptied the magazine with three bursts. By the third, there was nothing left to shoot at, the paper target was obliterated. Yuliana was laughing; I could hear her even with my ear protection on.

"Not a very subtle weapon, is it?" she said. She retreated to the bench behind us and came back with a Colt Cobra, a small, snub-nosed revolver that packed a .38 caliber wallop but was hard as hell to shoot straight at range distance—it was for close-in work. A Cobra was what Jack Ruby had used to kill Lee Harvey Oswald.

Yuliana chose a fresh target; another human silhouette. She took a shooter's stance, with both hands on the weapon. Six shots rang out, and she pushed a button to retrieve the target, which whirred toward us on an overhead cable.

The target was the same kind I'd used when I was a deputy. It had a circle in the center, where a shot would have hit the heart. Five of the six holes were neatly clustered within the circle, with the sixth about an inch outside of it.

"You missed one," I said. She awarded me another smile, and this time I decided that if I was going to be her love slave, I'd better pack my Kevlar pajamas.

*

I took the phone from my coat pocket as I drove the car back down Edson Hill Road. I owed my sweetheart a phone call. She didn't answer, and I remembered that she had classes all Wednesday afternoon. I would text her something apologetic when I wasn't at the wheel. My guilt had only increased after an hour of shooting bullets and the breeze with Yuliana Burleigh—just being in the presence of a woman that attractive made me feel like I was cheating. Barbara had very little to worry about in the looks department, and she'd been the one-and-only woman to sweep me off my feet after Glory, my spouse of twenty years, had been killed. This trip was the first time we had been apart since we'd met back in August. I loved Barbara, and I'd even grown to trust her. Now, the question was—could I trust myself?

My stomach was growling, and I stopped at a corner store to get a bag of locally-made tortilla chips and two tubs of Cabot's Ranch Dip. Vermont is one of the healthiest states in the national rankings, which is a small miracle seeing how it's the home of Ben & Jerry's, the Cabot Creamery, and, of course, maple syrup. I munched my way through half the bag of chips and scraped every last vestige of the dip from the first plastic container as I got back on the interstate. I had decided to travel north rather than south—back to Burlington, where I would get a hotel room and spend the night. I thought I might drop in at the Marriott and see my brother play, just for the hell of it. I was also tired, cold, and slightly horny, which surprised me. It would be a good thing if I could wrap this up fast and get back to Florida, and Barbara.

*

I checked into the hotel, which was above my usual price range but seemed to make sense if I was going to go to Junie's gig. I called my mother to explain that I wouldn't be sleeping there and to make sure she didn't need the car. She was relieved to hear that I had sprung my brother. I tried the cell number that Yuliana had given me for my sister, but there was no answer, and I didn't bother to leave a message. I lay on the bed with the second container of dip and began to polish it off, along with the rest of the bag of chips. Barbara would freak out— she had me running and working out again, and she supplied me with all sorts of repulsive, healthy crap in an attempt to get my weight back under two hundred. Not long after we'd started an official relationship, the effort to reinvent me had begun in earnest. I didn't protest—it was nice that someone would care enough to do it. I needed to break some of the bad habits I'd picked up after my wife had died.

The phone rang and I answered, with a mouthful of chips.

"What are you eating?"

"Busted," I said.

"I hear a crunching sound."

"They have food up here that would make a grown vegan cry," I said. "It's not fair."

"If you're going to get fat, don't bother to come back," Barbara said. "I don't do porky."

"Just as soon as I finish these chips, I'm going to do five hundred sit-ups," I said.

She laughed. "So, are you in the work mode?"

"Yes."

"Find anything?"

"Not really," I said. I decided I wouldn't confess to having spent most of the afternoon with Mata Hari. "How was school?"

"Bloody," she said. "We did anatomy stuff."

"Does it bother you?"

"I'm getting used to it. It's actually kind of fascinating."

"Cool."

"Speaking of cool, it's supposed to frost here tonight," she said.

"I won't even tell you how cold it is here."

"I really, really miss you."

"I know."

"You know?" she said. "What kind of an answer is that?"

I laughed. "Gotcha."

"I am going to have to spank you," she said.

"Get back to your books," I said. "I'll be home as soon as I can."

I hung up, and the phone rang immediately. I didn't recognize the number.

"Vince Tanzi," I said.

"It's Yuliana."

"So you even know my cell?"

"You called here this morning, remember?"

"Oh yeah," I said, and my paranoia receded. "Thank you for the target practice, I enjoyed it."

"So did I," she said, and there was silence.

I broke it. "So, what can I do for you?"

"I'm flying to Vero Beach tomorrow morning," she said. "Brooks is at the John's Island house, and the jet is up here. I'm going to pick him up and then fly back tomorrow night. I just wondered if there was anything I could do."

Sure, you could collect all my gear so that I could spy on you and your boss. Haha. "You have a private jet?"

"Yes."

"Do you ever pick up hitchhikers?"

"Certain ones," she said. The milky-soft voice got a little softer.

"I actually need to get some things from my house," I said. That, and I figured that time spent with this woman and her boss might be productive. So far, several roads were leading to the Burleighs.

"Where are you?" she asked.

"You don't know that?"

She laughed. "Not yet."

"I'm in a hotel in Burlington."

"The jet is at the Morrisville airport. Can you be there at eight thirty?"

"I'll be there," I said, and we hung up.

*

The clock radio said 8:30, and for a moment I thought I was going to be horribly late until it sank in that it was still night, not morning. I'd dozed off on the hotel bed, fully clothed and sated from my chip-and-dip orgy. Junie's gig had started half an hour ago.

I brushed my teeth, splashed water on my face, and put on a fresh shirt. It was an old wool flannel Pendleton, not something I'd usually wear to a restaurant, but Burlington was a college town and faux-lumberjack was perfectly acceptable evening attire. I found a seat at the bar across the room from where Junie sat with his guitar, illuminated by a single red spotlight. The tables were full, some of them with talky tourists, but others with quietly reverent locals. Junie had a following, especially among the guitar-playing community, and other musicians would often show up at his gigs just to be amazed and wonder how he did it. He played mostly jazz standards, but he could play anything. Someone could request a bluegrass tune, a Chopin étude, or a polka, and it made no difference, he'd just launch in like he'd played it all his life. Everything that came out of his guitar had a distinctive sound, nothing like what other guitarists did, and nobody could explain his technique, much less imitate it. He was in the middle of "Sweet Georgia Brown", and his solo Gibson archtop sounded like a whole band.

"Drink?" a bartender asked me.

"I'll have a Long Trail IPA. Got any oysters?"

"No, but we have steamers on special."

"Fine," I said. My digestive system was about to become a Super-fund site, but I intended to enjoy my freedom before reporting back to my girlfriend-slash-dietician. That reminded me, I might be able to see Barbara during my lightning-quick dash to Vero. I took out my phone.

U hv class tmrw?, I texted.

Of course, she sent back.

Feel like cutting? I'm in Vero noonish, just for a few hrs.

U R a bad influence but yes.

Pick me up at Vero airport. Will txt arrival time ltr ok?

What?? Private plane?

Private jet, I texted.

Oh forgive me, jet, of crse, she texted back. *La dee da.*

Haha see U tmrw, xo

Xo, she replied.

*

Junie finished his set and came over to the bar.

"Rumple Minze?" the bartender asked him.

"Yah," he said. The bartender handed him a glass with ice and poured a generous shot of the liqueur. "This is what the snowplow guys drink," Junie said to me. "They keep a bottle under the seat."

"I thought you had to yodel and wear lederhosen to drink that stuff," I said.

"Is that a request? I can do some yodeling next set."

I laughed. Junie smiled. This is where he was truly happy—at a gig. It was the only place I'd ever seen him beaming. The problem was that Junie didn't have an off switch, and if he was doing drugs or drinking Rumple Minze, he'd just keep on doing it until he was pie-eyed. That was the reason he only played solo—no one would put up with him after countless brief band stints that included missed gigs, fist fights, broken barstools, insulting the audience, or passing out cold in mid-song and collapsing backwards into the drum set. Everybody wanted to play with him, but everybody knew better.

"You sound awesome, as usual."

"Thanks, man."

"I'm staying here tonight," I said.

"You could have stayed on my couch."

"I didn't want to impose," I said. He was right, I could have, but it hadn't even crossed my mind. Is that what a good brother would have done? I downed the rest of my Long Trail and motioned to the bartender.

"I'll have what he's having," I said. He poured me a glass with as generous a shot as he'd served Junie. I took a swig and grimaced. "Tastes like toothpaste," I said.

"And it fights dental plaque," Junie said. We both laughed.

"I went up to the Burleigh place," I said.

Junie said nothing.

"Apparently they know all about the family," I said. "You ever meet the guy?"

"You don't want to mess with that dude, Vin," he said.

"What do you mean?"

"Just ask Carla," he said.

"I haven't talked to her yet."

"She's not exactly easy to reach. I can give you the address." He told it to me, and I entered it into my phone.

"Junie, what's going on? You're holding out on me."

"I don't owe you anything, bro."

"OK, I'll buy you a drink then, so you can owe me."

"I drink for free here. That's why I do the gig."

"What was Dad into? Were you in it too? And Carla?"

"The less you know, the better," he said.

"Come on, June. Give," I said.

My steamers arrived, and I picked at them while he sat there. He drained his glass, and the bartender topped it up.

"Gotta go start the second set," he said. He walked back to the stage, rested his drink on the top of his amplifier, and picked up the Gibson. His first song was "Giant Steps", a complicated John Coltrane tune that he transformed as he played into something barely recognizable but perfect. This time the whole room went quiet. I could see the glaze in his eyes as the Rumple Minze began to kick in. I decided I didn't want to watch him descend into inebriation—I'd stay for a few more tunes and then slip away. It's probably not what a good brother would have done, but I needed the sleep.

THURSDAY

I woke up at four AM feeling like I'd swallowed a whole tube of Crest. Once I'm awake, that's it—there's no going back to sleep, I can only choose between lying there, worrying about ridiculous, trivial things that are blown out of proportion in the funhouse mirror of half-sleep, or getting up and starting the day. I got up.

The night clerk at the Marriott was asleep in front of the TV, so I decided to just leave the room key on the desk. When the Subaru started on the first try, I realized the weather had actually warmed up some overnight. My inner thermostat said it had to be above zero. I checked the phone to confirm—plus one degree. I was just grateful to be back in the positive category.

I'd been putting off the obvious, which was to check out my father's apartment. It was in Waterbury, off the same interstate exit as Stowe. But Waterbury was no glitzy resort; it was a blue-collar town along the Winooski River that had seen the old lumber and textile mills gradually replaced by government offices and hipster industries like Green Mountain Coffee, Ben & Jerry's, and Alchemist Beer—makers of Heady Topper, a double-alcohol IPA that felled strong men like a just-sharpened chainsaw.

A few cars were on the streets when I pulled in to Waterbury—early birds, going to their jobs. The state mental hospital was there, or had been, before Hurricane Irene had washed away a good chunk of Vermont in August of 2011. When we were kids, the mental hospital was where our parents would threaten to ship us off to, if we didn't behave. The old hospital campus was already run down well before it got the coup de grace from Irene, and much of the population had been mainstreamed into the community in recent years, for better or for worse. Carla had actually been there for an evaluation when she was eighteen, but they determined that she was a pothead, not a psycho, and everyone calmed down. There are far more serious drug issues than marijuana use, and in my opinion the people who wrote the stupid laws ought to just roll a fat one, get the giggles and eat a whole bag of Pepperidge Farm Double Chocolate Milanos before they attempt any further legislation.

My dad's apartment was on the ground floor of a brick building that dated from the railroad days. I entered the hallway and was completely alone. It was still early in the morning; the sun wouldn't rise for another hour. I didn't have the key that Lieutenant Pallmeister had given my mother, but a quick look at the door hardware and I was unconcerned. The deadbolt wasn't set, and the door handle was a vintage Kwikset that I could eventually manage with a paper clip, but I noticed the doorjamb was loose, and all I needed was a quick slide of my Piggly Wiggly customer card and I was in. The Vero Beach Piggly Wiggly had closed years ago, but their card was the perfect thickness for certain jobs, so I kept it in a safe place in my wallet. I would collect the rest of my lock-picking tools in Vero in case I needed to get past anything more sophisticated.

Everything was neat and tidy inside. I left my gloves on, more out of habit than out of any concern for leaving prints. My father had lived a Spartan existence—there was hardly any furniture, no magazines, no books, nothing to play music on and a nearly-empty fridge except for some yoghurts and a bag of celery that was going limp. There was a water cooler in the living room, with a full glass bottle on top. Ex-alcoholics can't get enough water; I'd seen this in other people's houses. A closet held his clothes, which were neatly arranged. The same for his bureau. An old oak desk held pencils, writing paper, a few bills and some change. Two envelopes lay on top, addressed to "Betty Boop". I smiled—that had to be his pet name for my mother. I decided to just pocket the letters without reading them; I had no desire to embarrass my mom.

His bed was neatly made, his toothbrush was hung up, the floors were clean and the dishes were put away. Everything was way too perfect. Someone had sanitized the place.

I decided to take a fresh look. I turned out the lights, went back into the hall, and then re-entered the apartment. Reboot. I flicked on the light and started all over again. I was missing something.

When I found it, I knew it wasn't intended to be hidden; I had just missed it. A shiny, nearly-new MacBook Pro lay on top of the fridge, above my line of sight. It was the same model I had at home, except that mine was full of the snooping software that Roberto had helped me install. God knew what my 74-year-old father was doing with a fancy new Mac. God, and maybe a few other people. If they had already been here to sanitize the place, I could assume that the computer would also have been wiped clean. I put it in my coat, locked the door and left. If there was time, I'd get Roberto to check it over while I was in Vero. The kid could find things on computers that their owners thought were buried. He coaxed them from the grave like zombies. There are no secrets on hard drives; it's all in there, somewhere.

*

The Morrisville-Stowe airport had been updated in recent years to accommodate the private jet phenomenon—there were four of them on the tarmac, parked wingtip-to-wingtip, and a fifth, a big Bombardier 605, waited with the engines already running. I checked in at the small structure that was both control tower and flight lounge. A young man rose from his desk to greet me.

"How's it going?" he said.

"Good 'n' you?" I responded.

"You with Miss Burleigh?"

"Yes."

"She's on the aircraft, doing pre-flight. I'll take you out."

He put on a ski parka and led me to the big, shiny Bombardier. Yuliana smiled and waved from the cockpit window. There was a guy seated next to her wearing a hat and a white shirt with epaulets. She took off her headset, opened the door of the jet, and lowered the steps.

"This is Ed," she said as I stepped aboard. The pilot turned to greet me.

"Hi, Ed," I said.

"Hi, Mr. Tanzi," he said. "Sorry about your father."

"Thanks." I guess I was going have to get used to people saying that.

Yuliana wore tailored grey wool pants that hugged her hips, with a white blouse underneath a black Patagonia fleece vest. Steel-rimmed Ray-bans covered her dark eyes, and I noticed that today she wore makeup, including a deep red lipstick that provided a brilliant contrast to her otherwise monochrome outfit and made her lips the thing that I looked at first.

"Are we all set, Ed?" she said.

"Yes, Ms. Burleigh."

"Sit anywhere, Vince," she said, and she sat back down in the cockpit next to the pilot. She put her headset back on and began to flip switches and check dials as the jet's engines powered up. Apparently she knew how to fly one of these babies, and I added it to the list of surprising things about her. Brooks Burleigh had his own Bond Girl as a personal assistant. Maybe next week she'd take me spelunking, or we'd play polo, or go bungee-jumping, or do all three at the same time.

I strapped myself in to a beige leather seat that was bigger than a Barcalounger and stowed my bag underneath me. There were seven of the gigantic, cushy seats, and a bench at the back that I guessed would fold out to make a bed. I was surrounded by polished wood, sleek metal, and soft, tanned cowhide that must have come from some seriously pampered cows. This was not like flying first class; it was more like getting a massage.

The jet taxied, powered up fully, and then sprinted down the runway and shot into the sky at a forty-five degree angle. I watched the trees and hills get smaller as we passed over Mount Mansfield and swung in a long arc toward the south. This thing was a hot rod; a commercial jet was a school bus by comparison.

The plane leveled off, and Yuliana took her headphones off and came aft. She closed the double-paneled door that separated us from Ed, up front. It was just her and me.

"So, how long have you been flying?"

"Are you trying to guess how old I am?" she said. "I'm thirty seven."

"OK, let's try again," I said. "Where did you learn to fly?"

"Moldovan Air Force," she said. "I was twenty-four. The year before I met Brooks. He was a visiting VIP, and they assigned me to escort him." She sat in the seat facing me. "We're not lovers though."

"I didn't ask," I said.

"Your eyes asked."

She was right, but I wasn't going to acknowledge that.

"I have some work to do," she said. She withdrew a silver MacBook from her briefcase and powered it up. It looked exactly like my father's, which was in my own bag.

"There's Wi-Fi here?"

"Yes," she said. "And you can use your cell."

"Cool," I said, which sounded ridiculous. At least I didn't say gee whiz.

She busied herself on her computer. I decided to check out my father's, and found that it was protected by a password. Unlike Roberto, I have no clue about how to hack past those things, but just for the hell of it I typed in "bettyboop", and it worked. A slight chill ran through me as I realized I had divined my dead father's thought process.

I opened up Gmail and signed in. There were dozens of emails that I would read later. I wrote a quick message to Roberto to ask about his availability and described what I had in mind. He replied in less than a minute, telling me to type a URL into the Safari browser. I did what he said and a program opened, with a box that asked if it was all right to allow "MAD$KILZZ" to take over, and I accepted. That was one of his hacker ID's. My cellphone buzzed with a text, and I took it out of my pocket. Yuliana was busy, not paying me any attention.

Lv it running and I'll look arnd.

Aren't u in school? I sent back.

Home. Got mono.

Oh no, I texted.

Sucks.

Text me when you're done, I wrote, and put the phone back in my pocket.

"There's coffee in the back," Yuliana said, looking up from her computer.

"I'm downloading something," I said.

"I'll get us some," she said, and she walked to the back of the cabin. She returned with two mugs that had a "BB" monogram on them.

"Thanks."

"Do you have anything to do while we're in Vero?"

"A couple chores," I said.

"Do you need a car?"

"I have somebody meeting me," I said. I heard myself say *somebody*, not girlfriend.

"OK," she said. "I'm going to go take over for a while." She got up and went back through the partition doors into the cockpit.

I checked my father's computer. Roberto's cursor whizzed around and programs popped open and closed again like Fourth of July fireworks. He was in his element.

I took my knitting from my bag and went to work. I was part way through a watch cap that I wanted to have done for Roberto before his ski trip to Colorado in February. It was black, like everything else he currently wore, and the stitches were tightly spaced so I had to use size six circular needles, and the whole thing was a bitch. I have pretty good finger dexterity from picking locks, but I'd only started this hobby after Barbara hid my phone and my laptop when we were in

Key West and challenged me to live without them for a month. I'd produced three baby blankets for a friend, who was very pleased, although they only had one baby, not three.

My phone buzzed.

Done.

Find anything?

Porn, he wrote.

Yr kidding, right?

No.

Seriously?

Only looked bcuz it was heavily encrypted. Gov't quality encryption.

I'm home this afternoon. Will stop in, I texted.

Porn on my father's computer? Never too old, I guess. I didn't understand what he meant about government-quality encryption, but I'd ask him when I saw him. My afternoon was already filling up.

*

I knit while Yuliana flew. We cruised almost as high as the commercial jets, and the clouds scattered and thinned after we crossed the Mason-Dixon Line. I checked the Vero weather on my phone—it had warmed considerably and would be sunny and in the seventies when we landed. I looked forward to thawing out, even if it was only for one afternoon.

Yuliana came through the door as I was watching the coastline; I'd recognized the Jacksonville skyline and the high-rises along the beach.

"Landing in about twenty," she said. "I'm going to change."

She walked past me to the rear of the aircraft, shucked off the fleece vest, unbuttoned her blouse and exposed her tanned, sleek shoulders. Oops. I turned my head forward. I should be sticking, as it were, to my knitting. I picked up the needles and began the rhythmic motion. Yuliana gave out a small cry and I turned around, instinctively. She was struggling with the zipper of her pants, and her top half was exposed except for a lacy white bra. I snapped my head forward again and realized I'd lost count of the stitches. "Fuck," I said, too loud.

Her phone rang from the seat across from me. It was the oh-mama-mia-let-me-go melody from "Bohemian Rhapsody", by Queen. "That's Brooks," she said behind me, and she came forward, picked up the phone and sat across from me, clothed only in her bra and panties. My blood pressure rose to a level well above my IQ, and I tried my best to look downward into my yarn.

"Yes, he's with me," she said. "He's knitting a hat." She chuckled sweetly. "You didn't tell me he was handsome."

I dropped a stitch, and had to unwind part of the row.

"Sure. No, he has plans. OK. See you soon." She hung up the phone, and didn't get out of the seat.

"Is this what you used to wear in the Moldovan Air Force?" I asked.

"Underneath," she said, and gave me a you-are-my-prisoner smile. "Are you going to change?"

I had a short sleeve shirt in my bag, but enough flesh had been exposed for one flight. "I'll wait," I said.

Yuliana went back and slipped on a pair of white Capri pants and a striped top. She turned to me before re-entering the cockpit. "Remember to fasten your seatbelt," she said.

I heeded her advice and clipped it shut. I know when I'm about to be taken for a ride.

*

It may have been in the seventies in Vero, but the temperature was considerably cooler inside Barbara's Yukon, and the air conditioning wasn't even running. She had watched me get off the plane and cross the tarmac with Yuliana Burleigh, who, just to make it worse, had smiled and laughed the whole way to the general aviation terminal. I couldn't have been in any more trouble if I'd carried her in my arms.

I had introduced them briefly and attempted to steer Barbara to the exit as quickly as possible before anyone's eyeballs got scratched out. Miss Capri Pants, as Barbara now called her, had invited us to dinner before the flight back, but Barbara told her that we had other plans and gave her a theatrical wink. Yuliana caught my glance, and I rolled my eyes, which made her giggle, which in turn ratcheted up Barbara's anxiety level. Yuliana and I agreed to meet back at the airport by nine.

I drove, while Barbara simmered. "So who the hell is Miss Yooo-liana Burleigh?" she said, mimicking her Slavic accent.

"She was at the airport and looked kind of lost, so I offered her a ride," I said.

"Cut the bullshit, Vinny," she said. She only called me that when she wanted to piss me off.

"She's the personal assistant of a rich guy," I said. "My father worked for them."

"So why are they flying you around in a jet?"

"That's a very good question," I said. "Exactly what I'd like to find out. It smells funny."

"It smells like Clive Christian Number One."

"What?"

"It's a very expensive perfume. She was wearing it. You'd better not come home smelling like that."

"I usually come home smelling like food."

"I'm glad you're here, whatever you smell like," she said, and she put her hand on my arm. The interior of the car approached normal room temperature.

"So you're going to be nice to me now?"

"I'm going to take you home and put my scent on you," she said.

*

I noticed a car in the rearview mirror that had been there for a while as we'd made our way through town. I took a turn, and it followed. I took another, and it disappeared.

"Vince, where are you going?"

"Bear with me a sec," I said. I slowed, and the car appeared again. It was a Crown Vic. It could have been an unmarked cruiser, but it didn't have the usual giveaways like the cheap rims and big antenna. I turned into a Walgreens. "Be out in a minute," I said as I parked.

I waited inside the store and watched the lot. The Crown Vic parked across from us, and two very big guys got out. They didn't look like cops—more like muscle. I started looking for a rear exit.

They came up behind me and shoved me roughly into a storeroom, and one of them clipped me on the back of my head for good measure. I wasn't carrying; I'd left the Glock in Vermont. I swung a leg out and kicked Big Guy #1 in the shin, which made him double over, and I punched him, hard, in the solar plexus. The other guy went into a crouch, and I jumped sideways and kicked him in the neck—kind of a flashy Chuck Norris move, but it fooled him and he fell backward into some boxes. Both of them lay there and groaned, and I considered bolting, but I wanted to know who they were. I pulled a wallet out of Big Guy #2's pants and found his ID and a Border Patrol badge. Shit.

"Why didn't you identify yourself?"

"Fuck you," Big #2 said. Big #1 was still trying to get his wind back.

"You work for Robert Patton?"

"We're supposed to take you in," he said.

"I'm not going anywhere," I said. I had Robert Patton's card in my wallet, and I called his cell.

"Patton," he answered.

"Vince Tanzi," I said.

"What the hell are you doing flying on the Burleigh jet?"

"What the hell are you doing sending goons to pick me up? Don't these idiots have any training?"

"Where are they?"

"Lying in a heap at my feet," I said.

"I told you to stay clear," he said. "I'm going to have to detain you for a few days."

"If you're chasing Burleigh, how's that going to sound? I can't fly back with them because I've been picked up by the Border Patrol? Is that what you want?"

"You can't tell him that," he said.

"I have the feeling he knows already, and I haven't even met him."

"Fly back. Keep your mouth shut. Then go to your mother's and stay the fuck out of it."

"I'll give you two out of three," I said. "Tell your clods here to go away." I passed my phone to Big #2 and they talked. He handed it back to me and stood up, rubbing his neck.

"Rematch?" he said, "Without the pussy-kicks?"

"Fuck off," I said, and I left them there. I went out to the car, got in, and started it. Barbara saw my expression and didn't say anything. "I have to stop at Roberto's," I said. "Then let's get drunk and screw."

"You Vermonters sure know how to sweet talk a southern girl," she said.

*

Lilian, Roberto's mother, met me at the door. "Hi Vince," she said, with just a lingering trace of an accent. She was a phlebotomist at the Indian River Medical Center, where her husband Gustavo also worked in the accounting department. All of their relatives lived in Miami, but they had decided it was "too Cuban" and moved to Vero Beach, which was pretty much black or white back then. Now it has a fast-growing Latino population like anywhere else. There was even a Latino food section at the Publix, and I hung out there a lot because in my next life I want to be able to cook like Lilian—there wouldn't be enough time to master the subtleties of her stews, gumbos, and sauces in this one, but I was trying.

"What's that smell?"

"Witch doctor stuff," she said. "I'm trying to get Roberto to eat some."

"How is he?"

"Not good. The mononucleosis gave him a terrible sore throat," she said. "He'll be glad you're here. Go on back."

"Thanks," I said. "I won't stay long. Barbara's in the car."

"OK," she said.

I knocked on Roberto's bedroom door, and he croaked an acknowledgement.

"Dude," I said.

"Dude," he managed to say back. He sat up in his bed. "May have to text you. I can't speak."

"Take it easy," I said. "I brought the computer." I handed it to him, and he rose out of bed and put it on a desk in front of a gigantic computer of his own. He opened it and a security page appeared.

"Weird," he said.

"What?"

"This wasn't here before. You sure this is the same computer?"

I thought about that. "Actually, not a hundred percent." It was possible that I'd picked up Yuliana's laptop when I was leaving the plane.

Roberto tapped the keyboard with the same seemingly effortless virtuosity that my brother Junie applied to the guitar fret board. "It's here," he said. "The same porn vid. But this is a different computer."

"Show me," I said. He opened a file named STANDULL121312 .mov. The video player started and began to show raw, amateurish footage of a couple standing next to a four-poster bed. There was only one camera, and it appeared to be resting on something, not handheld. It had an audio track, but it was difficult to hear. A silver-haired man was naked, facing a much younger woman who held something in her hand. She was partially dressed. Partially, because her black, skintight outfit was missing fabric in the womanliest areas, and her breasts and pubic mound were clearly visible. She was exceptionally good-looking, and my first thought was that she was a pro, because although the john was handsome he was at least forty years her senior.

The fun began, and it involved what she held in her hand, which turned out to be a leather riding crop. Hi-ho Silver, and away! The audio track came to life, and the groaning and howling became loud. The door to Roberto's bedroom suddenly opened. It was Gustavo.

"Oh shit," I said, as if my own mother had caught me with a *Penthouse*.

"What's going on here?" Gustavo said.

"Let me explain," I said, and I went out into the hall with Gustavo and closed the door to the room.

"It's a case," I said. "I had no idea this was part of it. Roberto is checking out a computer for me, and that was on it."

"OK," Gustavo said. They liked me and trusted me, so he would cut me some slack. "It's not as if he doesn't see that stuff every day."

"I know," I said. "You have to wonder what the effect is going to be on these kids."

"Not good," he said.

We re-entered Roberto's room. "Vince says you're helping with a case," he said to his son.

Roberto was still facing the computer, typing. "No big deal, Dad."

"Let me watch," Gustavo said. "Replay it."

Roberto started the video again. I was twisting myself into a pretzel of awkwardness.

"That's Dulles Stanton," Gustavo said.

"What?" I said. I took a closer look at the patriarchal-looking naked guy. "Holy shit, you're right."

Dulles Stanton was the current chair of the Senate Committee on Homeland Security and Governmental Affairs. They were responsible for, among other things, the Border Patrol.

*

Barbara drove us the few blocks from Roberto's house to mine. The tires squealed as she pulled into my driveway and stopped the Yukon in front of the garage. I laughed.

"What's so funny?" she asked.

"Nothing," I said. "Do you have an agenda?"

"Yes. Get your ass upstairs and take off all your clothes."

"Can I at least get a drink of water?"

"Sorry, we don't have time," she said.

"We have all afternoon to make love," I said.

"Exactly," she said. She gave me her hundred-watt smile, and I got my ass upstairs.

*

Barbara was in the shower and I was alone in the bed with my guilt. My internal soundtrack was playing "Who Were You Thinking

Of", the Doug Sahm song that hit a little too close to what had just happened. Barbara was as sexy a woman as I had ever known, but my mind had been elsewhere. Specifically, my mind had been sitting on a soft leather seat in a private jet, watching something right out of Victoria's Secret. This one was going to take a lot more than a dozen Hail Marys and Our Fathers.

She came out, partially wrapped in a towel. Barbara was forty-five years old, and she kept in excellent shape. She didn't have the body of a twenty-year-old, but she didn't say "like, omigod" to begin every sentence, either. She was beautiful. She looked at me and frowned.

"You OK?"

"Yeah," I said.

"You don't look like a guy who just got lucky."

"Sorry. I'm…distracted."

"The case?"

"Yes," I said. *Good recovery.* "It's getting strange."

"How so?"

"My dad had a porn movie on his computer. Roberto found it."

"That's a little awkward," she said.

"You got that right," I said. "Gustavo was right there."

"Omigod," she said.

"It was a U.S. senator," I said. "It was also on Yuliana's computer. I think it's blackmail."

"Miss Capri Pants?"

"Yes."

"Good," she said. "Put her away for a long time, OK?"

"You're jealous?"

"Should I be?"

"No comment," I said. Barbara's mouth opened, and I realized I had just inserted my size-13 foot into my own mouth. "Barbara—"

"Are you fucking her?" she said, with the volume all the way up.

"Of course not."

"But you would, if she let you."

"Barbara—I—"

"Don't say it," she interrupted. "Don't start lying to me. If you want to fuck her, go ahead, just don't lie about it." She was hurrying into her clothes. She tugged on her top, and stuffed her bra into her pants pocket. Before I could get out of bed she was halfway down the stairs.

"Hey!" I yelled, but the only answer was the slam of the front door.

*

My phone buzzed on the bedside table while I lay there wondering how the hell I was going to fix this. The caller ID said it was Yuliana. Oh great, just what I needed.

"Hi," I said.

"I believe you have my laptop," she said. Her voice was flat.

"Oh," I said. "Sorry about that. It looks like mine."

"I'll be over to get it," she said.

"I'm here," I said. "I live at—"

"I know where you live."

"That figures."

*

I stared out the window at the cream-colored Bentley Continental GTC as it oozed into my driveway. Nothing like it had ever occupied that space, or ever would again. Yuliana had the top down, and her dark hair was tied in a ponytail that protruded from the back of an L.A. Dodgers baseball cap. The Dodgers had ditched Vero for spring training in Arizona some years ago, but their swag remained. She had changed, and wore a mint green, strapless tube top over the same white Capri pants, with a white leather jacket and shades that looked appropriately expensive for a woman driving a Bentley. I met her at the door.

"I'm not interrupting anything?" she asked.

"Come on in." She entered, and checked out the surroundings. "It's not much," I said.

"I'm not a spoiled brat," she said. "I grew up with nothing."

"Here's your computer," I said, and handed her the shiny silver laptop.

"Here's yours." She put a shopping bag that held my dead father's Mac on the kitchen counter. It felt like a prisoner exchange.

"Aren't we supposed to be doing this at the 38th parallel?"

She smiled. "Where's your friend?"

"She had to leave."

"She's very attractive," she said.

"Yes, she is," I said.

Yuliana took one of the chairs at my kitchen table and held it by the back. She was looking at it, not moving. I couldn't read her expression, but something was going on.

"Take a seat if you want," I said. "Limeade?"

"No," she said, as she sat down. "Sit." She pointed to the other chair. I took the seat across from her.

"How much do you know about us?" she said.

"Not much," I said.

"But you're investigating."

"No," I said. She frowned. "OK. Yes."

"Brooks is going to offer you a job," she said. "Probably on the plane, tonight. You need to tell him no. He won't like it, but just be firm."

"Why are you telling me this?"

"Because I like you," she said. She pushed the sunglasses back over her hat and looked straight at me. For the first time I saw some vulnerability in her dark eyes.

"Yuliana, what are you involved in?"

"I can't talk about it," she said.

"But you'd like to get out."

She waited a long time to answer. "It's all I have," she said.

"I can get you out," I said.

She stood up and walked toward the front door.

"No, you can't," she said. "Your father already tried."

*

She was gone, and I had learned nothing except that whatever was going on, my abusive, ex-lush of a father had apparently been deeply involved. The hardest part to accept was that people obviously liked him—at least Yuliana did. I couldn't get my head around that. I had long ago pushed him to a far corner of my mind; a sort of solitary confinement for people I detested. There weren't many in there, but there were a few. When you are a cop for as long as I was, you find out that not everyone has your well-being in mind, and that some people are evil, cruel, or stupid, and sometimes all of the above.

My cell rang. It was John Pallmeister.

"Tanzi," I said.

"Where are you?"

"Florida," I said. "Back tonight."

"Patton wouldn't say. He's apoplectic. He can barely speak."

"Apoplectic? That's an awfully big word for a cop."

"I'll ignore that," he said. "Bad news, Vince."

"What?"

"Your brother. We picked him up."

"For what?"

He paused a while before he spoke. "You know what. You saw the scratches on his arm."

"You got a DNA sample?"

"Not yet. They're going to rush it, but it'll be three weeks, which is fast by the usual standards. But there was definitely skin under your father's fingernails, and we found out from Burlington P.D. that Junie was in scrubs that night. The only break for him so far is that nobody ID'd him at the hospital. I'm not telling you this, by the way."

"Thank you," I said.

"There's more. He's on the security tape, both entering and exiting. Main lobby. The times line up."

"Shit," I said. "How do I get to look at those tapes?"

"Ask his lawyer," he said.

"Where is he?"

"Back in the South Burlington lockup," he said.

"He didn't do it. He told me, and I know when he's lying."

"I'll keep that in mind," he said. "You're back tonight?"

"Late," I said.

"Have you seen the weather?"

"No."

"It's warmed up to the thirties. Been raining for the last hour, and the roads are a sheet of ice. I'm in my cruiser and I've already run out of flares."

*

It was five o'clock, and I had a few hours to kill before I got a cab to the airport. I'd already packed my P.I. tool bag. No word from Barbara. I wasn't about to call her; I was somewhat peeved at her accusations and her fast exit. Normal people talked these things out. I take that back—normal people seldom talked these things out; they'd rather scream, throw crockery, stomp off and generally behave like four-year-olds. What I mean is that theoretically, according to the self-help book industry, people are supposed to be calm, ask the other person about their feelings, and not make judgments. It saves on the crockery damage, but I suppose it's not nearly as satisfying as the four-year-old approach.

I decided to organize my desk and look for any bills that I should pay now in case I stayed in Vermont longer than a few more days. Everything appeared to be under control. I found a black and white picture under a stack of papers that needed to be filed. Carla had sent it to me over a year ago, when I was in prison. There was no note attached and no return address, but I knew her handwriting. It was a photo of my parents, taken on their wedding day. They'd married in a Catholic church in Groton, Connecticut, where my father was stationed before they moved back to Vermont. He'd served two years in the Navy; he didn't get seasick and he could fix anything. But the M.P.s had dragged him home from the bars one too many times, and they discharged him. He looked young, handsome and full of hope in his uniform. Everyone does at some point, although the look eventually fades and becomes brittle around the edges like this old photograph. I tucked it into an envelope—my mother might want it.

*

I warmed up some salmon that was left over from the night before I'd left for Vermont, which seemed like an eternity ago. The phone buzzed in my pocket. It was Yuliana again.

"Can you leave early?" she said. "I don't mean to spoil your plans."

I didn't tell her that they had already been spoiled. "What's up?"

"Brooks wants to go now. Ed called from the airport. He said the weather is getting ugly up North."

"What time?"

"Pick you up in half an hour?"

"OK," I said.

"Do you have a passport?"

"Yes."

"Bring it with you," she said. "If we can't land, they might divert us to Montreal."

"OK," I said.

"Remember our conversation," she said. "Brooks is very persuasive."

"I can handle Brooks," I said, and we hung up.

*

I dialed my mother, and Mrs. Tomaselli picked up. "Oh Vinny!" she said, "My Vinny, I just love my Vinny!" It felt like I was getting hugged tight to her ample bosom, right over the phone. Mrs. Tomaselli doted on me, spoiled me, gave me candy (which was usually months past the sell-by date), sent me birthday cards, and I could do no wrong as far as she was concerned. Everyone should have someone like that.

"Is my mom there?"

"She's indisposed," she said.

"Would you please tell her I'm coming back late? And it may be tomorrow, if the weather gets bad."

"It's bad already," Mrs. Tomaselli said. "Horrible. You should see the cars, sliding all over. I don't even dare walk home, the ice, it's awful. Francine is going to make a bed for me on the couch."

"You girls stay out of trouble," I said.

She giggled. "You're lucky I'm too old to chase you, Vinny," she said. "I'd hunt you down like a jackrabbit."

I couldn't think of anything to say to that, so I just laughed.

"I could have had any man I wanted in my day," she said.

"I don't doubt you," I said. She'd shown me pictures, and she wasn't kidding—she'd been a hot peperoncino a few decades and dress sizes ago.

"Goodbye, Mrs. Tomaselli."

"Goodbye, my Vinny."

*

I was wrong about the Bentley being the fanciest machine that would ever park in my driveway. This one was a deep-green Maybach, and even in the fading afternoon sun the paint job shimmered like the northern lights. Brooks Burleigh was at the wheel, instantly recognizable by his shock of thick, white hair and bushy eyebrows. He wore chinos and a polo shirt, like he'd just been horseback riding or working outdoors. Yuliana got out of the passenger side, still in her Capri pants and leather jacket. In the rear seat were two people—a balding, somber-looking guy in a summer-weight grey suit that smelled slightly of cigarette smoke, and a young woman with short blonde hair who might have given Yuliana a run for my most-beautiful-creature-on-the-planet award, except she looked out of place, and a little scared. So far, Yuliana had never looked scared of anything.

"Vince, welcome aboard," Burleigh said, extending his hand as he got out. It sounded like in his mind he'd already hired me.

"Hi, Mr. Burleigh," I said, shaking it.

"Please, just Brooks," he said. He had a disarming smile. "This is my friend, Tomas, and his au pair, Jenny. They're getting a ride back with us."

"Nice to meet you," I said, through their open window.

"Yuliana, take the back seat," Brooks said. "Vince, up here." He motioned me to the front passenger seat. This was a guy who was used to giving orders.

I put my tool bag on the floor in front of the seat and got in. Even with the bag there, I had approximately an acre of legroom. The Maybach was a cocoon, decked out in leather, chrome, and walnut, and designed to meet even the most demanding corporate egomaniac's need to compensate for the fact that his parents hadn't bought him the Little Tikes Cozy Coupe he'd coveted when he was three.

Brooks Burleigh didn't look like he was compensating for anything. He seemed totally at ease, and his complete comfort was contagious. I began to relax.

"Nice whip, homie," I said. His brow furrowed, and then he laughed.

"You'll have to translate for me if you're going to speak police-talk."

"It means I like your ride," I said. "Rapper-talk, not police-talk. I hang out with fourteen-year-olds too much."

"I see," he said. "I have a fourteen-year-old, but she's in France, at boarding school."

"Where do you spend most of your time?" I asked, as he drove.

"I love it here in Vero," he said. "I'll have to get you out to the house. But I seem to be in New York or Washington most of the time, babysitting land deals. I'm becoming a full-time lobbyist."

"What sort of deals?"

"We buy and sell, parcel off timber rights, set up conservation easements, you name it. It's surprisingly complex, and the law is making it more so all the time."

"My father used to say buy land because they're not making any more of it," I said.

"Your father was a wise man," he said.

"Too bad he was a drunk and an abuser."

"It must have been very difficult growing up with him," he said. He turned and briefly looked at me. His expression was completely sincere.

"It was."

"I only knew the sober Jimmy Tanzi," he said. "But he told me everything."

I didn't respond; the conversation was beginning to stir up memories that I didn't want to revisit. I needed to get back to Vermont, bury my father, and get out of there. I was suddenly disinterested in whatever intrigue the Burleighs had going on, and even Junie was going to have to deal with his own problems. Something had pulled the plug and let the air out of me. I saw Yuliana looking at me from the back seat.

"You OK, Vince?" she said.

"Just a little tired, I guess," I said.

"Rest up," she said. "Ed's sick. He's going to lie down on the bench seat. You're my copilot."

"I've never flown anything bigger than a kite," I said.

"I'll do all the work," she said. "You can finish knitting your hat."

*

We were over Maryland, according to Yuliana. There was no cloud cover, and she pointed out the lights of the cities along the route. The storm stretched ahead of us, from New York to northern New England, and the Morrisville airport had already waved us off— we were going to Montreal, which was only a couple hours by car from Stowe. I wondered if I'd get any trouble from customs agents. I had some toys in my bag that I wouldn't want examined too closely by a curious inspector.

It was too dark to knit in the cockpit, so I just drank in the scenery—a starry sky, dozens of little LED lights and digital readouts, and of course, my copilot, who mostly kept her eyes on her work, but now and then would divert them in my direction and give me a quiet smile. I still felt badly about the scene with Barbara, but she was a grown-up. Like all fights, no matter how much I wanted to believe she was wrong, she was partly right. I was attracted to Yuliana Burleigh. I had been in a monogamous marriage for twenty years before Barbara, and maybe I had jumped back into monogamy too soon. Or maybe not. Barbara was a wonderful person and was everything I could want as a friend and lover. I was confused—I had about as clear an understanding of women as I did of the myriad buttons and dials on the cockpit dash in front of me.

"Take the controls," Yuliana said.

"Nah," I said.

"Just hold it. Keep it steady." I tentatively reached for the steering apparatus in front of me. Suddenly, I was flying a plane at four hundred miles an hour through a starlit night.

"That's it. Don't spill anyone's coffee."

"Where's the throttle on this thing?" I said. "I'm having fun. Let's see how fast it goes."

She smiled but did not respond. Instead, she took a clip out of her pony tail and shook loose her long hair. She rose partly from her seat and turned to me, then leaned over and put her mouth on mine. Her tongue darted inside, and she put an arm behind my head and held me tightly. I could barely breathe, partly from the pressure, and partly from the shock. Finally, she released me.

"Holy shit," I said.

"You didn't like it?"

"You just surprised me."

"Holy shit is not the reaction I've usually had when I've kissed someone," she said.

I laughed. "Try again," I said.

She tried again. This time, I kissed her back.

*

I woke up Ed before we landed. He looked gray, but he lumbered up to the cockpit and took his seat. Brooks wore half-glasses and was reading, and Tomas and Jenny sat across from each other, playing cards. I had hardly exchanged a word with them, other than to learn that Tomas was a diplomat, and Jenny was from Moldova, like Yuliana. Tomas had a house in Stowe, but said he'd probably stay the night in Montreal, and that we would too. He'd been on the phone looking for a limo that would take us to Vermont, but the State Police were telling people to stay off the roads, and no one he'd called would take the job.

Brooks put down his book. "If I can get a rental car, how do you feel about driving?" He was looking at me.

"I'm out of practice," I said. "We don't get many ice storms in Vero."

"Yuliana could do it, but she's been flying all night," he said. "And I don't drive."

"Really? You drove the Maybach."

"I was breaking the law. I lost my license. Too many DUIs," he said. "That's part of why I finally got sober."

"Oh," I said.

"Vince, can I ask you something personal?"

"Go ahead."

"How much money do you make?"

"It depends," I said. "Maybe forty thousand or so. And I have a pension from the Sheriff's Department."

"I see," he said. "I need a driver. Full-time, not just for tonight."

"Thanks, but I like it in Florida," I said.

"You could drive me there, too. You'd travel with me, and I'm down there most of the time. I'm thinking two hundred thousand."

"Two hundred thousand…a year?"

"I know. It's a lot for a driver. The money's not the issue with me. Your loyalty is, and I think I could trust you."

"It's a nice offer," I said. "But I'd get bored."

"No you wouldn't," he said. "You have a lot of valuable skills. I've done my due diligence. I'd keep you occupied."

"OK," I said. "I have a question for you, and I don't want any bullshit." He flinched. I wondered if anyone had ever addressed him that way. Probably not.

"Go on," he said.

"What you do," I said. "Is it legit?"

He thought for a moment before he responded, smiling slightly as he spoke. "The answer is mostly yes," he said.

"Mostly?"

"Mostly, as in the things in your bag over there. Most of them are legit."

"You looked?" I asked.

"No, I didn't," he said. "I didn't have to."

"I'll think about it," I said. Two hundred grand was nothing to sneeze at. Besides, I actually kind of liked the guy. However, I still wondered why two of his employees had a peep show on their computers that featured a U.S. senator. And what, if anything, that had to do with my father's death from unnatural causes.

Whatever had let the air out of me this afternoon had now blown it back in. Maybe it was Yuliana's kiss, or maybe Brooks' offer, or maybe it was just me being me. I don't like loose ends. My brother was in jail for a crime that I knew he didn't commit, and that was a major loose end. I suddenly had my mojo back, and I was eager to get back on the case.

And I liked getting kissed, although I had no clue what I was going to do about that.

FRIDAY

I lay on a bed at the Hôtel Le St-James, in the old part of the city, lights on, counting the fleur-de-lis on the wallpaper. It made a nice change from counting the water damage stains on the walls of the hotels I usually stayed in, when I was paying. The St-James was an old bank that had been converted into a super-luxury boutique hotel, and was a gem-among-gems in a city that was famous for great places to stay. A limo had whisked us here after a perfunctory customs check. Tomas had flashed his diplomatic passport, and we were suddenly transported through a bureaucratic wormhole into a different universe where there were no lines of sweaty, exhausted travelers with improperly filled-out paperwork and howling babies.

It was one AM and I couldn't sleep. Yuliana had ordered a whole chocolate cake from Gibby's which we'd eaten in Brooks' suite, and I had a slight stomachache. I hoped I wasn't getting what Ed had; he'd gone straight to bed. Brooks had booked a whole floor of the hotel, with a common salon and separate bedrooms for him, Ed, Yuliana, and me. Tomas and Jenny had decided to share a room. I figured they were probably just trying to save some money. Cough, cough.

My stomach tightened even more when I heard a soft knock. I had been thinking about Barbara and whether I should text her, but that would be admitting defeat as whoever texts first, loses. I put on a white terrycloth hotel robe and opened the door.

Yuliana stood at the threshold holding her phone in one hand, dressed in an identical robe, and from the look of it, nothing else.

"Why do you have the light on?"

"I couldn't sleep," I said.

"Have you considered that it might be because you left the light on?"

"I—" I began, but she put a hand across my mouth.

"Don't talk," she said. "Let's leave it on." She put her phone down on a dresser, loosened her robe and let it drop to the floor.

*

I woke up at six AM after a brief but deep sleep. I was alone in the huge bed except for the lingering scent of Yuliana Burleigh's expensive perfume. Just smelling it on the pillow gave me an erotic charge. I wasn't sure what she saw in me, to make her come on to me like that. I wasn't going to complain; our lovemaking had felt like one of those near-death experiences that people describe, complete with the harkening angels and the heavenly shaft of light. But whatever joy I'd had, I knew that my Catholic guilt would cancel it out before you could say hallelujah.

Brooks was in the salon and pointed me to a coffee urn. "Have you thought about my offer?" he asked.

"Not really," I said.

"Too distracted?" He gave me a conspiratorial wink. So much for my clandestine hookup with his personal assistant.

"What's the travel forecast?" I said, changing the subject.

"The Morrisville airport will be open soon," he said. "We can leave in a few hours."

"If it's OK with you, I think I'm going to rent a car and drive," I said. "I have a few stops to make before the wake. Are you still going to be there?"

"I'll be there," he said. "The concierge will get you a car."

"Thanks for everything," I said.

"Don't thank me. Just give my offer some serious thought. You'd be very well paid, very busy, and I'll treat you with respect."

"It's very generous," I said. "I'll let you know."

"At the wake?"

"All right," I said. I didn't appreciate the sales pressure, but I had already made up my mind anyway.

"I'm going to shower," he said, and I was alone in the big room. Brooks' smartphone was on a desk. No one else was awake.

I went back to my room and opened my bag of tricks. Inside was a little black box labeled "Radio Tactics Aceso", a high-tech, privacy-invading gizmo that was spreading like an epidemic around police departments all over the country. A cop could hook one up to your mobile phone and download your contacts, emails, texts, location records, and everything else. Scary. But for me, useful as hell. Everybody kept far too much personal information on their phone, and if the Devil ever got hold of one of these babies, St. Peter would be out of a job.

Fifteen minutes later I was downstairs, waiting for the rental car to arrive. I chatted with the concierge, who told me that the temperature was already back down to zero and the wind was coming up. So much for January Thaw. I asked him where I could find a pastry shop and he directed me down the block; there was one within easy walking distance—that is, if you were a penguin. I got as far as the front door and decided I'd just wait for the car; it wasn't worth freezing to death for a croissant.

*

The landscape between Montreal and the U.S. border is flat farmland dotted with silos, wildly-colored houses, and churches with metalclad steeples. The rain hadn't reached this far north, but as I approached Vermont, the trees began to shine with a thick coating of ice that was now chipping and crackling in the weak sun. The pine trees hung low with broken boughs littering the snow, and the more supple white birches were bent over in graceful arcs with their tops frozen to the ground. The storm's aftermath was as destructive as it was dazzling.

I got a major hassle at the Highgate Springs customs station over my gear. They analyzed and logged each piece, and ran checks on my driver's license, my Florida P.I. license, the rental car, you name it. I would have offered my dental records and my fourth grade report card, but any wiseguy behavior would have earned me a strip search, with the optional free prostate exam. Customs agents have a whole different attitude since 9/11, and no one could blame them. When I was a teenager we'd crossed the border to get Molson Brador beer, and they'd waved us through with a "have a nice day" like your local librarian. Now, they're badasses. Maybe they can keep out the truckloads of missiles and such, but if people really wanted to get into the country, they would find a way—which is part of what makes the United States so great, and so vulnerable.

The next town past Highgate Springs was Swanton. I took the exit and drove my little rental Chevy west through the village on Vermont 78, then wound my way across low-lying farmland and over bridges to North Hero, one of the Champlain Islands. The islands are mostly flat and are dotted with dairy cows, tiny villages, summer cottages, country stores, and state parks. At this time of year they are windswept and desolate, and the hardy full-time residents stay indoors, close to the woodstove.

I had Carla's address programmed into the GPS on my phone. The display led me across the island to the west shore, facing New York State across the now-frozen water. I drove down a long private lane to a two-story brown house with a detached garage and a large boathouse beyond it. There were several other outbuildings, some of which looked like little cabins, and vapor rose from the chimneys so somebody was keeping them heated. A white Subaru was parked in front of the main house under a porte cochere that was supported by stone pillars. It was like a family compound, and I guessed that if it were for sale it would fetch something-point-something. But many of these places never reached the market; they were handed down through the generations until the heirs started squabbling over who paid for what, and only then would they occasionally change ownership.

I saw movement inside the house as I got out of my car, but no one came out to greet me—not in this weather. However sunny and beautiful it was, the mercury still lingered at the bottom of a thermometer by the entrance. I knocked, and Carla opened a heavy wood door.

"Vince?" she said, apparently not sure it was me.

"Carla," I answered, and gave her a kiss on the cheek. She had a bruise on her forehead.

"How'd you get that?"

"Slipped," she said. "Icy walkway. You have a tan."

"I live in Florida."

"Oh. That's right. Sorry, I'm not really awake."

I smelled the faint odor of burning rope. Same old Carla, she'd probably just finished her morning joint.

"Come in," she said. I entered, and took off my shoes. It must have been ninety degrees inside, and a Vermont Castings woodstove was giving off waves of heat from a central, pine-paneled room. I wasn't about to complain.

"Where's Ginny?" Ginny was Carla's partner. I'd met her at my mother's house two Thanksgivings ago, and we hadn't hit it off. She had all the social graces of a feral dog guarding a carcass.

"She's not up yet," she said. "She sleeps in one of the cabins. I snore."

"All the Tanzis do," I said.

"You're here for Dad's thing?"

"Yeah."

"I'm not going."

"I'm not saying you should."

"I don't hate him," she said. "He was trying to be nice to me, after he stopped drinking." She poured a cup of coffee and handed it to me. "Take anything in it?"

"No," I said.

"Dad found me this place. They gave us both jobs, babysitting, and we stay for free."

"Who is they?"

"I'm not supposed to talk about it," she said. "They'd kick us out."

"What do you mean by babysitting?"

"They send some of the girls here. The au pairs, before they place them. We shop for them, feed them and so on. Some of them hardly speak English, and Ginny teaches them. She'd be super mad if she knew I was telling you this, so don't say anything."

Carla absently brushed a strand of hair from her forehead, reveal-ing the bruise. I wondered if she'd actually slipped, or if her friend Ginny was up to her old tricks. She'd gone gray, much more than I had—I still had more pepper than salt. She wore a pink, coffee-stained bathrobe and slippers. She was forty-eight; two years younger than me, but she was beginning to look like a bag lady. I suddenly wished I could wave a wand and get the old pre-drug Carla back. She'd been a vivacious and beautiful teenager, but it was gone now.

"Did you know that someone killed Dad?"

"No."

"They think it was Junie."

"That's impossible," she said.

"It's not impossible, but I don't think he did it."

"Where is he?"

"In jail," I said. "I'm working on it, don't worry."

"That guy," she said. "He had it in for Dad. I picked up a strange vibe. Dad used to stay in one of the cabins sometimes. They made Ginny and me go away, so we'd drive down to Burlington and stay in a hotel. They'd drop off a new girl, or sometimes two."

"What guy?"

"We came home too early one time, and they were still here. The guy was having an argument with Dad, outside. A couple months ago."

"Who is this guy?"

"The man who owns the au pair agency. Mean as a snake. His name's Tomas."

The front door opened, and Ginny appeared, stamping her feet on the hall rug. "What're you doing here?" she growled. Ginny was wispy-blonde, slender and pretty in a girly sort of way. She could have passed for Tinker Bell, with a kidney stone.

"I was in the neighborhood," I said. "Nice place you got here."

"Don't ruin it for us," she said. She turned to my sister. "What did you tell him?"

"Nothing," Carla lied.

"If you fuck this up for us, you're dead," Ginny said to me.

"You're a piece of work, Ginny."

"So are you," she said. "Finish your coffee and go. Carla doesn't need you to screw things up for her."

"Maybe I could ask Carla what she needs."

"Get out of here, Vince. You're trespassing."

I kissed Carla on the cheek and slipped on my shoes. "Thanks for the coffee, sweetie," I said. "I always have a place for you in Vero."

"Thanks, Vin," she said. "Maybe I'll come see you sometime."

"That would be great," I said. I didn't add that if she did visit, she would need to leave her junkyard dog at home.

*

The farther south I got the more trees there were down, and the power crews were everywhere. This is when nobody envied those guys—I couldn't imagine working in the intense cold, cutting up branches and hauling away brush. After the really big ice storms they'd bring crews in from all over the Northeast, and sometimes from the South and Midwest. It could take weeks to repair all of the lines, and meanwhile a lot of people had no water, no heat and a whole fridge full of food that was gradually going bad.

My cellphone buzzed in my pocket as I approached Burlington. I took a quick look. It was a text from Barbara.

I'm pregnant.

I laughed. I pulled over to the breakdown lane and texted back.

How pregnant?

Wicked pregnant.

Who's the father? I sent.

I'm serious, she replied.

Haha, I sent.

The phone rang, and it was her. "I really am serious," she said.

"Come on, you're forty-five."

"I thought I was starting menopause," she said. "I went to the doctor last week. They told me to take a pregnancy test but I didn't bother. I thought it was ridiculous. Then after I left your place yesterday, I got sick. I went out and got a test kit last night, and it was positive."

"Oh my God," I said. About sixteen bazillion different emotions were racing through my head. At the same time I knew that my next words would either preserve or kill off my relationship with Barbara, and I should choose them carefully. I paused and collected myself.

"That's wonderful," I said.

"Really?"

"Yes," I said. "Kind of a surprise though."

"No shit," she said. "I am so relieved. I didn't know how you'd take it. I was thinking you'd completely freak out and you'd want me to get an abortion."

"No," I said, although she was right about me freaking out. The cars were zooming by, and I suddenly knew how a moose must feel when it wanders into traffic.

"You don't have to be involved," she said. "I'm not going to lay that on you."

"Of course I'll be involved," I said. "It's mine, too."

"Oh Vince, I am so, so relieved. Get back here fast, OK?"

"I wish I could, babe," I said. "I have to see this through, though. It's going to be a few days."

"I can wait," she said. "I love you so much, Vince Tanzi."

"So don't I."

"What?"

"That's Vermont for I love you too."

"Oh," she said. "I'll let you go."

"Bye," I said. I put the phone down on the seat and sat there. I was going to be a father. When I was a kid, Harry Houdini, the escape artist, had been my idol. He could get out of anything, and I'd read every single book about him and learned most of his tricks.

I wondered how he'd get out of this one.

*

They wouldn't let me into the Foxtrot Room until visiting hours started at one PM, so I sat in the lobby and played with the Aceso while I waited. I had only tried it once before, on my own phone, and Roberto had been there to help, so I was a little lost. I could tell that a lot of data had been downloaded, but that was it. I called Roberto.

"Where are you?" he said.

"Jail," I said. "Just visiting. I need some help with the laptop. I'm trying to check out some things I downloaded from the new box."

"The Aceso?"

"Yeah."

"Let me remote in," he said. Soon I was looking at a group of folders on my desktop labeled Apps, Mail, Docs, Location and Texts. He had set the whole thing up in less than five minutes. I'd gotten my knitting out of my bag, but I hadn't even finished a row.

"You must be feeling better," I said.

"A little," he said, but his voice still sounded hoarse.

"Lay low," I said. "I'll bring you back some real maple syrup."

"I've never tried it," he said. "Just the Aunt Jemima stuff."

"I'm going to fix that," I said. "Friends don't let friends drink fake syrup."

He gave a weak laugh, and we hung up.

*

A guard opened the door to the Foxtrot Room and waved me in. Junie was already sitting at a table.

"We have to stop meeting like this," I said.

"You'd better get used to it, 'cause I'm fucked this time," he said. "They got me on videotape."

"But you didn't do it."

"No."

"I believe you," I said.

"That makes two of us then," he said. "Even my lawyer thinks I'm guilty."

"Who is he?"

"She," he said. "Jennifer Connelly. Public defender. Fresh out of law school, and she doesn't know squat."

"Great," I said. "So June…what were you doing there? I'll help you, but I need the whole story."

He looked away from me. "I'm still a fucking junkie, Vinny. It's pills this time. Painkillers."

"You and the rest of the world," I said. "I had a problem with them myself, not long ago."

"I got more than a problem. I was spending everything I made on them." He looked to see if the guard was listening, but he'd left the room. "I had a friend inside the hospital. They lock them up, but not that well. You taught me how to get past a lock."

"You were there to steal drugs?"

"Yes," he said. "I had a message on my phone that afternoon. Guy says he's a friend of my friend. He says to get to the hospital at six o'clock and it would be wide open. So I get my scrubs on and go to where I usually go, and there are people everywhere. No way can I break in to the cabinet I usually hit. I waited around for a while, but there were way too many people around. I usually go in later, like ten at night. Whoever called me was full of shit."

"Did you see Dad?"

"I didn't even know he was in there," he said.

"Do you still have that message on your phone?"

"I think so," he said.

"Good," I said. "Don't erase it. I might be able to use that. You may do some time for stealing pills, that's all."

"I can handle that," he said.

"There was skin under Dad's fingernails. They thought it was from the scratches on your arm."

"That was from the guy who pissed me off," he said. "He scratched me good, but I clocked the bastard."

"The DNA test will be done in a few weeks," I said. "You might be in here until then. I'll try to get you bailed out sooner."

"Whatever," he said. "At least I'm clean when I'm on the inside."

"I have to go to the wake," I said.

"Tell Mom I said hi," he said. "You're a good brother, Vin."

"You too, Junie."

*

Jennifer Connelly's office was in the old North End, the section of Burlington where most of her clients probably lived. It used to be an Italian and French Canadian neighborhood, but it had become the catchall for whatever ethnic groups were currently crazy enough to emigrate to the fearsome Vermont climate. Somalis, Cambodians, Haitians—people who had never even seen a picture of snow—were outdoors, scraping it from their walkways and chipping away at the ice.

I knocked on the glass of her door, and she looked up from her desk. It was a one-woman shop, no receptionist. She got up slowly and let me in. A Vermont Law School diploma was hanging on the wall; the ink still looked wet. I shook off the cold, removed my gloves and extended my hand. "Vince Tanzi," I said. "Junie's brother. I'm a private investigator."

"There's not much I can do for him," she said. "He's on the security tape, coming and going."

"He didn't do it, you know," I said. "So let's start with the presumption of innocence, just for the hell of it."

"I didn't say I thought he was guilty," she said. She had very short auburn hair and appeared to be about thirty. She was also pregnant. In fact, she was wicked pregnant, and I wondered if a new soul might burst forth while we were talking.

"He's not guilty," I said. "You'll know that in a few weeks when the DNA comes back."

"You're sure?"

"I'm sure."

"OK," she said. "Then what do you recommend?"

"How do I get the security tapes?"

"I have them on my computer," she said. "I can send you a link. They gave me everything from five PM until eight. You have to log in, but I can give you that too."

"Thanks," I said. "Here's my email." I extended a business card.

She rose, slowly, to take it. I was about to ask her about the baby, but "When are you due?" is potentially the most catastrophic phrase in the English language if you're wrong.

"Good luck," she said, as I left.

*

I had an hour to drive down to Barre, which was more than enough time. The wake started at three, and I'd told my mother I would pick her up on the way. Somehow I'd have to retrieve her car from the Morrisville airport, and turn in the rental car, but that seemed unimportant. I couldn't escape the sobering irony that just as I was about to bury my father I was about to become one myself. It was already changing the way I saw him. Yuliana said that Brooks Burleigh had tried to get him to reach out to me, but he couldn't, and that was because I had long ago put up an impenetrable wall. In the last two days I'd learned that James Tanzi had been trying to turn his life around—a little late, but he'd tried nonetheless.

My child would grow up without a grandfather. Somehow, thirty years of contempt for him was turning, very gradually, into a reluctant form of mourning. Not at all like I'd mourned my wife, but I realized I didn't hate him anymore. Maybe someday I'd even forgive him.

*

My phone buzzed. "We're on the way," Yuliana said.

"You're coming?"

"Yes, if that's all right," she said. "I'm driving your mother's car, and Brooks is in the Escalade. By the way, your gun is under the seat."

"Good," I said. "I wouldn't want to go to a wake without my piece."

She laughed. "So…how's everything?"

"Confusing," I said.

"Because of last night?"

"No, that was…unreal."

"Unreal?"

"Wrong word. It was insanely nice. I can't even think about it, or I'll run into a snowbank."

"I liked it too," she said.

"I have to stop and change at my mother's," I said. "She's riding with me."

"What are you wearing?"

"A dark suit."

"Sexy," she said.

"No flirting," I said. "This is a wake."

"Moldovans drink vodka and flirt at wakes. So watch out."

"Duly noted," I said.

"Are you playing hard to get?"

"Yuliana…I have a lot on my mind."

"Sorry," she said. "That was completely inappropriate."

"I'll see you there, OK?"

"OK," she said, and hung up.

*

A young guy in a wool Chesterfield coat and black gloves opened the door of the tiny rental Chevy and helped my mother out. We were at the funeral home early, and the only other person in the room where the wake would be held was Sheila. She stood next to my father's open casket, and had been crying. Sheila was only a few years older than I was, and used to babysit for us when we were little. She'd been something of a bombshell and had married and divorced twice, then inexplicably fell for my father when he was around sixty. She'd cleaned him up and made him stop drinking, but it didn't last, and they'd never married because he was old-school Catholic. Finally, a few years ago, she'd left him. Apparently that was right before he'd sobered up for good.

"Vince," she said, and gave me a huge hug, leaving me in a cloud of cheap perfume. "Look at him. So handsome. I can't believe it." She started sobbing again. My mother had been talking with the funeral home guys, but she crossed the room to join us.

"Hello, Sheila," she said.

"Hello, Francine. It's odd what brings people together, isn't it?"

"Yes," my mother said. "I was glad that he spent time with you. I always liked you."

"Thank you," Sheila said. "You're a kind woman."

I turned to look at my father, lying in his casket. It was a fancy one made of dark cherry wood with a white velvet lining, and it had a little plate at the bottom corner that said "#8082 Geneva Rose Gold—Made In America". That would be good to know, in case you really liked it and wanted to order one in advance of your own demise. My dad looked like a wax version of himself, with his cheeks powdered and toned with rouge. He still had all his hair and his strong nose. His eyes were closed, but somehow that didn't make him look at peace. It was like he could wake up any moment and whack me.

The last time I'd seen him, I'd whacked him, not the other way around. Actually, Junie did the whacking while I held Dad tight, with his arms behind him. I was a rookie Barre cop, and I'd had a call. It was from a neighbor of my parents, and there was a domestic disturbance in progress. I arrived in less than a minute and burst through the door. My mother had shut herself in the bathroom and was screaming. My father sat in his chair, drinking a beer and watching TV. Junie came in right behind me—it was when he still lived at home, and he'd just gotten off work.

I opened the bathroom door and found my mother, badly beaten, lying on the floor and crying. I radioed for an ambulance and then walked back into the living room. Junie had already started in on him, but my father was tough and he was swinging back with hard punches. I stepped in and grabbed him from behind, then held his arms while Junie landed blows. We left him slumped in front of the television, looking a lot worse than my mother. No charges were ever filed, but a week later the Barre P.D. was abuzz with rumors and my supervisor asked me what my plans were. I caught his drift and relocated to Florida. Junie's hands were so bruised he couldn't play the guitar for months.

The room began to fill with people. Rodney Quesnel had driven down from Burlington, and I greeted him, and then excused myself so I could circulate. Although I knew most of the people, I hadn't seen many of them for years, except for Mrs. Tomaselli, who wore an expansive black dress with a lace veil and looked like she was the grieving widow. She made a beeline as soon as she spotted me and stuck to my side like a conjoined twin.

Yuliana and Brooks entered the room, and the crowd parted before them. Brooks wore a suit that probably cost ten times what mine did, and Yuliana looked like she'd stepped off the cover of the Neiman Marcus catalog in her floor-length black sable coat and leather boots with heels. The nobility had just arrived, and the rest of us, the peasants, went quiet. They proceeded straight to my mother, introduced themselves, and offered their condolences. Yuliana caught my eye, and I felt a jolt of electricity as if I'd stuck my finger in a socket.

"Who are those two?" Mrs. Tomaselli whispered, too close, into my ear.

"Friends of Dad," I said. "He worked for them."

"She's a looker," she said.

Yuliana broke free and came over. I introduced her, and she took Mrs. Tomaselli's hand. Yuliana looked at me. "You have the prettiest date here, Vince," and Mrs. Tomaselli laughed.

"No, your gentleman friend does," Mrs. Tomaselli said, pointing over to Brooks. "You are lovely, dearie."

"He's my boss, not my date, but thank you." Yuliana leaned into my other ear. "Are you holding up OK?"

"Yeah," I said.

"Ready for a drink?"

"God, yes," I said. I'd been laying off since the Rumple Minze episode, but I was ready now.

"Come with me," she said, and she led me toward the door. I put on my coat and we went out into the frigid late afternoon, across the parking lot to a white Cadillac Escalade that was spattered with streaks of road salt. Yuliana pushed a button on her key, which started the engine, and the interior of the SUV lit up like a concert hall. She opened a rear passenger door, and we climbed in.

"Where's the pool table?" I said.

"The seat folds down and makes a bed," she said.

"I see," I said. "This model must be very popular with homeless people."

She laughed and sat next to me on the back seat. She opened a purse and produced an engraved silver flask. "Vodka?" She pronounced it "Wodka".

"*Da*," I said. I took a swig. I don't usually drink vodka, so I had no way to tell whether it was the good stuff or the cheap stuff, but I figured it was top-shelf even if Brooks didn't partake any more.

She took a sip, and we passed it back and forth, not talking, letting the alcohol defrost us. The car's lights had automatically dimmed, and the faint remnants of afternoon sun provided a weak glow to accompany the booze.

"So what's on your mind, Vince? What's the matter?"

"Well, my father's inside, lying in his casket."

"But that's not what it is." She went silent, and waited.

"OK," I said. "I got a call. The woman I see—is pregnant."

"Barbara? She's mid-forties, right?"

"Right."

"Congratulations," she said. She tipped the flask to her lips and drank some more.

"I'm scared shitless," I said.

"Nothing scares you."

"This does," I said.

"You can handle it," she said.

"How do you know that?"

"You're strong. You're smart. And you're kind."

"I don't feel very smart," I said. "I feel like a fool."

"Because you slept with me, then found out your girlfriend was pregnant?"

"Yes. I don't think I've been very honest with you."

"Don't worry about it," she said. "I prefer kindness over honesty. Here, have some more." She extended the flask, and I took a long swig. I finally looked her directly in the eyes. The sable coat covered everything but her face and hands, and I wanted to just open it up, climb in there with her, and sleep until the spring like a couple of hibernating bears.

"Yuliana, you are so gorgeous," I said.

"No flirting at wakes, remember?"

"Oh. Right," I said.

"Are you going to take the job?"

I had made up my mind the night before. I was going to turn him down, despite the money. It didn't smell right, Yuliana had warned me not to take it, and I had a case to work on. Everything about it said no.

"Yes," I said.

"Why?"

"The money," I said. Kids were expensive. Barbara would probably want to stay home, and I'd want to support that decision. Two hundred grand would go a long way, even if I didn't stay for long. Also, I figured I had my best chance of finding out what happened to my father by sticking close to Brooks Burleigh.

"It's very seductive," she said. "You're honest, at least."

"Are you going to stay?"

"I'll come back after my maternity leave," she said. "I'm pregnant."

"What? Really?"

"Yes," she said. "You knocked me up last night."

I looked at her, puzzled, and then smiled when I realized she was teasing.

"Two can play that game," she said.

"Jeezum crow," I said. "You women. I think I'd better just give up and go gay."

"They're worse," she said. We laughed, then drained the rest of the flask and went back inside.

*

Brooks had asked me to start tonight, but I told him no. I wanted a little alone time with my mother, and he understood. I also needed to check out everything on his phone that I'd downloaded, but I didn't mention that. And if I had time, I was going to watch the security tapes from the hospital, which could take hours. What I really wanted to do was to just chill in one of my mother's living room chairs and knit, but I'd had a little too much "wodka", and I didn't want Roberto's hat to come out looking like Mickey Mouse's ears.

My mother was in the kitchen making American chop suey. She used fresh pasta and plenty of garlic, and the whole house filled with the smell. I had the laptop open and started with Brooks' *Mail* folder. It was almost all business-related. Land deals—correspondence between attorneys, regulators, bankers, surveyors, tax accountants, soil engineers, timber buyers, hedge fund investors, foundations, environmental groups, bureaucrats, and politicians. It was dense reading, and after half an hour I knew I wasn't going to find anything juicy in his emails, he was too careful. The *Apps* folder held nothing, unless it had any meaning to Roberto. The *Docs* folder was empty except for a legal agreement pertaining to a timber deal in Chile. I open the *Texts* folder and began to read.

Lots of them were to and from Yuliana. She was very brief with him, and professional. He flirted a little, and teased a lot, but she deflected it. It was largely domestic stuff like what's for dinner, don't forget to pick up some half-and-half, and so on. Yuliana had said that they weren't lovers, but their texts had the casual intimacy of a long-married couple.

There were also quite a few exchanges between Brooks and Tomas, whose cell number I made a note of. I understood very little of it. It wasn't personal correspondence; more like messages between a field commander and a platoon leader—brief, serious, and possibly coded. A lot of it didn't make sense, and I decided that Brooks and Tomas had a language of their own. I was going to have to find out more about Tomas, especially after Carla had mentioned her connection to him. She had described him as a "snake". If she could tolerate someone like Ginny, then Tomas must be some kind of serious badass.

I read the cryptic texts chronologically. The last one was yesterday afternoon, about the time I was having it out with Barbara after our hasty lovemaking.

PRGM HACKD. That was Tomas, who apparently was one of those annoying people who wrote in all caps.

Which one, Brooks had sent back.

VID.

DK wht yr refrng to.

STNDUL

Sht. Source?

TRACING NOW

Let me kno, Brooks wrote.

I read it three times. I'd figured it out the first time, even with the after effects of splitting the flask with Yuliana. I just wanted to make sure it was what I thought it was, because it was bad, and I was scared shitless for the second time in a day.

I dialed Gustavo's cell, and he answered on the first ring.

"It's Vince," I said.

"Hi," he said.

"Listen…do you have anywhere that you could go for the weekend?"

"What do you mean?"

"That video. I think someone traced it. It might have been protected somehow, and someone might be able to find out who got into it."

"Lilian's sister will take us. She's in Miami."

"Tell Roberto to stay off the computer."

"That's not going to be easy," he said.

"Sorry about this," I said.

"Not your fault."

"Yes it is," I said, and we hung up.

OK, now I was pissed. A threat to Roberto, of any kind, was unacceptable. I was glad about one thing though, which was that I'd taken the driving job. I'd have a better chance of figuring out what the fuck was going on, which I needed to do, fast.

SATURDAY

I got up at sunrise, which in late January occurs around seven thirty. My back was sore from the old bunk bed mattress, which should have been thrown out years ago. My childhood bedroom certainly made a change from the previous night's accommodations at the Hôtel Le St-James.

I looked for something to eat in the kitchen and found a box of Shredded Wheat that was relatively fresh. I crumbled up two cakes, poured some milk on them and sat down in front of my laptop.

I had downloaded the security videos while I'd slept. The files were huge, and I figured that my next AT&T data bill would come in somewhere in the neighborhood of a really bad night at the poker table. There were sixteen cameras: two at the main entrance, two at the emergency room drop-off, four in the lobby, two in the parking lots, and six others scattered around various exterior locations. I was able to view all sixteen on the screen at the same time, and I could slow down the frames-per-second rate whenever someone appeared at any of the locations. Almost all the traffic was in and out of the front door, and it didn't take me long to find Junie. He'd gone in alone just before six, and came back out the same way about fifteen minutes later. I could see the pant legs of his hospital scrubs protruding from his cheap parka, and he wore no hat. James Tanzi Junior, master of disguise.

Everyone else looked like visitors. I saw Sheila returning, at six thirty. There were no emergency admissions that I could see. Things got busy at seven PM when the nurses' shifts changed and most of them went out the front door to the parking lot. I ran the tapes right up until they stopped at eight PM. I'd seen nothing that piqued my curiosity—no hit men, just a bunch of good old Vermont folks coming to see their sick relatives on a Sunday evening.

I decided to rewind the tapes and try again. My mother had entered the kitchen and was making coffee, but she could see that I was engrossed, and she left me alone. I was missing something. If this had been a pro job they would have been in and out, quickly. I focused on the front door, trying to see if anyone in the six-to-six-thirty window had both entered and left during that time.

Zero. It took me half an hour to view it three more times, speeded up. Still nothing.

My mother put a cup down in front of me. She watched, over my shoulder.

"Is that the hospital?"

"Yes."

"When was that taken?"

"Sunday night," I said. "Right around when Dad was killed."

"They pick up garbage on Sunday night?" she said. "That's strange." She pointed to one of the video feeds I had ignored. It was a back entrance labeled "KITCHEN". A garbage truck was pulling up to it, and a guy got out of the driver's side and entered the building. I zoomed in.

The camera had been placed up high so that I could only see his profile from above, but it was clear that he was a very large man. He wore a dark wool coat and leather gloves, and was seriously overdressed for his job.

Another man stepped out of the truck from the passenger's side. This one had an overcoat on also, and his face was briefly illuminated as he lit a cigarette and waited for his friend to return. The overhead camera revealed a bald spot on his hatless head. I recognized him, even though the image was grainy.

It was Tomas. Tomas the Snake. My sister Carla was right.

Less than ten minutes later, according to the clock on the security tape, the big dude returned, and they got into the truck and left. Nobody had picked up any garbage.

But they'd done their work.

*

My call to Lieutenant John Pallmeister went to voicemail, but he called back within minutes. "Everything OK?" he asked. "You sounded like something was up."

"You can let Junie go," I said. "I found your killer."

"What?"

"Two guys on the security tapes. One of them is muscle, and I've met the other one."

"Do you have a name?"

"Tomas. I flew up from Florida in Burleigh's private jet with him, Thursday night. I don't know his last name but I'll get it."

"Don't bother," he said. "It's Schultheiss."

"You know him?"

"You'd better check in with Patton," he said. "He's going to go ape shit."

"He's not too fond of me."

"That's an understatement."

"Are you going to spring Junie?"

"I doubt it. We have to wait for the DNA results."

"Look at the tape," I said. "Kitchen door, just after six PM. Two guys in dress overcoats, riding in a garbage truck."

"Good catch, Vince. You want a gig with us?"

"I just took one. I'm Brooks Burleigh's new driver."

*

When I don't know what to do next, I clean my gun. I retrieved it from the floor of my mother's Subaru after leaving it there all night, which was dumb, but I'd been distracted by the whole Roberto thing, and then the security tapes, and oh-by-the-way, my girlfriend was pregnant. I didn't have any gun oil, but there was some 3-In-One in my mother's closet and that would do the job. My Glock is an ugly piece of weaponry, but it has never jammed or given me an ounce of trouble, knock on wood. I gave it a fresh coat of oil and came to a decision. I needed to get some backup.

Roberto's hacking skills were way beyond my comprehension, and in all likelihood he'd be fine. He had explained to me before how he could hide behind strings of untraceable IP addresses through proxy servers and so-on, and anyone looking for him would think he was in China. He said that's what all the kids did, as nobody trusted the Chinese, and when a trace led there, the pursuers threw up their hands. Maybe that was what would happen if Tomas tried to track Roberto's hacking, but maybe not. I don't like having to call the authorities in on a case; it's an invitation to screw things up. I was a cop for twenty-five years, and I know. But it was time. I dialed Robert Patton's number on my cell.

"I don't believe you have the balls to call me," he said.

"Take it easy, Patton, this is important."

"Take it easy?" he said, the pitch of his voice rising. "Three years and a couple million bucks in resources, down the shithole? One guy, one fucking guy shows up uninvited, and the whole fucking investigation gets ruined. You got some big stones calling me, Tanzi."

"I need your help," I said.

"Fuck you," he said. "Call the Red Cross."

"If you're investigating Tomas Schultheiss, I have him on tape. He was an accessory to my father's murder."

"I'm not investigating anyone. The investigation got called off, yesterday afternoon. They said we were using up valuable resources and wasting taxpayer money."

"What? Who said?"

"The fuckheads at Homeland Security. They pulled the plug. They blame the assholes in Congress."

"Is your line recorded?"

"Why?"

"Is it?"

"No," he said.

"I have a video of Dulles Stanton getting laid. Your boss. He doesn't look all that good in his birthday suit."

"Where?"

"On my father's computer. It was buried—a pro encryption job."

"Who's the woman?"

"More like a girl," I said. "Young and beautiful. I think he was set up."

"Honey trap," he said. "Interesting."

"Your investigation got cancelled out of the blue?"

"No warning. We were totally blindsided."

"Maybe there's a connection."

There was a silence. "Maybe you're right," he said.

"I just took a job as Brooks Burleigh's driver."

"OK," he said. I could hear him calming down. "That's good. I can work with that."

"I thought you were shut down," I said. "They'll reassign you, right?"

"I've got four weeks of vacation time that I haven't taken," he said. "Let's get a beer."

"The Skinny Pancake, in Montpelier?"

"That's a hippie joint."

"They serve Heady Topper beer," I said.

"Fine," he said. "I'll wear my Birkenstocks."

I laughed. "It's a little cold for sandals."

"Noon," he said. "If I nail Brooks Burleigh, you'll be out of a job."

"I can take care of myself," I said.

*

Barbara texted me a link, and I went to the URL on my phone. It was an ad for a maple crib and changing table set, posted on the Treasure Coast Craigslist for $200. I laughed and texted back.

Aren't we getting a little ahead of ourslvs?

Those go for $700 in the store, she replied.

Fine with me, I replied.

Going to OBGYN on Monday.

Cool, I sent.

Everything ok?

Dandy. Going 2 be here a while. Don't wait up, I added.

OK. MissU.

XO, I sent.

XO2.

*

Two days after the storm the trees were shedding their icy glaze as the temperature rose. The power crews had worked nonstop, and only a few hundred homes were still in the dark. I switched on the radio on the way to Montpelier in time to hear the weatherman say that the fun wasn't over—it was supposed to warm up even more in the evening, and then snow. Twelve to eighteen inches were possible for the northern half of the state, with more at the higher elevations. That much snow would cripple most parts of the country, but in Vermont they just called it "good sledding" and dug out.

Montpelier has a population of 7,868, making it the smallest of all the state capitals in the United States. Approximately 7,813 of them are java-sipping, granola-crunching, PETA-supporting, Warren Zevon-listening, Pete #2-recycling, Prius-driving hippies, and the other 55 are the minority Republican members of the state legislature who are in town for several months each winter to debate everything from the mundane, like regulating tanning beds, to the cutting-edge, like coming up with a health care system that covered everyone—which actually happened in 2011. The state legislature is a surprisingly nimble and effective group, and it draws its legitimacy and its tone directly from Vermont's town meeting tradition in which local officials can get an earful, directly from the citizens, about the potholes on Route 116 and the skunks under the library porch. Being small has its virtues.

I found a parking spot on Main Street across from the restaurant. Robert Patton rose as I entered the door, and gestured me over. "They have illegals in the kitchen here," he said.

"I thought you were on vacation."

"I'm always working."

"Those are just college kids," I said. "It's cool to look like a migrant worker these days."

A very white, very tall young woman brought us menus. Her sandy-colored hair was tied behind her head, and she wore a tight gray T-shirt that revealed a little silver loop through her belly button. She had what my mother called a "cute figure", meaning that she had large breasts. Patton, in typical cop fashion, spoke directly to her tits.

"Cup of coffee and some eggs, OK sweetheart?"

"We have the Noah's Ark," she said.

"What's that?"

"Two eggs, two slices of bacon, and two frumple cakes," she said. She tugged her shirt down to cover her exposed middle and frowned at Patton.

"Over light on the eggs," Patton said, and handed her the menu with a too-late smile.

"Crêpadilla," I said. "And a coffee." A crêpadilla, according to the menu, was some kind of Mexican crêpe. Everything looked good, and I was thinking I'd better bulk up before I reported back to Florida for daddy-duty.

"Schultheiss is German, but he has a Moldovan passport," he said. "He's with the Ministry of Culture, which is bullshit. He's some kind of spook."

"Have you checked with the CIA?"

"Oh yeah, they know him, but they think he's a joke. They say he's just a wannabe. He's an influence peddler, and he sees himself as a big cheese."

"What's his background?"

"Born in East Germany, back before the Wall came down. Married a Moldovan and relocated there, God-knows why, it's a piss-poor country."

"What are you after him for?"

"People-moving. His reputation is for getting anyone in or out of the country, unnoticed by us. We've never caught him doing it, but we suspect he's behind literally dozens of cases. If you do something bad and want to go to Brazil, he'll get you out."

"Where does the sex tape fit into this?"

"That's Burleigh. Have you ever wondered how he made all his money?"

"Not really," I said.

"He can take a land deal that's dead in the water, and suddenly, once he controls it, everything starts going right. Whether it's a permit problem, zoning, environmental whackos, whatever. He makes a killing every time."

"So he's a good businessman."

"No, he's an extortionist. I don't have a speck of proof. But whenever I've talked to one the victims, they're scared shitless. That's what your video is—it's a honey trap. They can just imagine themselves up there doing an Elliot Spitzer in front of the press, crying wife at their side, explaining how they were fucking some twenty-year old."

Two women at the table next to us turned and glowered. "Sorry, ladies," Patton said. They tut-tutted him, and resumed their lunch. "I've picked apart some of his land deals, found out who the road-block was, and then I visit them, usually at home. I don't have to say much, and they turn white as a fucking sheet. I offer all kinds of immunity, whatever, but they don't want to risk it. I've met Burleigh, and the funny thing is he strikes you as a genuinely nice guy. But he's a tough son-of-a-bitch."

The two ladies called a waitress over and loudly asked to be moved. That was fine with me, now we could talk. "You want to see it? I have the computer in this bag."

"Right here in the restaurant?"

"Everybody around us has left," I said.

"What the hell," he said.

I booted up the computer and opened the file. The video started and Patton watched, his face not moving, until I noticed a flicker in his eyes.

"You can close it," he said. "That's Stanton all right. And I know the girl. We followed her when she was up here. She worked for Burleigh for a while until she fell in love with your brother. Melissa-something. A Slav, like Burleigh's pilot."

"What? Junie?"

"Yeah. She stayed at his place a lot, and they were tight for most of last year, then she hasn't been seen. At least not by us."

"Junie with a girlfriend? He's a junkie."

"Even junkies need some pussy now and then," Patton said, right as the waitress returned with our coffees. She put his down and immediately knocked it over. The hot liquid raced across the table, onto his lap.

"Fuck!" he yelled, jumping to his feet.

"Oh, sorry sir," she said, but she couldn't help smiling.

Patton cleaned himself off with a napkin and sat back down. "This is the computer from your father's apartment?"

"Yes," I said.

"We checked it, and we didn't find that."

"It was heavily encrypted," I said.

"How do you know that? You a computer geek?"

"No," I said. "I have a kid who helps me. And I think that when he found it, Mr. Schultheiss got tipped off. I'm worried about the kid. He might need protection."

"I have people who will help us," he said. "Lots of people were pissed when this thing got shut down."

"I'm thinking of reporting for my new job today," I said.

"Good," he said. "We've never had anyone on the inside."

"I'll work with you," I said. "But I want a favor."

"Fucking A," he said. "OK, what is it?"

"Get Junie out."

"Done," he said.

"Impressive," I said.

"The judge is my cousin," he said. "I get him cigars from Cuba."

"Everyone's got a hustle," I said, and he smiled.

*

I called Yuliana and told her I was on the way. She said Brooks was out cross-country skiing, and she'd show me around. There was a room for me down in the bunker for now, but they would eventually find me a pied-à-terre somewhere, as Brooks was in Vermont every few weeks, and I'd need my own digs.

The clouds were gathering as I drove up the Mountain Road, with no sign of snow, yet. My little Chevy had tired-looking all-season tires on it and would be useless if it got truly nasty out. I chugged up Edson Hill Road and stopped at the gate, which magically opened for me. Yuliana must have been waiting.

I parked in the dooryard, near a barn—suitably out of the way, as I wouldn't want to clutter the picturesque setting with my ratty rental car. Yuliana met me at the door.

"Welcome back," she said, and gave me a peck on the cheek. Her manner was cool, not passionate, which was good—I needed some breathing room. At the same time, I was blown away once again by her beauty. She wore a white wool sweater with a cowl neck and black stretch pants—the Bond Girl look. She was way too perfect.

"You have a little piece of something, right here." I showed my teeth and pointed with a finger.

"Where?" She looked horrified.

"Over one," I said. "That's it."

She removed her finger from her mouth. "I don't see anything."

"I was teasing," I said. "You're flawless."

"Ohh," she said. "I'll make you pay for that." We laughed, and she took my coat.

"The weather's about to turn bad."

"So I heard," she said. "We may need to fly out Sunday night. I hope it's done snowing by then."

"Where to?"

"Washington," she said. "You're coming. He'll want you to drive while he's there. He has some meetings on Monday."

"I don't know my way around D.C.," I said.

"I've rented a Town Car," she said. "It will have navigation."

"OK," I said. "If you can fly us, I guess I can drive us around."

"We're staying at the Willard. Have you been there?"

"Not unless it's a Best Western," I said.

She laughed. "It's nice. They have really big beds."

"Hey, no flirting with the help," I said. Maybe I was wrong about her interest cooling.

"The wake's over," she said. "You're my prisoner now."

I picked up my bag. "Show me to my cell," I said. "I have some knitting to attend to."

"Right this way," she said, and led me downstairs.

*

Yuliana left me alone, and I unpacked and started to settle in. I was making progress on Roberto's hat. With everything that was going on I should have been padding around the house in a black turtleneck, opening drawers and planting listening bugs, but I decided I'd just be a loyal employee for a while, and would let things come to me. Junie was getting out of jail soon, my father was already dead, and there was no great rush. I was even starting to relax about Roberto—maybe I'd panicked a little on that one. I put down my knitting and texted him, just to check in.

You in Miami?

Yah, he sent back, immediately. His phone was hard-wired to his body.

You sound bored.

Just sick.

Sorry. I freaked. Saw a txt from somebody about the vid being hacked into.

NBD.

Can they trace you?

Not a chance.

You sure?

100%, he replied.

Cocky little bastard, I sent.

LOL.

Tell your folks I calmed down, I wrote. *Prob OK to go home. I hv a friend who can provide security.*

Kinda like it here, he sent. *Thong season on South Beach.*

Haha, I replied, *Don't burn yr eyeballs out.*

Haha bye.

Roberto was pushing fifteen, and it appeared that the testosterone was already flowing. I would have envied him, but fifteen is when boys are at their clumsiest, socially, and the girls basically run the show. Come to think of it, that also applies to being twenty. And thirty. And fifty. And...

*

Brooks Burleigh knocked on the door of my cell and I let him in.

"Vince," he said. "I am so glad you're here. Welcome." He gave me a hearty, varsity-squad handshake.

"Thanks," I said.

His cheeks were bright pink from being outside, which set off his bushy, silver eyebrows and thick mane. He was a very handsome man, and he radiated confidence. "It's so nice out there."

"Looks like snow coming," I said.

"Yes," he said. "Hey. We have time for a quick loop before dark. Would you like to ski?"

"Cross-country?"

"Yes," he said. "I've had trails put in. What size are your feet?"

"Thirteen," I said.

"Same as my son. He has banana-boats, like yours. Come on up-stairs and I'll kit you out."

"Never tried it," I said.

"You'll love it." He led me to the second floor of the house where the bedrooms were. We rummaged through one of his kid's drawers and found a set of long johns, socks, gloves and a skin-tight, orange-striped spandex outfit that made me look like I'd been run over by one of those trucks that painted the lines on a highway. Thank God nobody I knew could see me now.

We went outside and Brooks helped me into my skis. They were the backcountry style; not as skinny as true cross-country skis, and he assured me that they were a little more stable. "This way," he said, as he cruised down a slope behind the house. I followed, but I felt like I was riding a skateboard down a roller coaster. I'd skied the usual way when I was a kid in Barre, but the narrow backcountry skis were nothing like the normal kind and they wobbled like toothpicks as I prepared to crash into the nearest tree and end up in a #8082 Geneva Rose Gold box like my father.

We were picking up speed as we coasted down the hill. I tried my best to control the wobble, and I wondered if the best way to ap-proach this sport might be by watching it on TV. Brooks turned and yelled. "You have to jump here!"

The trail had widened, and I watched him lift up, thirty yards ahead of me, and fly through the air. Before I could do anything, I came to a slight lip, and without thinking about it my body reacted and I was airborne. Below me was a frozen stream that had cut through the built-up snow. It was a good ten feet down, but I cleared it and landed on the other side. I was so scared and thrilled at the same time that I whooped with joy, and promptly crashed in a jumble of skis, poles, and snow.

Brooks herringboned his way back up the slope to help me. "You're doing great!"

"This is fucking nuts," I said.

"Really," he said. "You're a natural."

"Next time we're in Florida, I'm going to take you dike-jumping."

"What's that?"

"I have a friend with an airboat," I said. "I won't spoil the sur-prise. But you'd better be wearing your titanium jockstrap."

He laughed and skied off. The terrain flattened and we came to an open, snow-covered field with Mount Mansfield in the backdrop. The clouds obscured the peak, and you could see the new snow approaching across the valley. It was like a painting, except that no artist dead or alive could capture it. Not even an IMAX movie could make you see and feel what you do when your heart is pounding, your skin stings from the cold, and you are way out in the wilderness with the deer, the bears, and the gods of winter.

Brooks stopped in the middle of the snowy field and waited for me to catch up. "Amazing, isn't it?"

"Yes," I said, getting my breath.

"I hear you're going to be a father," he said. "Does that affect your willingness to take this job?"

"To be honest, I don't know."

"I'd understand if you couldn't do it," he said. "Fatherhood is a calling."

"I'm here for now," I said. "I hope that's OK."

"It is," he said. "I really like you, Vince, and I'll take whatever you can give."

"Thanks."

"We're going to D.C. on Sunday."

"Yuliana told me," I said. "That's cool."

"I could just hire a limousine," he said. "But I like to be able to hold a phone conversation and know that whatever I say, it's not going to be repeated."

"You got it," I lied.

"People can so easily misinterpret things."

"Right."

"I'm going to hold you to that, Vince," he said. He looked me straight in the eye. It was the equivalent of a polygraph, and I put on my cop face.

"I understand," I said.

He skied off, and I followed. I began to get the hang of the skis, and tried to mimic the way he set his poles and then did a long glide forward with alternating legs. It took me a while, but I got the rhythm. A few snowflakes started to fall out of the increasingly damp air. By the time we huffed and puffed our way back up the long hill to the house there was an inch of powder on the ground, and the flakes stuck to our clothes and faces, making us look like a couple of snowy owls.

"Dinner is at seven," Brooks said, as we put away our skis and stomped the snow off our feet in his hallway. "You don't have to dress."

"I'll just come like this," I said, as Yuliana rounded the corner. She stifled a laugh when she got a look at my Day-Glo outfit.

"No you won't," she said. "He hired a driver, not David Bowie."

*

I lay on my bed and thought about Barbara. For some reason I was avoiding the huge bomb she'd dropped, via text, the previous morning. I hadn't even told her about taking the job. Given what Robert Patton had told me, it might not matter, as I could be unemployed again in a couple of days. My new boss had a highly illegal game going, if, like Patton said, he'd done some arm-twisting to get his deals done. Arm-twisting, as in dangling some juicy female bait in front of influential, middle-aged johns, and then getting it on camera. I wondered how many other tapes like Dulles Stanton's were out there, and how many guys were lying awake at night, hoping that Burleigh wouldn't ruin them with a few keystrokes on a computer and an email to the *National Enquirer*.

My bedroom had a small casement window at one end that was at ground level, and the snow had already piled up high enough to cover it. We were going to get whomped; the farm was at enough elevation to collect even more snow than what would fall in the valleys. I used to get excited about a big snowfall when I was a little kid. It meant that school would be closed, and we could play outside the whole day, making snow forts, staging battles with snowballs, and then coming into the house, soaking wet, for hot chocolate with marshmallows. The older you get, the more the snow becomes a pain in the ass, but there's still that feeling of anticipation as you watch it pile up.

Yuliana came to collect me. I'd put on a fresh shirt, but I was running out of clothes fast. She had changed again, and she wore a powder-blue knit dress that hugged her figure and would make any sensible man want to gnaw off his wedding ring and drop to his knees. We went upstairs, and she introduced me to Kermit, who was holding forth in the kitchen, and his wife Eunice, who was putting out the place settings. They lived in town, she said, and came in to cook whenever Brooks had company. I looked into the living room and saw Tomas, puffing on a smelly, black-tobacco cigarette with Jenny at his side. They sat on a plush couch, and I noticed that Jenny's duties as an au pair included absentmindedly rubbing her hand up and down his pant leg. He smiled, and gave me a little wave. We were old pals now. I waved back.

"Got some nice leg-a-lamb in the oven," Kermit said to me. "They raise 'em over ta Charlotte." He pronounced it Sha-lott, which is how the locals did.

"Smells great," I said. "You ever cook it outside?"

"Yes sir, Mister Dooley," he said. "That's the real way. Butterflied lamb over lump charcoal. Did one last summah, and the god-danged dog pulled it right off the fire when I wasn't payin' attention. Sixty bucks worth of lamb, gone in a jiffy."

"Too bad," I said. Kermit looked like he'd weigh in at around 120, and Eunice was about double that. You see them all over the state—skinny guys in tractor hats with a big wad of keys on their belts, pushing the shopping cart for momma, who was so big she made a beep-beep noise when she backed up. Ah, love.

My phone buzzed. It was a text from Junie. I had no idea he even knew how to do that.

I'm out, it said. *Thanks.*

I crossed the kitchen, over to a window where I could watch the snow falling outside. *No prob*, I wrote back.

Going to the bar to celebrate. Wanna come?

I'm at Burleighs, I texted. *Took a job driving.*

CALL ME, he wrote.

Can't, I sent back. *Supper on table.*

GET OUT OF THERE NOW.

Will call U later, I wrote, and I put the phone away.

*

Kermit's lamb was as good as you could get in any restaurant in the world. He used an ancho chile marinade according to Eunice, who listed the ingredients for me in a squeaky-doll voice. She said he'd found the recipe in *Bon Appétit*, which she pronounced Bone Appetite. There would be no leftovers, and I would need to be careful not to back up after the huge portion I'd had or I'd be beep-beeping myself.

Jenny sat at my left side, with Yuliana at my right. The au pair barely spoke, and when I tried to draw her into conversation, Tomas would run interference. He was pretty good at it, so I started to make it into a game. I'd thrust, he'd parry, and after a while he realized what I was doing and laughed.

"You're quite the inquisitor, Vince," he said.

"I'm just a curious guy," I said.

"Next time we meet I'll have Jenny bring her résumé."

"That would be a time-saver," I said, and he smiled. He had a small mouth, and his slightly-crooked teeth were stained with tobacco.

"Too bad about your father," he said. "And your brother. I'm sure he's innocent."

"He's out already," I said. "They suspect someone else." I dangled that out there to see if I'd get a reaction. Nothing. Tomas had as good of a cop-face as I did—not even an eyelash moved.

"Well, that's welcome news," he said. "How do you know this?"

"They picked up two people on the surveillance tape. Professionals. The state cops are looking for them now."

"Any idea who they are?" Man, he was good. But I was holding the cards, and I could either lay down some aces or raise the pot. I decided to see if I could make him squirm.

"I forgot to ask," I said. "But the lieutenant I spoke with said he thought they'd pick them up within a few hours."

This time I got a reaction. Fear. I couldn't exactly see it, but I could smell it. It was as strong as the lingering smell of the marinade on the lamb bones that covered my plate. I almost expected him to push his chair back from the table and bolt for the exit, but he was way too cool for that. Instead, we finished our entrée and chatted over coffee and Eunice's maple bread pudding, which was so sweet and rich that I could already hear the scales groaning in the morning as the needle hit the danger zone.

"Everyone's tired from a long day," Brooks announced. He was right; I was ready for bed. "Tomas, you're staying over, yes?"

"No, thank you," Tomas said. "We have to be up early."

"You can't go out in this weather," Yuliana said.

"We must, I'm afraid," he replied. "Thank you for a lovely evening."

"Why not have Vince drive you in the Escalade?" Brooks said.

"We'll be fine," he said. "The Audi has all-wheel drive."

"Give me your keys," I said. "I'll get the snow off and start it for you."

"Thank you," he said, and he handed them to me.

"I'll just grab my coat," I said, and I bounded downstairs. It was snowing like hell now, and I'd need my coat, hat, and gloves. I also needed something else—something from my little bag of tricks. It was a battery-powered GPS tracker, with magnets that would hold it onto the underside of his Audi. The unit would send me a signal which I could track from a program that Roberto had installed on my computer. I had put a scare into Tomas Schultheiss, my fencing partner, and if he was going to run, I wanted to know where.

*

I woke up at midnight, thinking about Junie. I'd forgotten all about calling him back. I checked my phone in the dark, to see if he had called me. Nothing. Whatever it was he was so worried about could wait. Maybe he was hitting the bars and was still awake—but I nixed the idea of calling him. I was groggy with the effects of the huge meal, and snowstorms make me extra-sleepy, as if Nature was covering me up in a soft white blanket. I'd try him in the morning.

SUNDAY

I was up before the sun, and the first order of business was to boot up the laptop and see where Tomas' Audi was. He'd wasted no time—the car was a long way from his house in Stowe. It was in North Hero, and I recognized the address: Carla's. It must have been quite a drive in the storm; I'd apparently provided him some motivation. I inwardly laughed my Evil Laugh.

Yuliana was in the kitchen, still in her robe, making coffee.

"What time do we leave for D.C.?" I asked.

"Late afternoon. Assuming they have the runway plowed."

I looked out at the landscape. The farm was buried under at least a foot of fluffy white stuff. It was powdery and it hadn't stuck to the trees, which was fortunate because it would have significantly added to the damage from the ice storm. The dawn cast a pink glow, and a gusty wind was blowing the new snow into drifts against the outbuildings. Someone had already plowed the driveway, and I guessed that the roads would be open. Vermonters don't let snow stay on the road for more than a few hours; it would be an affront to civilization.

"Looks like the driving will be OK," I said.

"The snow stopped a few hours ago," she said. "It's supposed to be sunny and cold." She put a mug down in front of me. "Missed you last night."

She was dangling the prize again. I wasn't quite sure how to react. I laughed my non-evil laugh. "As if we could have done anything, with all that food in us."

"I felt like I'd swallowed a whole sheep," she said.

"Somehow I have to get my rental car back to Montreal," I said. "Does Brooks have anything going on today?"

"Not that I know of," she said. "He was going to stay in and plan for his meetings."

"Maybe I'll drive it up there this morning," I said. *With a side trip to North Hero.*

"I could change the flight plan and pick you up in Montreal," she said.

"I don't want to inconvenience you," I said. "I can get a bus back."

"It's twenty minutes from here in the jet. I'll hardly even get to altitude."

"If it's OK with Brooks," I said.

"He does what I tell him," she said, and smiled. "And you will too, eventually."

I laughed, but I already knew her well enough to know that she wasn't kidding.

*

I inched down the hill in the Chevy. After a few miles I got my snow-driving mojo back and was negotiating the curves without slipping, even with the car's balding tires. You have to just pretend you're on skates, not in a car, and you'll be all right as long as you don't make any jerky movements and leave plenty of room to stop.

The interstate was almost clear of cars, and I was able to travel at about fifty miles an hour—slow, but I'd get there. I was on the island in a little over an hour, and used my phone's GPS to lead me back to Carla's place. I got out at the end of their driveway to take a look. There was one set of tire tracks in, superimposed over an older set from a different car that had gone out. I could tell by the direction of the tread pattern. Normally I can't track for shit, and it always makes me laugh in the old movies when the Indian sees a broken twig and says, "He went that-a-way." But fresh snow makes tracking easy. I called Carla from my cell.

"Hello?"

"It's Vince."

"Oh, hi," she said.

"Where are you?"

"Burlington," she said. "That guy made us leave last night, in the middle of the storm."

"Does he own the place?"

"It's some kind of non-profit. They give money to marine research, and they do this international exchange program thing. They get girls from Europe and place them with families. Like a work-study deal."

"Who else comes there?"

"Just him, and Mr. Burleigh sometimes. Dad's boss." I heard her talking to someone in the background.

"What are you doing calling her?" It was Ginny, who had snatched the phone.

"Is that any of your business?" I was getting my fill of Ginny.

"Where are you?"

"North Hero," I said.

"For God's sake, get the hell out of there," she screamed. I held the phone away from my ear.

"I have a question for you," I said. There was no response, so I continued. "What do you call it when a man mistreats a woman? Yells at her, smacks her around, you know."

"That's abuse," she said.

"Right," I said. "Felony domestic abuse. And it doesn't have to be a man."

"Yes it does."

"No it doesn't. You can ask some of the people I've put in jail. They're not all men."

"What are you implying?"

"What I'm implying is that I'd like you to give the fucking phone back to my sister before I report you."

There was a silence. "Vinny?" It was Carla again.

"It's OK, Carla."

"You're just making things worse," she said.

"If I am, I'm sorry," I said. "But if she's abusing you, you should think about your situation, and call me if you need anything."

"OK," she said, and we hung up.

*

There was no sign of life from the house or any of the outbuildings. The Audi's tracks led to a garage, and I parked the Chevy in front of it and tried the door. It was unlocked, and I raised it overhead, enough to see that the sleek German car was inside. A single set of footprints led from the garage to the large boathouse that I'd seen earlier, down the slope to where the water—now ice—met the edge of the shore. The footprints ended at a door on the side of the boathouse. It was secured by a keypad lock—my nemesis, as none of my lock-picking tools could crack it, and I'd left them in Stowe anyway. The boathouse exterior had no windows and looked fairly new and solidly built. I couldn't detect any heat coming from within it, or any signs of life. Whoever had gone in hadn't come out, and if they were still in there they must be damn cold by now. Strange.

I walked around to the lakeshore side and checked out the huge overhead door that was positioned to let a boat in or out. It met the surface of the ice with a firm seal, but I noticed some slight melting around the edge. Some people paid to have heating installed inside their boathouses, along the waterline, so that they didn't have to have their vessels removed in the winter to prevent them from being encased (and ruined) by the powerful ice. It was an expensive type of boat storage, but if Brooks and Tomas controlled this place there would be money to burn.

I was puzzled by the fact that no tracks led out. Whoever had gone in must still be in there? No. It was clear that the building was empty. I tried to come up with some kind of theory, but it was escaping me. Tomas had done a Houdini, and I was pissed off, but I was also impressed. I needed to get on the road to Montreal, but I'd have to revisit this little non-profit Shangri-la, and the next time I'd bring my more persuasive door-opening tools, like a big-ass chainsaw.

*

Yuliana waved at me from the cockpit window as I approached the plane. There wasn't as much snow in Montreal, but the wind had whipped up to a fury and I sprinted across the freshly plowed taxiway. The interior of the big Bombardier was cozy and warm. I felt like I'd re-entered the womb, and I began to wonder if that wasn't the primal, driving desire behind all human activity.

She was alone in the plane—no Ed. "You can fly these things so-lo?"

"There's so much technology onboard you hardly need a pilot," she said.

She had yet another Bond Girl outfit on, this time a uniform like Ed's, but with strategic pleats and tucks in the right places. One of these days I wanted to see her in a dirty T-shirt and sweatpants. Forget it—she'd probably still look great.

"Back to Morrisville," she said. "Do you want to try a takeoff?"

"No way," I said. "Those dials look like a video game from hell."

She laughed, and busied herself with her preflight routine. I took the seat next to her and tried to stay out of her way. The big engines roared as she taxied out to a runway, accelerated, and pulled the jet up at a steep angle into the crisp winter sky, leaving the Canadian snow-fields behind.

"In the event of a water landing, I'll be your flotation device," she said. Her dark hair was tied behind her back, but it still glowed from the light of the LEDs.

"Let's not try that," I said. "The water isn't too welcoming right now."

"I have a confession," she said.

"What?"

"It's not what you want to hear."

"Try me."

"I like you."

"Thank you."

"I'm not complimenting you, I'm confessing," she said.

"Is there something wrong with liking me?"

"Yes," she said. "I'm a little terrified about the whole thing."

"That makes two of us."

"You are going to be a father. I know that you're off-limits."

"I was reading about it while I waited for you," I said. "In the airport. It says on the net that there are all kinds of risks at Barbara's age."

"What's she like?"

"She's gutsy," I said. "She had kind of a rough start in life, but now she's studying to be a nurse."

"Commendable," she said. "People can reinvent themselves in this country, which is a great privilege. Second chances are a gift."

I thought about what she'd said while she adjusted dials and spoke into her headset microphone. She was talking to air traffic control, and she sounded cool and professional.

"Like I said, I can get you out," I said, and she took the headset off.

"What do you know about your father and me?"

"Not much," I said. "Except that you both have the same video of Dulles Stanton on your computers."

She stiffened in the seat. "Not possible," she said.

"You thought you'd wiped it?"

"I was the first person in his apartment," she said. "I'm nothing if not thorough."

"Hard drives don't lie."

She banked the plane into a slow turn toward the south. The sky was an azure blue, dotted with clouds that were outlined by a creamsicle sunset.

"I don't know what to say," she said.

"You already said it. Second chances are a gift."

*

I had a number of phone calls to make, so I stayed in the jet while Yuliana went into the Morrisville air facility to stretch her legs and wait for Brooks. The first was to Carla. I realized that she was on the other side of a number of loose ends. Rodney Quesnel had told me that she was the "trustee", and was responsible for paying the premiums on my father's insurance policy. I didn't understand that, and I'd missed the opportunity to ask her when Ginny had shooed me off. I also wanted to know what was in the boathouse. Her phone went to voicemail, despite several tries. I left a brief message.

Next was Junie, who was not answering either. Probably still sleeping it off—he was a night owl. I was extremely curious about his girlfriend who had co-starred in the Dulles Stanton video. I was glad that he had had a romance going, even if it was over. I had the feeling that Junie was deep into whatever was going on, and he was holding back. If I couldn't reach him on the phone, I'd go see him, which was probably a better way to get him to open up anyway. Face-to-face is always the most effective way to get to the truth.

I got Patton on the first ring. "I'm just coming out of the shower," he said.

"Thanks for the visual," I said. "I'll have nightmares for weeks."

"Sorry about that," he laughed.

"Can you track Tomas Schultheiss' cell?"

"You have the number?"

"Yeah." I gave it to him. "He may be far away. I spooked him a little."

"How?"

"I told him the cops had ID'd two guys on the security video, and they were about to pick them up."

"Subtle," he said. "We'll probably never see him again."

"That solves your problem," I said. "But not mine. I want his ass in jail."

"Pallmeister's on it. They saw what you saw on the tapes, and they may be able to ID the garbage truck."

"Good."

"They re-interviewed all the people at the hospital, but nobody saw the big guy in the dark coat."

"That figures," I said.

"Yeah. Oh, and I pulled some strings and got the DNA results, about half an hour ago."

"And?"

"No match," he said. "If it was the big guy, he's not in the database."

"At least it's not Junie," I said.

"Yeah," he said. "Pallmeister said to say he's sorry for the fuck-up."

I saw Yuliana approaching the plane with Ed and Brooks in tow. They were carrying several pieces of the type of luggage that I could only afford if I took out a second mortgage.

"Gotta go," I said. "I'm flying to our nation's capital."

*

Brooks was too busy to talk. He'd opened his briefcase upon entering the plane and was studying some papers. He'd smiled and greeted me, but his body language said to leave him alone. I worked on Roberto's hat for a while, and then got out my phone to check in with Barbara.

So how much do kids cost anyway? I sent.

$500K incldg college, per Newsweek, she replied. *Better start saving.*

Up here they give you five cents for returning your beer bottles.

That's not what I'd call a financial plan, she wrote.

You doing OK?

Nervous.

About what?

Everything. You.

Me?

Miss Capri Pants, she sent.

No worries, I wrote.

She's way too hot.

Hadn't noticed.

Yah, right.

I love you Barbara.

Oh shit, she wrote back, after a long pause.

You OK?

You made me start crying.

Sorry.

Don't be, she wrote. *Just come home.*

ASAP, I sent. *It's getting complicated.*

Be careful.

XO, I sent back.

*

Yuliana and Ed prepared to land us at Ronald Reagan, which I took as a sign of Brooks' clout. Ed had told me during a pee break that most of the private flights to D.C. went to Dulles, twenty-five miles out of the city, while Reagan was right near the downtown area, and that's where we were touching down. I wondered if some poor FAA guy had been caught on a video with his pants around his ankles.

I'd squeezed into the plane's bathroom and changed into the same suit I had worn for my father's wake. I'd recycled the white shirt, but if this gig lasted for any amount of time, I would need to check in at a men's shop. We were escorted to an area where the rental cars were kept and a valet handed me the keys to a black limo. I loaded the bags, set the GPS, and headed into town, toward the Willard.

The hotel was a Washington landmark, and like the rest of the city, polished marble was everywhere. I wondered if the stone had come from Vermont, and if the great-grandfathers of the kids I'd grown up with had quarried it, shaped it, and sent it down by rail. I offloaded my boss and his entourage, and was directed to the garage by a doorman. Several other chauffeurs were gathered at one end, smoking cigarettes and gabbing. I grabbed my own bag, locked the car, and headed for the lobby.

A bellhop took my suitcase and escorted me to the room. Brooks had reserved four of them, and if mine was any indication, his must have looked like the interior of Versailles. I was starting to get used to this jet-set thing. The Best Western would never look the same.

Yuliana texted me.

R U hungry?

Yes.

Oysters?

Hell yes.

Be ready in 5 mins, she wrote.

*

Ten minutes later there was a knock on my door. She was dressed for the city: black pants, a silver-grey blouse, and a medium-weight black leather jacket. "You clean up good," I told her.

"You look nice, too," she said. Her voice was quiet, and oddly shy.

"Are you all right?"

"Tired from the flying," she said. "It wears me out. You have to really concentrate."

"Let's go," I said, and we took the elevator down to the lobby, not talking. I was a little tired too, but I figured that some oysters would perk me up.

*

The Oceanaire was two blocks away on F Street. It was an expense-account kind of place with well-dressed patrons who were picking at seafood and drinking. Washington is foreign turf to me, but from what I've been told, most of the important business is done in restaurants like this.

A waiter seated us and gave us menus. I ordered a dozen Wellfleets, my favorites, and Yuliana chose the Malpeques from Prince Edward Island. She picked the wine, a New Zealand chardonnay that I'd never heard of.

"How did you know I love oysters?"

"I did my homework on you, remember?"

"So what other dark secrets do you know about me?"

"That's all," she said.

"Come on."

She looked away, at the other diners. "I recognize that guy," she said. "Over there. He's on CNN, right?"

"Yuliana, are you dodging my question?"

"All right. I know a lot. Brooks had me do the research, before he made you the offer."

"Like what?"

"I know about your wife," she said. "Glory. I read about it in the *Press Journal* archives. Your father had told me about it, too. He was so sad for you."

I felt a stab, as if somebody had inserted a dull knife and tried to shuck me open, like the oysters we were about to have. "It's been over a year now," I said. "It seems like last week."

"Do you miss her?"

"Of course," I said.

"Are you still...how do I say this?"

"Mourning? Yes."

"No," she said. "The word I was searching for was healing."

The waiter arrived and poured us each a glass of wine. I took a sip, which turned into a gulp. I was thirsty. "Yes," I said. "I'm still healing."

"Is that why you're not sure about Barbara?"

"How do you know that? That didn't come up in your background check."

"I'm a woman, Vince."

"I've noticed," I said.

She took a tiny sip from her glass.

"Let's change the subject," I said.

"OK," she said.

"Do you want out?"

She looked at me. "Of us?"

"No," I said. "Of Brooks. The second chance."

She took another sip of the wine and looked back into her glass as she spoke. "Your father was going to blow the whistle," she said. "I was the one who gave him the video. In fact, I gave him the computer. He didn't have a complete understanding of what they were really doing, but when he did, he came to me. We were going to try to get out."

"But they killed him first."

"Yes," she said. "And I'm responsible."

"No you're not," I said. Her eyes were welling up with tears. I was getting pretty good at making women cry.

"It's even worse now," she said. "He's dead, and I'm falling in love with his son."

"Yuliana—"

"Please don't say anything."

"Shit," I said.

"Especially that," she said.

"That's not what I meant," I said.

We were quiet for a while. Our oysters arrived, and I devoured one while she picked at hers with a little two-tined spear.

"I'm a lost cause, Vince. I don't know why you'd even bother."

"I have this damsel-in-distress thing," I said. "It can get me into trouble."

She pierced one of her Malpeques and dangled it near her lips, without putting it in her mouth. That was, without question, the sexiest thing that a woman could ever do in the presence of a man who loved oysters.

"So," she said, "you're saying you want to save me? Then what happens? You get me pregnant like Barbara, and then you dump me?"

"Jesus Christ."

She saw my face drop. "Vince. That was awful. I'm so sorry."

"No, I deserved it," I said. "I'm in an unfamiliar place. Meeting you has kind of moved the furniture around."

"So you have feelings for me?"

"That depends on what you mean by feelings," I said. "I'm intimidated. I'm in awe. I'm completely turned on. And I feel like I'll go straight to hell if I ever touch you again."

"You're such a Catholic," she said.

I laughed. "You did your homework, all right. You know me way too well."

"No, I don't," she said. "No one really knows anyone else, and they know even less about themselves."

"Damn right," I said.

"I'm not going to knock on your door tonight," she said. "If you want me, you have to come to mine." She took a big gulp of her wine.

"Finish your oysters," I said, and I waved at the waiter for the bill.

*

I didn't have to knock on her door because we went directly to her room. It was larger than mine and was littered with her clothes. "Sorry about the mess," she said. "I was trying on outfits."

I unbuttoned her blouse and pushed it back off her shoulders. She wore a patterned bra, and I reached behind her and undid it with only a little fumbling. She unbuttoned my twice-worn shirt and stroked the hair on my chest. I put my fingertips on her breasts. They were small and delicate, and her erect nipples pointed at me like a firing squad.

"I'm built like a boy," she said. "Your tits are bigger than mine."

"You are very beautiful, Yuliana," I said. "You know you are. No more apologizing." I reached for the switch on the wall, and stopped.

"Do you want me to leave the light on again?"

"No," she said. "Not this time."

"Tell me what you want," I said.

"I want you," she said, and I made the room go dark.

*

It wasn't about being Catholic. I hadn't been to church in years except for weddings and funerals. It was about being a human being. I had made a decision, and no visits to the confessional, no penance, nothing would get me off the hook. Somebody was about to get hurt. It could be Yuliana, or Barbara, or me, or all three of us, and the responsibility would be mine.

I held Yuliana in my arms while she slept. Her skin was still moist from our lovemaking, and just touching her made me want her all over again.

Harry Houdini, where the hell are you when I need you?

MONDAY

Brooks' seven AM meeting was cancelled and he was pissed. I was driving him to the Rayburn House, and he had just received a call from Yuliana. I only heard his side of the conversation, but apparently a staffer had called her and said that his boss was not feeling well and had to cancel. He sputtered in the back seat while I watched him in the rearview mirror.

"Set the navigation system for Leesburg," he said. "Here's the address." He passed his phone to me and I punched the information into the limo's GPS. We were going to Octavio Muñoz's house. Muñoz was a congressman from Florida's 18th Congressional district, which covered Miami, the Keys, and a chunk of the Everglades.

I didn't know much about Muñoz except that he was a freshman congressman who played polo and had married rich. His wife's family was Cuban, and they owned a big piece of southern Florida, especially around Coral Gables where you only needed to own a small piece of it to be wealthy. Even with the real estate crash the big land-owning families had hardly felt the pinch.

We took the Dulles Toll Road out of town. The traffic, despite the early hour, was a nightmare. The road coming in was a parking lot, and even going away from town it was worse than anything I'd seen in other cities. The D.C. area had been a sleepy tidal backwater until air conditioning had become ubiquitous and changed everything. Now the city and its environs hummed year-round, and in the last thirty years the population had exploded, while the infrastructure had not kept up. I knew a retiree in Vero who had commuted ten miles to the Pentagon every morning and had to leave for work at five AM, otherwise it would take hours.

Brooks made calls while I drove. It was all business, and all about deals. He had an interesting style on the phone—he knew when to shut up. He listened for long periods, and then he would respond with a few carefully chosen words. Good listeners are the best negotiators.

He put down his phone and asked me how far away we were.

"The nav system says twenty more minutes, but it'll be longer unless this traffic thins out."

"I hate to waste the goddamn day in the car."

"It's nice out, at least," I said. It was well above freezing and there was no snow, just brown grass and bare trees. We finally got off the Toll Road and into horse country, with mini-estates dotting the low hills, and miles of whitewashed fence. The GPS led me around Leesburg and south down Highway 15, then onto a back road which turned to gravel. The houses were set farther apart here, and it looked like the equivalent of Brooks' neighborhood in Stowe. The Blue Ridge Mountains spread out in the background, and if they weren't as dramatic as the backdrop of Mount Mansfield, they had a subtle beauty all their own.

"Mind if I ask you something?"

"What?" he said.

"My father had an insurance policy," I said.

"I can't discuss that right now," he said. He picked up his phone. "Octavio? It's Brooks Burleigh. Listen, I'm on the way to your house. I'll be there in a few minutes." He was quiet for a little while. "No, it can't wait. Waiting would be very risky for you."

He put the phone down and caught my eyes in the mirror. "I'll have Yuliana wire your first month's pay to your bank today. Sixteen thousand and change. Let's round it off to twenty. Call it a signing bonus."

"Thanks," I said. And I got the message. No more questions. I was his now, bought and paid for.

*

I waited in the car while he went into the house, carrying only a slim tablet computer. The place was a McMansion, oversized, with zero personality. It was probably built in the 1990's real estate boom, and it had all the hallmarks of new wealth—a pool, a horse barn, a multi-bay garage for the toys, and at least 10,000 square feet of house. I bet they used less than a thousand of it to actually live in.

I have the cop habit of counting the security cameras and checking out the alarm system whenever I approach a place. This one was fully wired. It figured—a U.S. congressman was a big deal, and even if I could not see any evidence of bodyguard-types, they probably weren't far away.

I had no idea how long he would be in there, but I thought I'd make some calls. The first one was to Robert Patton. I'd had an idea when Brooks had handed me his phone, earlier.

"Patton,"

"Tanzi."

"What's up?"

"Do you know what a Radio Tactics Aceso is?"

"We just ordered ten more of them last week."

"I have some files to send you. Give me your email address. Your personal one."

He gave it to me. "What do you have?"

"Brooks Burleigh's contacts, emails, and texts."

"Damn," he said. "You looking for a job?"

"I have one, for the time being. Pallmeister asked me the same thing."

"We have better benefits," he said.

"I'll get the files to you later," I said. "I don't have my laptop. I'm working."

"Watch out," he said. "If they find out what you're doing, you're in trouble."

"I know," I said. The proof of that was lying in a funeral home basement waiting for the ground to thaw.

The phone had buzzed twice while I'd had it to my ear, talking to Patton. One was a text from Yuliana. Right below it was a text from Barbara. Even my phone was trying to mess with me. I answered Barbara's first.

Where R U? she'd sent.

Virginia, I replied.

What? On the way home?

Not yet. Business here.

Srsly?

I took a job with that guy. The one with the jet.

U took a JOB? When were U going 2 tell me this??

Not permanent.

Call me.

Can't talk now, I sent.

She didn't send an answer, but the lack of one conveyed her message.

Yuliana had simply written: *I'm sore.*

Me too, I sent back.

I'm in the Jacuzzi, she sent.

Don't drop the phone.

Haha, she sent back. *Where R U?*

I shivered. I had just received the exact same text from Barbara.

Leesburg, I wrote. *Some rich guy's house.*

When do U get back?

Don't know.

When U do, come straight to my rm.

Ur nt my boss.

Yes I am LOL.

Then that's harassment LOL.

Maybe U shld take a vacation. Fly off w me 4 a few days.

I've been wrkng less than 2 days.

I want U, she wrote.

Hold that thought, I sent back, and I put the phone away. Brooks was coming out.

*

"Coming out" was something of an understatement. It was more like he had been fired from a cannon. The door had burst open, and Brooks was sprinting across the gravel driveway toward me. Not far behind him was a middle-aged man in an untucked flannel shirt, with thick white hair like Brooks' and a deep tan. It was Octavio Muñoz, and he was gaining on Brooks. The tablet computer was nowhere to be seen.

Brooks opened the limo door and jumped in. "Go!" he yelled, and I stepped on the gas, leaving the enraged congressman in the driveway, screaming obscenities that you wouldn't find in a Spanish-English dictionary. "Fucking madman," Brooks said, as he wiped his forehead with a napkin from the limo's bar.

I tried not to smile, and I knew better than to speak unless spoken to. But I was quietly laughing my ass off. Brooks had tried to squeeze the guy, obviously, and the congressman had not taken it well. I couldn't help myself—I had to ask him something.

"Did you leave your computer there, sir?" I heard myself calling him sir, and realized that the dynamic between us had changed.

"I meant to leave it," he said. He appeared to be calming down, and was getting his breath back. "That didn't go so well," he said, and I couldn't help but laugh out loud.

"Sorry," I said.

"He'll come around," he said. "They always do."

"He just needs to find a way to save face," I agreed.

Brooks looked at my eyes in the mirror. "Exactly," he said. "You know something about negotiating."

"I was a cop. We negotiated with people who had guns."

"I want you to start carrying your gun, Vince. Things have been a little out of control lately."

"Are you in danger?"

"Not specifically," he said, and he took out his phone to signal that our conversation was done. "Back to the hotel," he said, before dialing.

*

We got back to D.C. at noon. Brooks told me we had some downtime, that the plane wouldn't leave until four. I thought about Yuliana's directive to come straight to her room, but I decided I needed a little downtime to myself. I took off the suit and my now three-day-old shirt and lay on the bed in my undershorts. It was time to change not only my outfit but also my persona, from newly-hired lackey back to Vince Tanzi, Private Eye. The combination of my new job and my philandering (and the ensuing guilt-fest) had left me little time to concentrate on the reason that I had gone to Vermont in the first place—my father was dead, and my siblings were somehow involved in whatever enterprise had been responsible for his death. I had tried to reach both Junie and Carla numerous times by cell and text, without success. That was beginning to worry me. The first thing I would do when we touched back down in Vermont would be to go find them.

It was also time to connect with Barbara. Her words had been as clear as if they'd been tattooed on my chest. *If you want to fuck her, go ahead, just don't lie about it.* I had, against my better judgment, fucked Yuliana. That certainly wasn't the nicest way to put it, but it had happened, and it had happened the second time with the full knowledge that Barbara was pregnant. I could just see the therapist saying "And how does that make you feel?" And I'd say it makes me feel like a worthless scumbag, and I deserve to be eating out of dumpsters, not spearing Wellfleet oysters and sipping chardonnay with Ms. James Bond.

I was about to make it even worse. I was going to lie.

Barbara answered on the first ring. "Hi," she said.

"Hi," I said back. There was a silence, and all I heard was the humming of the minibar fridge in my room.

"Why didn't you say you were taking a job?"

"Most of the time I'll be in Vero," I said. "He's paying me two hundred thousand a year."

"What? Why?"

"He has it to spend. He said he pays people a lot to keep them from talking about his business."

"He must have something to hide."

"He does."

"Why are you doing this, Vince? We can live on what we have."

"It's not the money," I said. "At first I thought that if he was legit, the money might be great. Stash it away for the baby's college fund."

"Oh," she said. "That's sweet."

"He's not clean," I said. "I saw him in action today. And I'm ninety percent sure that he or one of his friends is responsible for my dad being murdered."

"Oh my God," she said.

"Yeah."

"Is your friend involved?"

"Who?"

"You know. The babe."

"Yes and no," I said. "She wants out."

"And so you're riding to the rescue."

"She and my father tried to get out, and that's what got him killed."

"Oh God," she said. "I'm sorry. I'm jumping to conclusions that I shouldn't. I…"

"You what?"

"I just…get nervous about you and her," she said.

"It's under control," I said.

Every time you lie an angel cries, as the nuns at school used to say.

*

I had tried Junie and Carla several more times with no results, and I'd finally turned the phone off, as the battery was low and I'd left my charger in the plane. I had *General Hospital* on, which was one of the last remaining soap operas—all but a handful had folded. It made me wonder what was wrong with the world. Losing the soaps was a loss of innocence, even though their plot lines were about nothing resembling innocence. Glory used to tape *All My Children*, and we'd watch it at night, in bed. The characters became our friends. They had left without even saying goodbye.

I pondered my own personal soap opera, and decided I was making too big a deal out of it. I'd fucked up before and lived. And it wasn't as if I was trying to hurt Barbara, nor was I just looking for a friend-with-benefits in Yuliana. My feelings for her ran deeper than that, otherwise I wouldn't be in such a predicament. But I needed to give it a rest.

I had a Perrier open and was halfway through a tin of Pringles from the minibar. I'd worked on my knitting project for a few minutes, but my eyes had closed, and I was drifting in and out of sleep while the TV show played. It was a perfect way to spend an afternoon, and for the first time in days I was completely relaxed.

There was a knock at my door. I got up and put a robe on. It was Yuliana.

She entered the room and closed the door behind her. "Where have you been?"

"Right here," I said. "I dozed off."

"Your brother is in the hospital," she said. "He's in rough shape."

"What happened?"

"Somebody beat him up," she said. "They smashed his hands, with a hammer. Brooks told me."

"Oh my God," I said. "How did Brooks find out?"

"He didn't say," she said. "But he's panicking. We couldn't reach you."

"I turned the phone off."

"Don't do that again," she said, and she gave me a hard look. "I didn't even think to try your room."

"Jesus Christ," I said. I looked at my hands, and wondered what my brother was going through.

"The plane's ready," she said. "Brooks wanted to get you back as soon as he could."

"Thank you," I said. "I'll be ready in five and will get the car."

"It's out front," she said, and she went out the door.

*

Ed had already taken a cab to Ronald Reagan, and the plane was waiting for us with the engines running. I helped load the bags and was the last aboard. Yuliana took the copilot seat, and Brooks and I took the Barcaloungers in the main cabin. He hadn't said anything on the way over except that he was horrified and would do whatever he could to help. Here he was being a super-nice guy again, as if the hard-ass extortionist from our morning sojourn was someone else. I wondered which one was the real Brooks.

I decided, since he was being the Nice Brooks, that I would do some digging. I felt sick to my stomach about Junie, but if I was going to help my family, I needed to dig.

"Do you have time for a question?"

"OK," he said. The jet was now moving, and I reckoned we'd be taking off soon.

"The insurance policy," I said. "Who funded it?"

He took a while, as if he was deciding whether to answer. Like I said, smart negotiators say as little as they can get away with. "There's a foundation," he said. "A tax thing."

"The foundation paid?"

"Yes," he said. "It's quite complicated."

"Intentionally?"

He looked at me. "In a way," he said. "Money is fluid, like water. It has to find a route to the sea."

"I doubt that the IRS would appreciate such a poetic description," I said.

Brooks smiled. "You're too smart to be my driver," he said.

"How deep into all this are you?"

The jet's engines began to whine as we prepared to take off. "Deep," he said.

"Too deep?"

"Meaning what?" he asked.

"You said things were a little out of control, and that I should start carrying."

"Just a precaution," he said.

"Brooks, you can fire me for asking this, but I need to know something. My brother is in the hospital. Are you connected to that?"

"No," he said.

"But you know who did it."

"Yes," he said. "And I will help you. Just be patient."

"Frankly, I'm not feeling too fucking patient right now," I said.

"I'm sorry, Vince," he said. "I'll fix it."

"We'll both fix it," I said, and I got my knitting out of my bag. I was ending the conversation this time. Two days of being somebody's lapdog was about as long as I could stand.

*

Yuliana lent me her car and rode home with Brooks. It was a sleek little BMW, like Glory's convertible, but it had a hardtop and all-wheel drive, which was fortunate as there was a thin layer of snow on the road from flurries that came and went in the dark Vermont evening. I made it to Fletcher Allen hospital in Burlington in less than an hour.

Junie's room was as dark as the night outside, and he was surrounded by pulsating machines that looked no less complicated than the cockpit of Brooks' jet. I approached his bed and looked at him. He was sound asleep, with an IV in his arm that was probably loaded with pain drugs. My sad, profane, genius, addict brother had finally latched onto a free supply of his favorite junk. His hands were wrapped in surgical gauntlets that were crossed over his chest. I could only imagine the damage within.

The nurse who had directed me to his room came in and stood by my side. She was quiet, and we watched him breathe. "I saw him at the Flynn Theatre, back in the '90s," she said. "I never knew a guitar could sound like that."

"Nobody did," I said.

"Did you talk to the doctor?" she asked.

"Not yet," I said.

"There are more than thirty fractures," she said. "They operated on him all day. But they're worried about infection, and they may have to amputate."

"OK," I said. "Is he going to wake up?"

"We have him on a heavy dose of meds," she said. "Probably not tonight."

"I'm going to sleep here, if that's all right."

"That chair folds out," she said. "I'll bring you some bedding."

She left, and I looked at my brother. He was snoring, like the Tanzis do. I put aside my thoughts about my fatherhood, or my infidelity, or my infatuation, or the whole soap opera. I had only one thing in mind now. I was going to find whoever did this, and he would regret being born.

*

I lay under a blanket on the chair-bed, listening to the gurgling of Junie's IV and wondering if I was too stupid to be doing what I did for a living. I hadn't even seen my father's killers on the security tapes until my 74-year-old mother pointed them out. And I'd totally missed the connection about the phone call that Junie had received, telling him to go to the hospital, and that there would be an opportunity to steal some drugs. As soon as he'd arrived he had realized that whoever had called him was full of shit, as he'd put it.

It was a setup, pure and simple. The person who'd called him had intended him to be seen on the security cameras. They'd lured him there, right at the same time that someone had suffocated my dad. They probably knew about Junie's temper, and his animosity toward James Tanzi Senior. A smart person would have figured this out days ago.

The other aspect of it was that Junie would have gone to jail, were it not for the DNA evidence, and that would have put him out of the way for years, or maybe life. I wondered if the frame job was intended to neutralize both of them at once. Junie knew things, and someone was covering their tracks. It was surprising that they hadn't killed him, like they had my father. Maybe I'd figure that one out in a few weeks.

I wondered what else I was missing.

TUESDAY

I used the hospital room bath to shave and clean up. It was a Florida-like temperature on Junie's floor so I dressed in a fresh T-shirt from my bag. I called Pallmeister's cell, figuring he was an early riser like most cops.

"Is your brother OK?" he asked.

"No," I said. "It's bad."

"Is he able to talk?"

"He's still asleep. They have him loaded with pain meds."

"Vince, I don't know what to say."

"We're going to get the motherfucker, that's what you can say."

"We're all over it. He was attacked in his apartment. Do you already know all this?"

"None of it. I flew in last night."

"We think it happened late Saturday night. He was in there for a long time before he was found. Someone heard him screaming on Sunday, around noon. He couldn't pick up the phone, or open the door."

I shuddered, thinking about it. "Any evidence? Leads?"

"Not much. A bloody hammer, but no prints. No forced entry. He might have known whoever did it."

"I'll be talking to him as soon as he wakes up."

"Call me if you find out, and we'll collar the guy."

"I'm not going to give you the chance," I said.

"Don't do that, Vince. We'll put him away, don't worry."

"Right," I said. "And whoever did it will be out in three months for good behavior."

"Please, Vince."

"You won't even know about it, John," I said. "I'll clean up my mess when I'm done."

I hung up, just as Junie's eyelids opened.

*

"Melissa?"

"No. It's Vince," I said. Melissa was the name that Robert Patton had mentioned. Junie's ex-girlfriend.

"Vince," he said. "I'm fucked."

"You're going to be OK," I said.

"No, I'm not."

"Do you want me to find Melissa?"

His eyes were just slits, but they suddenly opened. "You know Melissa?"

"You just thought I was her. Your ex."

"Oh fuck. Fuck, fuck, fuck."

"Who did this to you?"

"Did what?" he was slurring his words and spoke in a near-whisper. I guessed he'd be back asleep in a short time.

"Beat you up."

"Fucking guy," he said.

"What guy?"

"Can't tell you," he said. "He said he'd break my hands."

I realized he was totally delirious. I tried another way in.

"Is Melissa in danger?"

"Uhhhh," he said.

"What?"

"They won't kill her."

"Junie—"

"Bro," he said, "Can't talk. She got them to let me—Melissa."

"Say that again?"

"Drink of water," he said.

"Sorry," I said. I held a cup with a straw to his mouth, and he sipped at it for a full minute.

"I'm beginning to fuckin' wake up," he said. "What were we talking about?"

"The guy who smashed your hands," I said. "I need his name."

"They did it to shut me up," he said. "And it worked. I'm not going to tell you a thing."

"Why didn't they kill you? Like Dad?"

"I can't talk, Vince."

"Did Melissa stop them?"

"What the fuck? How do you know her name?"

"I know a lot, Junie. I'm going to get you some protection. And then I'm going after them."

"They'll kill you," he said.

"No, they won't. Who did this?"

"They're scared," he said. "They're closing down the whole thing. I was a loose end."

"What about Carla?" I said. "Is she a loose end?"

"Carla doesn't know shit."

"She must know something. Ginny was telling her not to talk to me."

"Fucking Ginny," he said. "Talk about a bitch on wheels. They wouldn't go after Carla."

"How do you know that?"

He took a long time to answer. "Shit. You better check on Carla," he said. "They're ruthless."

"Junie," I said. "Who did this?"

Junie's eyes were glassy from the early hour and the drugs, but he finally looked directly at me. "It was Ginny that got me to open the door. The big guy had the hammer."

"Ginny's the one who had you beat up?"

"They only let me live because of Melissa. I had a long time to think about it while I lay on the floor in my apartment. If they killed me and Melissa found out, she would bail. If they lose her, they're fucked."

"What were you doing for them?"

"Talked enough," he said. "Leave it alone, Vin. I told you too much already. I'm dead."

"No, you're not," I said. "I'm going to have a cop outside this door."

"Find Carla," he said, and his head dropped back. He was asleep.

*

I called the hospital administration office but they were "in a meeting". I doubted they knew shit about protecting patients anyway. After all, my own father had been killed in a hospital a little more than a week ago. I dialed Pallmeister again.

"Hello Vince," he said.

"I need your help," I said. "I want a cop outside his door. They may want to finish the job."

"Done. But I want something in return."

"What?"

"You don't kill anyone until you talk to me."

"I'll call you when I find him," I said. "But I don't guarantee that he'll have much of a pulse."

"You're no use to anyone in jail," he said.

*

A young state trooper arrived about ten minutes after I'd hung up with John Pallmeister. He looked about the age of Roberto, but with a little more facial hair, and he had the whole state cop outfit, complete with the shaved head. "Trooper Desmuelles," he said. "Lieutenant Pallmeister said to take special care of your brother. I'll honor that."

"How long have you been on the force?"

"This is my third month," he said. "I was Trooper of the Month in December. Sixty-two moving violations and I broke up two bar fights."

"Very impressive, trooper," I said. "Now let me clue you in on this situation. Some very bad guys may want to come kill my brother. If they do, just draw and shoot them."

"That's not what we're supposed to do," he said. "We have a protocol."

"If somebody shows up here and you don't like the looks of him, draw your fucking weapon," I said. "Trust your instincts."

He looked at me, and then looked at Junie, lying on the hospital bed with his arms wrapped and crossed over his chest like King Tut.

"I understand," he said.

*

I badly needed to find Carla. I tried her cell one more time, and it went to voicemail one more time. She was in the hermit crab mode. I only hoped that it was because she'd had the good sense to know that she was in danger and had crawled into a shell somewhere.

I decided to drive down to my mother's in Barre before driving up to North Hero. Even she could be a target. The roads were now dry, and the BMW cruised effortlessly at 100 mph. If the cops stopped me, I'd call in a favor from Pallmeister. I was in no mood to waste time. I made it in less than half an hour, scaring a few truckers along the way, and pulled into her driveway.

My mother was in the shower, and I waited in her kitchen until she came out, smelling of Yardley soap, which is what she and my father had both always used.

"Vinny? Is everything OK?"

"No, Mom," I said. "Junie's in the hospital in Burlington. Somebody smashed his hands."

"Oh no."

"I want you to move in with Mrs. Tomaselli for a few days," I said. "I'll let you know when it's OK to come back here."

"My plants will die."

"Did you hear what I said? You're in danger, Mom, and your son is in a hospital bed."

"I heard you," she said. "I'm sorry. Things don't always sink in at my age."

"We can take the plants," I said. "Pack up some clothes."

"What's happening, Vinny?"

"Somebody is messing with our family," I said. "I'll take care of it."

"They are going to regret it," she said, her expression changing.

"Damn right," I said.

*

Sometimes when I'm driving I don't play the radio, I don't talk on the phone, and the passing scenery hardly registers. The road is a place where I can go and just Zen out, like when I'm knitting, or walking behind the lawn mower. I start thinking about all kinds of things—some of them bad, like people I've hurt or disappointed; some of them good, like the way Yuliana giggled softly in her sleep after we'd made love at the Willard; some totally random, like what I would spend the money on if I won the Megabucks; and some downright evil, like what I would do to Junie's attacker when I caught him.

It was about an hour and a half drive to North Hero, and the time passed quickly with my musings. The sun doesn't get very high in January, and it was behind me most of the way, making me squint whenever I caught it in the side-view mirror. The temperature had warmed up again, to just above the freezing mark. In a few weeks the weather would shift to cold nights and warmer days, and the maple sap would begin to run. I thought about Roberto, and the syrup I'd promised him. I hoped he was OK, and I reminded myself to text him and check in when I wasn't driving.

*

The white Subaru was parked in the driveway but no one answered my knock, and no smoke rose from the chimney. I checked some of the outbuildings and cabins, but no tracks led in or out. The girls were gone—maybe they were in a hotel in Burlington. Carla had said they did that when Tomas periodically kicked them out. I hoped they weren't together, because I now knew that Ginny was deeply involved—to the point of helping them destroy Junie's hands and livelihood. It was painful to think about his future, but my mental anguish was nothing like the intense physical pain that he was going to be enduring, once the drugs were taken away. Fingers are full of nerve endings, and if you break them it can be excruciating. Thank God for the drugs, for once.

Tomas' Audi was not in the garage where I'd seen it the last time. I realized that a whole day had passed since I'd checked the tracker, and wondered again how I could be so sloppy. Perhaps I took after my mother—there was too much going on, and things didn't always register. I'd check it now. The laptop was in my car, and I booted up the tracking program.

I waited, but nothing happened. Something was wrong with the transmitter—either it had malfunctioned, or Tomas had discovered it. It definitely wasn't the batteries because they were fresh. I'd learned that lesson a while back.

There were several sets of tracks leading down the slope to the boathouse. Something had been dragged there. As I got closer to the boathouse door I noticed several tiny dark spots on the snow that could have been snow fleas, which you sometimes see jumping across the surface on the warmer days. I bent down to take a closer look.

It was dried blood. Little specks, everywhere.

There was no chainsaw in any of the outbuildings, but there was a maul, which is like a combination of an axe and a sledge hammer. It's a convenient tool for splitting logs—simpler than driving metal wedges into the wood with a sledge. I took one swing, and the maul pulverized the keypad lock on the boathouse door. On the second swing the door opened.

At first I thought somebody had dropped their parka into the water. The inside of the boathouse was about twenty feet wide by twenty-five long; there was enough room for two big boats, but there were none inside. Instead, I was looking at a pool of unfrozen water, thawed by electric heating elements that were submerged along the side of the wooden docks. At the far corner a light blue parka floated at the surface, and when I went to the end of the dock to retrieve it, I realized that there was a body inside. I grabbed the floating corpse under the arms and lifted it onto the dock, careful not to fall into the icy water myself.

Underneath a wet tangle of blonde hair was the bloated, blue face of Ginny, Carla's lover.

*

A resident trooper on North Hero was the first on the scene. He'd already been briefed by Pallmeister: he knew my name, and he understood that I was neither a suspect nor dumb enough to foul up the crime scene. I'd left Ginny's body on the dock and had gone back out to the driveway, stepping in my own tracks. Within thirty minutes a forensic team arrived from St. Albans, and Pallmeister, who had been at Junie's apartment in Burlington, got to the scene a half hour after they did. Pretty soon the tracks to and from the boathouse looked like there had been a stampede. So much for my careful preservation.

Pallmeister was in the boathouse for a while, and I sat in my car and listened to the radio. Vermont Public Radio has a second, all-classical station, and I was listening to Brahms' Hungarian Dance Number 5, which reminded me of the background music for the Looney Tunes cartoons that I had watched as a kid. That had been the extent of my classical music education.

The lieutenant emerged from the boathouse and walked up to the BMW. I turned down the music and lowered the window.

"So, who is she?"

"She was my sister's girlfriend," I said.

"Where's your sister?"

"I wish I knew."

"What do you know about this?"

"I came here to look for them. Junie told me that Ginny—your floater—was the one who talked him into opening his door, then some goon did the dirty work. I don't know the guy, but I suspect he's the same one who was with Tomas Schultheiss on the hospital security video. The garbage truck driver."

"Did she live here?" he asked.

"Yes," I said. "House-sitting, or something like that. My sister said it's owned by some kind of non-profit and they do marine research. They also use it as a residence for the girls in the au pair program."

"What au pair program?"

"Schultheiss controls it. I don't know much about it except I'm pretty sure it's dirty."

"What does that mean?"

"I think they're hookers. Honey-trap girls. I think they're placed with political VIP's, and then they run an extortion racket."

"Is Patton in the loop?"

"Sort of," I said. "I was just about to call him."

"You can go if you need to."

"Thanks," I said. "If I think of anything I've forgotten, I'll call you."

"What else did you get from Junie?"

"He's delirious," I said. "And scared. They threatened to finish him off if he talks."

"OK. Where are you going now?"

"I'm going to look for Carla. If you could put out a search, I'd appreciate it. I'll email you a photo."

"You got it," he said, and I rolled up my window and drove back down the long driveway to the road.

*

The phone rang in my pocket just as I was crossing over the Winooski River, approaching Burlington. "Vince?"

"Yes?"

"Rod Quesnel. You'd better come here."

"Your office?"

"My house. Robinson Parkway, on the hill. Third on the left."

"I'm maybe ten minutes from there."

"The sooner the better," he said, and hung up.

*

My phone's GPS led me to Rodney Quesnel's house. It was a 1940s brick colonial in a neighborhood near the University of Vermont, and the driveways were populated with Audis and Saabs, most of them encrusted in overlapping layers of dirty-white frosting from road salt. If you lived in Vermont, you pretty much gave up washing your car until April, then you obsessed about it for a few months, then you gave it up again in November. Rod saw me pull in, and he opened the door.

"You all right, Vince?" he said. He could read my anxiety, and I felt his.

"Not so good. Junie's hurt, and I'm trying to locate Carla."

"That's why I called," he said. "She's upstairs. Scared out of her wits. She said she hitchhiked here from North Hero."

"Seriously?"

"That's what she said. She showed up at the office looking like a rag doll. I brought her here, gave her some tea, and put her to bed."

"Thank you. Who knows she's here?"

"Only my girl at the office."

"Keep it quiet," I said. "Can she stay with you for a while?"

"Long as she likes."

"I'm going upstairs," I said. I found Carla lying on her side in a four-poster bed, covered up to her shoulders with a patchwork quilt.

"Carla," I said, and she opened her eyes but didn't raise her head.

"I ran," she said. "I didn't know what else to do."

"From who?"

"Günter," she said. "Tomas' man. We never saw him unless something bad was happening."

I sat down next to her on the bed and put my hand on her shoulder. "Carla—"

"I already know she's dead."

"You saw her?"

"No. I ran as soon as he came into the house. I could tell what was going to happen. Ginny screamed, and I was in the back. I don't think he saw me; I got out the back door and ran for the road. I didn't even have a coat on."

"How did you get here?"

"A guy in a van picked me up. He saw me running, and he stopped."

"Jesus," I said.

"Somebody was looking out for me," she said. "The guy in the van actually tried to hit on me. He wanted to take me to a hotel. I said no, and then he apologized and got real embarrassed about it."

"He took you to Rodney's?"

"He said he was going to Burlington. He had to park in the Cherry Street garage. I walked around for a while and ended up at Rod's office."

"Do you know Günter's last name?"

"Schramm," she said. "I had to wire money to him once."

"Very big guy?"

"Yes. He has a really short haircut, and a big nose that has a lot of veins on it. He speaks with an accent."

"Carla, I want you to stay here for a few days. No phone calls, no computer. Don't take any calls from Tomas, or Brooks, or anyone else. Just me, OK?"

"OK," she said.

"Are you going to be all right?"

"I guess," she said. She turned her head and looked at the ceiling. "Did you see her?"

"Yes," I said. "She was in the boathouse."

"I shouldn't have run away," she said. "I loved her."

"Get some rest," I said. "I'll be back."

*

I called both Pallmeister and Patton from the hospital to give them Günter Schramm's name and description. They said they'd get back to me, and I put the phone away and worked on Roberto's hat while I watched Junie sleep. Dr. Kinney, the hand surgeon, had just left. She had told me that the infection was under control now, and there would be no amputation, but that Junie wouldn't be able to even feed himself for a long time. I asked if they had any psychological counselors, and she said yes, she'd arrange some time with one when he was in better shape. She said that within a day or so they'd move him into a skilled nursing facility; she just wanted to make sure the infection was gone, and they also had to wean him off the IV drugs. I told her about his history with that, and she thanked me, and made some notes.

If it wasn't for the calming effect of the knitting, I think I might have started picking up furniture and throwing it against the walls. A quiet rage had come over me. My father—my ex-alcoholic, ex-wife-beating father—had somehow drawn his entire family into a snake's den. Junie was lying there with his hands crushed, Carla was hiding in Rodney Quesnel's house, and my mother was staying at a neighbor's, probably terrified. I decided that I needed to end this, fast. It was time for the direct approach. I was going to go knock on the door of the snake den.

*

My mother called me on my cell as I turned off the Stowe exit. I pulled the BMW over and stopped next to a gray snowbank.

"Are you all right, Vinny?"

"Mom, I should be asking you that."

"I'm OK. Mrs. Tomaselli is cheering me up."

"I found Carla," I said. "She's safe. Her friend Ginny got killed."

There was a silence on the other end of the line. "I won't say anything bad about her," she said. "But she worried me. She was up to something. I worried for Carla."

"She'll be safe, Mom. She's at Rod Quesnel's."

"That's good," she said. "The one I really worry about is you, Vinny. What's the matter?"

"Me? You should be worrying about Junie, not me."

"I just talked with the nurses. I'm going up tomorrow. There's not much I can do for him, but you I can help. Tell me what it is."

"I don't know if I can talk about it," I said. My mother could read me like the newspaper.

"Who else are you going to talk to? You don't go to church."

She was right. "Barbara is pregnant," I said.

"That's wonderful," she said. "Isn't it?"

"I guess," I said. "I'm not sure I'm ready to be a father."

"Vinny. Everybody feels that way. Then you go ahead and it happens, and you never regret having children, not even the difficult ones like your brother."

"There's something else," I said.

"The woman at the wake," she said, not skipping a beat.

"Yes."

"She's very pretty."

"It's more than that," I said.

"Vincent, you've only known her for a few days."

"I know."

"Have you told Barbara?"

"No," I said. "I don't know if I'm going to tell her."

"She'll know," she said. "You can't lie to her."

"I sort of already did."

"Lying is abuse," my mother said. "No different from how your father used to hit me. Sometimes it's worse."

"No, Mom. Hitting you was totally off limits," I said.

"He never lied to me," she said. "He hit me, and I put up with it, and that was a mistake. But if he'd lied to me, I would have thrown him out."

"I have to go."

"I want to go back to my house," she said.

"Not yet," I said. "I have some things to take care of first."

*

Patton's call had gone to voicemail while I was talking to my mom. I called him back. "We found him," he said. "He was in the Interpol records."

"That was fast," I said.

"He's German," he said. "He was picked up in France a few years ago for a murder rap, but he got off. Here's the interesting part."

"What?"

"He's never been to this country. No border crossings, no flights, in or out."

"Are you surprised? I thought that was Tomas' specialty."

"Tell me about it. Vince, what can I do here?"

"I need Schultheiss' address," I said.

He gave it to me. "Don't get killed," he said.

"I'm not planning to."

"These guys are psycho," he said. "That boathouse thing was fucked up."

"When this is done, I'm going to take you out and get you drunk," I said.

"Please don't," he said. "Not unless you want to watch me sing 'Sweet Caroline' on the karaoke with my pants off. I'm kind of a liability after a few beers."

"Thanks for another great visual," I said.

*

Tomas Schultheiss' driveway would have been a challenge for a mountain goat. It was several miles out the Moscow Road, and it didn't just have a view of Mount Mansfield, it had a view of the whole goddamn state. Yuliana's BMW kept on climbing and climbing like a steady little packhorse, and I made it to the top. I parked behind a garage, out of sight of the main house, and looked in a window—no cars. The driveway was empty, and I saw no signs of life. No one was home—I hoped.

The house was angular with lots of glass and was perched like a peregrine on a craggy ledge, overlooking the valley below. It was also fully wired, with cameras, alarms, and God knows what else. Maybe land mines. I tiptoed toward the front door with my bag of tools. I didn't give a damn about the security cameras. I was going to let myself in and see what I could find, and if I got caught, it would be a crime, but I didn't care. These guys were murderers, and I wasn't going to wait for cops with warrants.

I was working a tension wrench and a short hook into the tumbler on his big front door, and was concentrating so hard that I almost fell in when it opened unexpectedly. It was Jenny, the au pair, in a T-shirt with no bra. She gave me a cute smile and invited me in. I hurriedly packed my tools into the bag and left it outside.

Tomas rounded the corner of his foyer as I entered. He did not give me a cute smile.

"Vince," he said. "What brings you here? With your tool set?"

"You might as well call the police, Tomas," I said. "You caught me, fair and square."

"So you came to burglarize the house?"

"What can I say?"

"You can tell me what you were really doing here."

I decided to lay down an ace. "I was looking for Günter Schramm," I said. "When I find him, I'm going to kill him."

"He's not here." His face didn't betray anything.

"So you know him?"

"He's out of the country," he said. "Too bad. He'd probably love to hear from you."

"Do you have a hammer in the house? I could demonstrate what he did to my brother."

"I know nothing about that," he said.

"Bullshit."

"You need to leave," he said. "I'll let you go this time. No police."

"Gee, thanks," I said, and I left.

*

I was frustrated, having gotten nowhere with my home invasion. I suppose I could have reached out and clubbed the bastard, but he had taken me by surprise, and Jenny was right there. I would deal with him later—right now I had my sights set on Günter. Eventually I would kill them both. I don't usually shoot unless shot at, but the usual rules don't apply when it's my family that's at risk.

Brooks Burleigh's farm was across the valley, and the Stowe skiers were heading away from the mountain in a steady stream of cars in the opposing traffic. The lifts had closed and it was either time for an après-ski beer, or to get back to their condos. I climbed up Edson Hill Road just as the sun began to dim behind the peak, leaving pink smudges against the deep blue sky. Florida is flat, and I love it there, but if you are born in mountain country there is a piece of you that feels exposed without the vertical scenery around you.

Once again the magic gates opened for the BMW without me having to get out. Yuliana, or someone, was waiting. I thought about what my mother had said as I drove the long half-mile to the house. She was right, as mothers tend to be. Lying to Barbara was wrong—dead wrong. If I lied to her, then I was no better than my father. That was kind of a shock, and I saw him in a new way, and my mother too. I'd never heard her say a single word about being beaten. Then again, I'd never really asked.

*

Kermit pulled into the driveway right behind me. He looked jovial as he got out of the car, and I helped him with his shopping bags.

"They had some of them quahogs at Mac's Market," he said. "Hard to find them things this time a year."

"You're making chowder?"

"Yes sir, Mister Dooley," he said. "Got the salt pork and the rest of it. It'll be ready in a jiffy."

"Where's Eunice?"

"She's taken ill," he said. "She has the bursitis wicked bad. I'm gonna be doin' the cookin' and the servin' too."

"Let's just do buffet-style," I suggested. "We don't need you spilling the soup on your maid outfit."

He laughed, showing me his teeth. My mom used to call them "summer" teeth. Some are in, some are out.

*

I was downstairs packing up my things, including the Glock 30, which I hadn't worn for almost a week. Brooks had asked me to start carrying. I was going to carry, but not for Brooks' sake. He had plenty of his own guns. I would be telling him tonight that I was done as his driver, effective now, and that I'd return the money. I doubted that he would be surprised. Then, we were going to have a talk about what was going on, and this time I wanted some answers.

Yuliana stood at the door to my room. She wore jeans and a red turtleneck that had specks of food on the front. "I've been cutting up potatoes with Kermit," she said. "Sorry if I'm a mess."

"You're never a mess," I said. I motioned for her to sit down, and she sat on the edge of my bed while I packed.

"I want out, Vince," she said. "Even if I go to jail."

"I'm leaving tonight," I said. "You can go with me."

"I'm not ready. I have things I need to discuss with Brooks."

"Me too."

"He's out skiing," she said. "He's been very sad. He knows he has a big decision ahead."

"He's getting closed down, one way or the other," I said.

"I think he's starting to realize that. He's a complicated man."

"You're a complicated woman," I said.

"No, I'm not," she said. "I'm very simple. But I seem to have gotten myself into a very complicated relationship."

"Likewise," I said.

"What are you going to do about it?"

"If I was a heartless bastard, I'd just shut the door and take off your clothes."

"You are anything but a heartless bastard."

"It would be a lot easier if I was one," I said. I sat down next to her and took her in my arms. We lingered for a long time over our kiss as if we both knew that it might be the last one.

She stood up and, on her way out of the room, turned to me. "You are going to be a good father."

"Thank you," I said. I couldn't think of anything else to say. I had come to a crossroads, like Brooks. And for the second time today, I felt like smashing some furniture against the wall.

*

Supper was Kermit's fabulous, insane, hold-me clam chowder, with Westminster crackers and a side salad of greens, crumbled feta cheese, and caramelized walnuts. Brooks drank a Pellegrino, and Yuliana had opened a bottle of Riesling from Washington State. She poured me a generous glass. Brooks looked ruddy from skiing and was very quiet. Yuliana finally broke the silence.

"Tell us about your brother," she said.

"No amputation," I said. "But he'll be in nursing care for weeks, and he'll never play the guitar again."

Brooks looked at me. "I'm partially responsible for this, Vince. Not directly, but responsible all the same. I'm going to set up a trust for your brother."

"Please don't," I said. "You set up an insurance policy for my father, and it got him killed."

"He wanted the policy," he said. "It was money I would have paid him, but he said he didn't need it, and he wanted to provide for your mother and the three of you."

"What was your angle?"

"I was buying his loyalty, to be perfectly frank. And I was able to launder some funds in the process."

"Through Canada?"

"We have a foundation. Theoretically, it's for marine research."

"What else does it do?"

"I can't answer all your questions, Vince. I'm sorry. I'm going to see some attorneys in D.C. soon, and I'm about to make some changes."

"What if the cops pick you up before that?"

"Then the attorneys will have to come to me."

"So, how many girls are there?"

"Girls?"

"Au pairs. The honey traps," I said.

"Seven, at the moment," he said.

"Wow," I said. "Where did my brother fit in?"

"Ginny had him do transportation when your father was away."

"Ginny ran it?"

"Yes," he said. "When they killed her, I realized we were next."

"I can't be your driver anymore."

"I know. You can stay here, and we'll get you a cab in the morning."

"I'll take him," Yuliana said. She looked at me from across the table. "You can leave tonight if you want to." She'd changed into a black dress. It wasn't fancy, or sexy—just simple, and stunning.

"Vince, Yuliana told me you want to return the money," Brooks said. "Please keep it."

"I can't."

"For your child."

"Shit," I said. "Let's stop talking about my child." They went silent. I was going to bust this guy, and here we were breaking bread together, being all nice as if we were the oldest of friends. I couldn't help but like Brooks Burleigh, and I would have even felt sorry for him, but he was right. He was responsible for this. At least he was man enough to accept that, unlike many of the other powerful people I'd met in my life. Being rich usually meant that you had a ready supply of excuses, lawyers, and other people to blame.

Yuliana poured herself a generous glass of the Riesling and drank half of it. "You're driving," I reminded her.

"I drive just fine with a buzz," she said.

As good as the chowder was, I had lost my appetite. I didn't stay at the table to see what Kermit had made for dessert. I had some more packing to do.

*

There was no moon out, and the sky was clouded over. Neither of us talked while Yuliana steered through the darkness down the long hill to the Mountain Road. I took out my phone and saw three missed calls from Robert Patton and one from Barbara. I didn't feel like talking to anyone, so I put the phone back into my pocket.

I had been thinking about spending another night in Junie's room, but I was tired and needed a real bed, so I'd asked Yuliana to take me to my mother's where I could also borrow the Subaru. She had drunk most of the Riesling and was concentrating hard, but she weaved a little once we hit the interstate.

"I can drive," I said.

"I can fly a jet," she said.

"I know."

"I'm flying him to D.C. the day after tomorrow. We discussed it while you were packing."

"He's going to turn himself in?"

"Hardly," she said. "He's going to negotiate."

"What about you?"

"He said it's all contingent on me not being charged with anything."

"He may not be able to just dictate things like that."

"You haven't seen him negotiate," she said. "I'm not worried about me. More about you."

"Me?"

"Yes. I don't want you to be killed."

"I won't be," I said. "People have tried."

"I saw the scars," she said. "The time we left the lights on."

"Cut myself shaving," I said.

She laughed, and then turned serious. "Günter Schramm is a psychopath."

"You know him?"

"I was married to him," she said. "It took me eighteen months to find out he was mentally unstable. He and Tomas were on loan to the Moldovan security agency. They were spies, in East Germany, before the Wall went down. Tomas has his hands in lots of things, and Günter just likes to threaten people. Or kill them."

"Border Patrol says that according to their records he's never been in this country."

"I believe it," she said. "Borders mean nothing to those two."

"How did Brooks meet Tomas?"

"When he met me. I was twenty-four, and just divorced from Günter. I was in the Air Force, but they paid us nothing. I was desperate for money."

"Meaning what?"

"I was the first. You call them the honey traps."

"With Brooks?"

"Yes. They made me his au pair, back when his kids were young. He brought me here, and we carried on for a while. Then Tomas put the pressure on him, and so Brooks simply told his wife. That was two wives ago. He and Tomas had a big laugh over it, and they ended up being friends."

"Amazing."

"The seven girls are in incredibly high places," she said. "Politicians, CEOs, lawyers, bureaucrats, all married, with families. There's going to be a lot of damage done."

"They have it coming," I said.

"Don't be too quick to judge," she said.

She was right. I knew how easy it was to fall for a Moldovan girl.

*

Yuliana turned off the BMW and took my bag from the trunk. She and I walked across my mother's driveway to the darkened front door. This might be the last time I saw her, and I couldn't raise my eyes to look.

"I'm sorry about everything," I said.

"I'm not," she said. "Please invite me in."

"You can come in," I said. But—"

"You don't have to say it," she said. We entered the house and turned on the lights.

"Does she have any wine in here?"

"If you can call it that," I said. The Carlo Rossi Paisano bottle was still two-thirds full. It would probably still be here when I returned on the next Thanksgiving. I poured her a glass, and she tasted it and winced.

"You have to be pretty desperate to drink this," she said.

"It's good after about the tenth glass," I said.

She put the wine to her lips and drank the entire glass. "Nine more to go," she said, wiping the red liquid from her lips.

"Are you trying to get drunk?"

"Yes," she said. "I won't touch you, I promise. But I'm not ready to leave you yet."

"It's late," I said.

"I'll sleep right here," she said. She took off her shoes and lay down on the same couch where Mrs. Tomaselli slept. I left the lights on, and watched her until she dozed off.

*

Having Yuliana in the next room was not restful. I could hear her snoring through the thin wall—she would have made a good Tanzi. I tossed and turned, got up, had a glass of milk, knit a few rows of Roberto's hat, looked at the weather on my phone, recapped the entire day's events (especially the things I'd bungled), got mad at myself, felt sorry for myself, forgave myself, and then began the whole cycle all over again. I finally drifted off into a fragile truce between anger, sorrow, absolution, and sleep.

*

Someone was in the room. The Glock was at the side of the bed, and I reached for it, groping in the dark.

"Please don't shoot me," Yuliana said. She got under the covers and lay next to me, and I put the gun back on the table. She was naked and I was in my boxer shorts.

"I can't do this," I said.

"I know," she said. "I promised I wouldn't touch you." Her breath smelled of the cheap wine but was still sweet.

"That's not possible in this bed," I said.

"I'm a little tipsy."

"Maybe more than a little."

"Am I slurring my words?"

"No," I said.

"I was supposed to be keeping an eye on you," she said.

"You're doing an excellent job."

"No, I'm not," she said. "It wasn't supposed to feel like this."

We didn't make love, although I couldn't see the difference. Just lying there with my arms around her and feeling her warm softness was as much making love as it was anything else.

WEDNESDAY

I showered for longer than usual, hoping to clean everything including my conscience. It didn't work. Yuliana had left before I woke, and I heard my mother and Mrs. Tomaselli bustling through the front door as I toweled off.

"Hello, dearie," Mrs. Tomaselli yelled, through the door of the bathroom. "We're just here to pick some things up. Then we're going to the hospital to see your brother."

"OK," I yelled back. I shaved and dressed, and when I emerged into the kitchen my mother was standing at the stove making a sausage-and-egg scramble. She added some sharp cheddar cheese and mixed in her homemade garlic-and-onion croutons, which she had fried in olive oil. I poured a cup of coffee and descended on my plate before it got to the table.

"This is unbelievable," I said, between mouthfuls.

"Thanks," my mother said.

Mrs. Tomaselli sat across the table and watched me eat. "Would you like some?" I asked her.

"I don't have breakfast," she said. "But I make up for it at lunch and dinner, unfortunately."

"You look great, Mrs. Tomaselli," I said.

"You're such a flirt, Vinny," she said, giving me a coquettish bat of her eyes. "So, whose perfume did I smell on the way in?"

When it comes to perfume, women can detect a stranger quicker than a police dog can sniff out a joint under a car seat. "Just a friend," I said.

"Ooh-la-la," Mrs. Tomaselli said.

"It's none of your business, Donna," my mother said. "So that means you've decided to stay with her?" she said to me. "The new girl?"

"No, Mom," I said. She had her back to me, and it was clear that I was on her shit list.

"I hear you're going to be a daddy," Mrs. Tomaselli said.

"Yes," I said, trying to fend off the questions by keeping my mouth full of the scramble.

"You'll make a good father," she said.

"That's what my friend said," I said.

"You can't have any more of those kinds of friends, Vinny," Mrs. Tomaselli said. "You have a child to think about. You have to decide, one or the other."

"I've decided already," I said. "I'm going back to Vero, soon. I just have some things to finish up first."

"When can I move back in?" my mother asked.

"Soon, Mom," I said. I figured that with some luck I could wrap it up today. I'd had a revelation while I'd lain awake with Yuliana sleeping in my arms. I was pretty sure I'd figured out exactly what Tomas and Günter were up to. After I finished my breakfast, I was going to do some research on the computer, and then make a phone call.

*

I was Googling on my laptop in the peace of my mother's house. She and Mrs. Tomaselli had left, but the smell of the scramble lingered. My phone vibrated.

It was Roberto. *U still up there?*

Yes. Tell your folks it's OK 2 go hm. I think I'm almost done.

Cool, he sent back. *Miss U!*

I miss U 2! I sent. I loved that young man like a son. Maybe I would be able to handle being a dad, and if I didn't fuck him or her up too much, my kid might turn out to be awesome like Roberto.

*

An hour later I was on I-89 again, heading north. More than two days had passed since I'd heard from Barbara or she'd heard from me. I wasn't ready to call her. My current excuse was that I was too busy trying to nail Günter and Tomas, but there was more to it than that. I'm good at avoiding things, but I'm even better at realizing that I'm avoiding things. I figured I would have time to call her while I waited for Günter. He might not show up for hours, but I was pretty sure he'd show up. It was time to put my plan into gear.

I called the number I had for Tomas that I had taken from Brooks' cellphone.

"Who is this?" he said.

"I have a message for Günter Schramm," I said.

"I'm not his answering service," he said. He'd recognized my voice.

"I'll be at the house in North Hero," I said. "I'm waiting for him."

"I told you he was out of the country," he said. "You'll have a long wait."

"I don't think so," I said, and I hung up.

*

No one was home at Brooks Burleigh's and the front gate was closed. I parked my mother's Subaru on the road and began the long walk up the hill toward the house. I had my tool bag with me, just in case the place was locked up.

I don't get nearly enough exercise at home, and I needed to do something about that. If I was going to start lugging children around, it was time to add some muscle. I'd seen some of the thirty-something dads in airports or on the beach looking like a Sherpa under the weight of the folding stroller, playpen, bottle bag, diaper bag, changing pad, and car seat, with little Junior strapped to their bellies in a pouch. From a distance fatherhood looked like an expedition. I had twenty years on most dads, and I decided I'd better get the weights out as soon as I got home.

The sun was on the ski trails across the valley, and I could see the chairlifts and gondolas in the distance, ferrying people up the slopes. I was breathing hard, but I was energized, and the crisp winter air felt good. I reached the house in a few minutes and knocked, not expecting an answer. There was none, so I got out my tools.

The front door lock was a high-end Medeco, which took more than fifteen minutes to pop. By the time I was done my fingers were frozen and I was glad to get inside. An alarm had been activated, but it didn't bother me. I was going to be in and out, fast.

Five minutes later I was jogging back down the driveway carrying my tool bag, three full magazines of ammunition, and the beige FN SCAR I'd fired at Brooks' range the first time I'd met Yuliana Burleigh. I was hustling because the alarm might be wired to the Stowe cops, and I didn't want to have to explain what I was doing running down a road with an assault rifle.

A little over an hour later I was at the house in North Hero. I parked the Subaru in the driveway where it would be seen. I looked around briefly, but was confident that I had arrived first. There was no one in the house or the other buildings. It was time to sit and wait.

I found a plastic patio chair in the garage and took it down to the boathouse. I took it around behind the structure to the side that faced away from the main house, cleared away some snow and sat down. I rested the rifle against the side of the building, and then opened my bag and took out my knitting. Sooner or later I was going to have to finish this fucking hat.

*

The sunlight had faded to near-dusk when I heard the noise. My feet were frozen solid and I needed to pee, but I stayed absolutely still in my plastic chair. It was a rumbling sound, coming from inside the boathouse. Shortly after it stopped, I heard the door open on the other side of the building. Günter Schramm had arrived, after a five-hour wait.

I gave him a minute, and then cautiously looked around the edge of the boathouse to watch him. He carried his own rifle, a Kalashnikov, and he wore winter-camouflage fatigues and a white hat. There were several canisters looped to his belt, along with an extra magazine for the rifle. He trod slowly and quietly up the slope like a hunter.

First, he checked out the car, which he quickly dismissed. Then he approached the house and smashed open a downstairs window with the butt of his rifle. He tossed in two of the canisters; a flashbang grenade which echoed across the surface of the frozen lake, followed by an incendiary grenade that produced a halo of fire from the windows and soon engulfed the whole downstairs in flames. Anyone inside would be deaf, blind, and roasted like my mother's garlic croutons.

He waited with his gun raised, expecting me to emerge from the flaming house. I backed up from my position and picked up the FN SCAR. I was in no hurry; eventually he'd come back to the boathouse, and I'd empty a full magazine, which would probably saw him in two. I raised my weapon and prepared to execute the man who had murdered my father and had destroyed my brother's hands.

He began walking back, slowly, the fire behind him outlining his huge frame. So this was Yuliana's ex-husband. He must have outweighed her by two hundred pounds. His eyes were blinking from the smoke and flash of the grenades, which was to my advantage, since I hoped to remain unseen at the corner of the boathouse. I let him get to twenty feet from me and then flicked the safety off my gun.

I couldn't do it. It would be killing in cold blood, no matter if he'd attacked my family or not. Günter Schramm opened the boathouse door, not seeing me, and stepped inside the building.

I stood there wondering what the fuck was wrong with me. I was angrier at myself than I had ever been. I entered the brightly-lit structure in time to see Schramm lowering himself into the hatch of a yellow-and-blue research submarine that was floating alongside a wooden dock. He saw me approaching with the gun, and he quickly closed a Lexan dome over his head and started the boat. He looked like a gigantic astronaut, and he smiled and gave me the finger as the sub began a slow descent into the dark water. My quarry was slipping away before my eyes and would soon be under the ice, far away from the boathouse.

Cold blood or not—instinct took over, and I fired. A half-dozen rounds deflected off the thick dome and ricocheted around the building before the gun jammed. Furious, I threw it at the disappearing sub and it bounced off and sank into the water.

The splitting maul I'd used to break the lock was still inside the boathouse, leaning against a wall. I grabbed it and ran out the dock to the submarine. I swung the maul in an arc over my head and crashed it down on the hard surface of the dome. It bounced off, almost taking me into the water. I swung again, harder, and I felt a stab of pain in my wrists when it bounced off the glass again. I only had time for one more swing before the submarine would be out of my reach. I swung hard with the pointed side of the maul facing downward, and the dome shattered. Water poured through the hole as the sub sank lower. Günter Schramm's smile turned to horror as the frigid water began to engulf him, and he struggled with the hatch cover, but it was too late.

I watched him drown.

The sleek blue submarine settled to the bottom and stayed there. I threw my extra magazines in after it and left the boathouse, and then walked up the slope toward the main house, which was now fully engulfed in flames. I stood in front of the fire, warming my frozen limbs, and for the second time in two days I called Lieutenant John Pallmeister to report a death.

*

I sat in my car, bathed in flashing red and blue lights as the embers of the house hissed under the streams of water from the firemen's hoses. There was almost nothing left except for a tall stone chimney.

John Pallmeister emerged from the boathouse and walked up the hill over to my Subaru.

"Get inside," I said, and he took the passenger seat.

"What is that thing?"

"It's a Hawkes Deepflight," I said. "A rich man's toy."

"It's somebody's coffin now."

"That's Günter Schramm."

"I figured," he said. "I have to book you."

"Whatever," I said.

"That your assault rifle?"

"No," I lied. "He had two of them." Just carrying that weapon could get me a nice long sentence.

"I'll get you in front of Patton's cousin, and we'll try to have you out tonight."

"You know about the Cuban cigars?"

"Yeah," he said.

"I might have to hit Patton up for one," I said. "I have a baby on the way."

*

Jennifer Connelly and I waited in the holding area of the Edward J. Costello Courthouse in Burlington, a few blocks down Cherry Street from Rod Quesnel's office. We had appeared before Robert Patton's cousin, who had agreed to see us in the evening, and Patton himself had shown up and watched from the gallery while I was arraigned. I was released on my own recognizance, given my background as a cop and the "extraordinary" circumstances, as the judge had called them. Give that man a cigar. My new attorney signed some paperwork and showed me where to sign, and we were out on the street. Patton was waiting for us.

"Ready for that beer?" he said.

"Yes," I said. "But no karaoke."

"Fair enough," he said. "Join us, counselor?" he asked, turning to Jennifer.

"I can't drink," she said, pointing to her belly.

"Tea, then?"

"I think I'm having contractions," she said. "They started in the courtroom."

"Oh my God," Patton said. "You want an ambulance?"

"No, thank you," she said. "I already texted my husband. He's parked right over there." She pointed toward a guy waiting in a green

Subaru Outback with all the correct bumper stickers along with some that I'd never seen before. We said our goodbyes and watched as she waddled across the street to the car.

*

Patton chose Leunig's, a bistro around the corner on Church Street. The waiter seated us right in front of two musicians: a woman double bass player with long gray hair, and a short guy on a stool with a jazz guitar that was almost as big as he was. They were between songs, tuning up and chatting. The guitar player gave me a look like he'd recognized me. I could pass for a larger version of Junie, except I keep my hair shorter and I have a tan, unlike my brother.

"He's my older brother," I volunteered.

"I heard all about it," he said. "We're going to do a benefit for him."

"Thanks," I said.

"Can he have visitors?"

"Not sure," I said. "I'm going over there tonight."

"Please tell him we send our love," the woman said. "What a fucking nightmare."

What had happened to Junie was probably any musician's worst fear. The pair started a song that I recognized from Junie's repertoire: a ballad called "Here's That Rainy Day". They traded solos, and I couldn't even look at the menu, I was so distracted by the sad, beautiful music and the duo's virtuosity. Burlington may excel in bumper stickers, but its real treasure was a community of musicians and artists who brought heat to the frigid climate.

We ordered two beers and I downed the first half of mine in a hurry. "I figured it out last night," I said. "There's a website for an organization called the Canadian-American Maritime Research Foundation. It's a cover, but it described what they supposedly did—zebra mussel study, underwater archeology and so on. They own a sub, called a Deepflight, and when I saw that it all came together. My father was in the Navy, at the Groton sub base. Tomas went into the boathouse that time, and he just vaporized. And they kept the boathouse water defrosted, but there was no boat."

"That explains a lot," he said. "Fucking guy came and went as he pleased. Any idea what they were moving back and forth?"

"It could have been anything," I said. "The sub was big enough for several people. It could have been people, cash, drugs, whatever they wanted."

"Under the ice," he said. "Slick. We have satellites, radar, ground sensors, all that stuff, but we'd never see a submarine under a foot of ice."

"There must be another location across the border."

"Yeah," he said.

"What do you have on Tomas Schultheiss? Can you pick him up?"

"There's the accessory thing—to your dad's murder—but it's thin. He's supposedly a diplomat, which makes it a lot harder. Other than that, nothing."

"The guy's a former spy," I said. "East Germany, before the Wall. Now he's an extortionist, a smuggler, and a killer."

"We'll get him," he said. "Sooner or later, don't worry."

"I'm worried," I said. "I don't think he's finished cleaning up."

"He changed phones," he said. "We found the old one in a dumpster in Stowe. Everything was wiped."

"When?"

This afternoon. I had a guy tracking the phone after you gave me the number. Something must have tipped him off."

"It was me," I said. "I called him, to draw Günter out."

"You got balls," he said.

"I might have moved up a notch on his to-do list."

The waiter came and we ordered. Patton said he was paying and to order whatever I wanted. He chose the duck tacos, and I had the poutine, my father's favorite.

"That stuff will kill you faster than some spook can," he said.

"Yes, but what a way to go," I said.

*

Junie's hospital room was dark except for the LEDs on the machines. My mother and Mrs. Tomaselli had been there all day and food and flowers were everywhere. A nurse and I were making up the chair-bed when he stirred. "Vin?"

"Junie," I said. "Everything's going to be all right."

"No, it isn't," he said.

"I found Carla, and she's safe. Günter is dead."

He blinked his eyes a few times, and I couldn't tell whether he was completely awake. "What about Tomas?" he said.

"He's next," I said, and he fell back to sleep.

*

The front of my phone lit up, on the small table next to my rock-hard chair-bed. It was almost midnight, but sleep had eluded me. I had too much to process before I could drift off. It was a text from Barbara.

So hv I just ceased to exist?

Damn. I was way late in contacting her, with no excuse. I dialed her cell.

"Sorry," I said. "It's been crazy here."

"I thought you'd at least want to know what the doctor said," she said. "And that was two days ago."

"What did he say?"

"She."

"Sorry," I said. "She."

"She said I'm healthy as a horse, and that the baby should be fine. They're going to do some kind of special test at twelve weeks, because of my age."

"That's awesome," I said.

"Where are you?"

"My brother's hospital room. He's asleep."

"Hospital?"

"Somebody smashed all his fingers," I said. "On both hands."

"Oh my God," she said. "Who would do that to him?"

"A very bad person," I said. "He's out of the picture now."

"Meaning what?"

"I killed him."

She didn't say anything for a long time. "Vince, I want you to get on a plane and come home. I can't handle this."

"I can't. I have to finish it. My family is in danger."

"Your family is here, too," she said.

"I know," I said. "Barbara—"

"What?"

The poutine was bunched in a tight ball at the bottom of my stomach, and I felt like I was about to be sick. But it was time to stop lying.

"I had an affair. It's over."

"Her?"

"Yes," I said.

"I knew it," she said. "How many times did you fuck her?"

I took a deep breath. "Two," I said. "Actually, two and a half."

"Before or after you knew I was pregnant?"

"Both."

She said nothing.

"I promised I wouldn't lie to you," I said. "I feel like a worm."

"Fuck you, Vince Tanzi," she said. "Don't ever call me again."

"Barbara—"

"Just stay the hell out of my life," she said.

"We have a child on the way."

"The hell we do," she said. "You can go fuck somebody else if you want a child. This one's mine."

She hung up. You can't slam down a cell phone like you could the old kind, but if you could have, it would have been ringing in my ears.

THURSDAY

Yuliana texted me at five AM. I was wide awake. I had slept on and off, in what felt like ten-minute bursts that were punctuated by the mini-explosions and reverberations from Barbara's words that would jolt me awake every time I fell asleep. *Stay the hell out of my life.* Bang! Then I'd drift off again, and another shell would explode. *Fuck you, Vince Tanzi.* Blam! No one had ever said anything like that to me. I've had a few enemies over the course of my life and have heard some things that would make most people's ears curl, but I'd never heard words like that from someone I loved. It hurt.

U awake? Yuliana had sent.

I talked with Barbara.

Uh oh.

Right.

She went crazy?

She and I are over, I sent.

Not a chance, she sent back.

What are u talking about?

Makeup sex is the best.

Not going 2 happen this time.

Why not?

She told me to never call her again.

Right. I'll give her 24 hrs.

She'll never forgive me.

That's not the point, she texted.

What?

Forgiveness is a guy thing, she sent.

Meaning?

She'll take u back. And no, she won't evr forgive U.

Why not?

B cause she can use this for ammunition for the rest of your life.

Wish U were right, I sent.

I'm a woman, she sent back, *I'm always right.*
Wish U were here.
Ur in enuf trouble.
Damn straight.
Can you drive us 2 Morrisville airpt this afternoon?
Guess so, I sent. I thought I had quit as Brooks' driver.
TX, she wrote. *Dnt want 2 leave a car there. We may be gone a long time.*
Hope not, I sent.
Ulterior motive…I want 2 see U.
Why?
Just want to look at U.
Ditto, I sent back.
Meet us at the house at 4 PM, OK?
OK.

*

I went down the hall to the nurses' station for coffee and then chatted with the state cop who was outside Junie's room, half-asleep but trying to look awake. He was another rookie, but he appeared to be a lot more rough-and-ready than the one I'd met two mornings ago. I made a mental note to call John Pallmeister and tell him to relieve these poor guys. I didn't think Junie was in as much danger anymore. Tomas, if he saw the newspapers, would have read about the demise of his associate. If he had a brain in his head, he'd be on the run, and I would be right behind him.

I was washing my face in Junie's bathroom when my mother and Mrs. Tomaselli arrived. My mom was carrying a big bag that I knew would contain more food, and Mrs. Tomaselli had a bouquet of flowers wrapped up in newspapers so that they wouldn't freeze.

"We're taking over here," Mrs. Tomaselli said. "You can scoot. You have much more important things to attend to."

"Hi, Mrs. Tomaselli," I said, as I toweled off my face. "Hi, Mom."

"Good morning, Vincent," my mother said.

"Mom, just so you know, I told Barbara everything."

"I hope she read you the riot act."

"Worse than that," I said. "I hardly got any sleep."

"I wish I could feel sorry for you," my mother said. "Let's keep our voices down." She turned to Junie. "The poor child. He needs his rest."

"He's not a child," I said.

"When your baby is born, you'll know what I mean," she said. "They're always your children. Even the unfaithful ones."

"Francine, give him a break," Mrs. Tomaselli said.

"It's OK, Mrs. T.," I said. A nurse entered the room with a breakfast tray for Junie.

"I'll feed him," my mother said to the nurse. "You run along now." The young woman put down the tray and left.

Junie began to stir. "What's going on here?" he said.

"Some kind of weird reality show," I said. "Good luck."

"Don't leave me, Vince," he said, with a faint smile. It was good to see him smiling. Maybe we'd survive this, somehow.

"You're on your own, bro," I said. I got my clothes and started to dress. Mrs. Tomaselli was ogling me like I was one of the Chippendales.

"Where are you going?" Junie said.

"To find Tomas," I said.

"What are you going to do to him?"

"Later," I said. "You rest up."

*

My cheer about Junie turned to gloom over Barbara as soon as I walked across the hospital parking lot and a cold wind off the lake hit me in the face. Yuliana was wrong. There would be no make-up sex. My relationship with Barbara was beyond redemption because I had crossed the ultimate line. I had no excuses. It was over. Between the lack of sleep and the knowledge that I had truly screwed up, I felt like I might have been better off if Günter Schramm had just barbecued me in the house on North Hero.

I also had very mixed feelings about seeing Yuliana again, even if it was for a few minutes in the rearview mirror of the Escalade. I wished that they would just call a cab. I was a free man again, and technically, I could start seeing her, provided they didn't lock her up. But as much as I cared about her, I just didn't feel up to it. I wanted to crawl off to a dark place somewhere and lick my wounds.

That would have to wait. I had some work to do first.

*

My mother's old Subaru was not intimidated by Tomas' steep driveway. It climbed to the top as nimbly as Yuliana's BMW had, and I felt like patting it on the nose and giving it a carrot. I parked in the middle of the driveway, which was empty. There were no cars in the garage, and this time the place really did look deserted. Just to be sure, I drew the Glock from my holster and rang the front bell.

No response. I guessed that Tomas was far away; perhaps in Canada, or further. I'd called Patton on the way to ask him to alert me if Tomas crossed a border, but even without the submarine I figured he could find an alternate, anonymous route.

I got in the hard way. The front lock was a polished-steel Baldwin, and it didn't want to budge despite my best efforts. Instead, I climbed up a porch railing in the rear of the house where there was a sliding glass door. It had a cheap lock and I was in in less than a minute, no doubt tripping the motion-detecting alarm units that I noticed in the corners.

I found a Sony laptop in an upstairs bedroom on top of a dresser. It was plugged in and fully charged. I sat down on the side of a king bed and opened it up. Someone had conveniently left it in "sleep" mode, so there was no login or password necessary. I sent Roberto a text message from my phone.

U in school?

Still sick, he sent right back. *Week 2.*

Ur voice working?

Can talk a little, he sent.

I called him. "I'm on someone's computer. I need you to have a look around."

He gave me a URL to type in, and guided me through the process of letting him in.

"What are you looking for?" he asked.

"I'm trying to locate somebody. I think this computer belongs to him. I can't track his car or his phone. He's probably gone underground, and may be out of the country."

I watched as Roberto navigated for several minutes. "There's a lot of crazy stuff in here," he said.

"Like what?"

"More videos, like the one you had. A lot of them."

"Encrypted?"

"Yeah," he said. "About half of what's on here is in a different language. Looks like German."

"He's German."

"OK," he said. "Here's something. Check it out."

"I can't. That print's too small. I don't have my reading glasses."

"Somebody rented a van. From a place called LaBounty Car Rental."

"When?"

"Last night," he said. "The credit card says 'Rudolf Meijer'. The address is in Stowe, Vermont."

"You mean the guy's address or the rental agency's?"

"Both. The guy has a Stowe P.O. box, and the car rental place says Mountain Road, Stowe."

"The person I'm looking for is called Tomas, not Rudolf," I said.

"Let me look around," he said. I waited while the cursor flew back and forth across the screen by itself, opening windows and searching files. "Here's a picture," he finally said. A small photograph opened on the screen. It was Tomas, wearing tinted glasses.

"That's Tomas," I said.

"The file name is MEIJER3.jpg," he said.

"Interesting," I said, and Roberto started coughing. "You get back to bed."

"Don't forget the syrup," he said, and we hung up.

I decided to borrow Tomas Schultheiss' computer for a while. I'm not into porn, especially when it involves old, fat politicians, but this thing was a treasure trove. I wondered how many land deals and God knows what else had gone exceedingly smoothly thanks to Tomas' smut collection. I would hand it over to Patton as soon as I saw him. Whatever was on there would surely get his closed-down investigation opened again, and some cow pies would be hittin' the windmill, yes sir Mister Dooley.

*

The LaBounty Car Rental office was inside a tiny building at the far end of a gas station on the Mountain Road. It looked closed, and I was about to give up when a young man pulled into the lot in a rusty Dodge pickup that was peppered with bumper stickers. The stickers appeared to be the only things that were keeping the pockmarked tailgate from disintegrating.

"Help ya?" he said.

"I was supposed to meet Rudy here," I said. "Not sure if I got the time wrong."

"Rudolf Meijer? You sure did, Mister. He left last night."

"Nuts," I said. "I was supposed to go with him. I'm going to lose my job."

"You were going to Canada too?" he said.

"Yeah," I said. "But I have no idea where. He was going to drive me. I'm screwed."

"Wait right there," he said, and he opened the hut and went in-side. I saw him working on a computer, and a few minutes later he came out with a slip of paper in his hand.

"Here's the address," he said. "You didn't get it from me, OK? I don't want anybody to lose their job, includin' me."

"He gave you the address?"

"Nope," he said. "Don't tell anyone, but we have trackers on all our vehicles. We got ripped off one too many times."

"Smart," I said.

"That address is where the car is, right now," he said. "Can you, like, make up a story, so you didn't get this from me?"

"Oh yeah," I said. "I'm pretty good at that."

*

I was passing through Burlington on the way north, wishing that I had time to stop and check on Carla and Junie. It would be something of a squeeze already; it was almost noon, my destination was an hour north, and then I had a two-hour ride back to Brooks' house and I needed to get there by four. The phone's GPS program led me across a bridge over the lake to Alburg, and then over another bridge to Rouses Point, in New York State, just below the Canadian border. I took Route 11 north a few miles and stopped at the Canadian customs building, where the agent waved me through after I'd shown him my passport. I'd called Robert Patton again as I'd passed through Burling-ton, and he had cleared the way. I was carrying the Glock, and that was a no-no, but I wasn't about to visit Tomas Schultheiss unarmed.

A few miles past the border I turned onto a gravel road that bi-sected a snow-covered farm field. It led me to Rang de la Barbotte, a paved road that ran along the western shore of Lake Champlain and served a string of cottages and small estates. I was now heading due south, parallel to the way I had come, and I wondered if the GPS was playing tricks as it sometimes does. I decided to trust it, and the blinking dot led me to a lakeside estate that was within sight of the U.S. border. The wrought iron gate was secured with a chain and a padlock.

I got out of the car and fumbled with my tools in the icy wind. I had the lock open in a short time, but as the gate had been chained and locked from the outside I didn't expect to find "Rudolf Meijer" or anyone else within.

My expectation proved to be correct. There was no rented van and the place was deserted. It looked similar to the house in North

Hero—isolated from its neighbors, with several outbuildings and a large, new-looking boathouse. I walked down a frozen slope to check the boathouse out.

It had the same keyless lock system as its Vermont counterpart. I didn't want to leave a record of my visit with any splitting-maul antics. I figured I already knew what was inside—wooden docks, unfrozen water, and no submarine—I'd already taken care of that.

I called Robert Patton. "I found the Canadian side," I said. "It's just over the border from Rouses Point. He rented a van under a different name and it was here a while ago, but now the place is locked up and he's gone."

"You'd better get back here, Vince," he said.

"What's up?"

"Your sister is gone. Pallmeister sent someone to check on her. She's gone, and so is Rod Quesnel, and his secretary doesn't know where he is."

"Where are you?"

"My office," he said. "We're at the Burlington airport."

"I'll be there as soon as I can. Do me a favor and get someone to guard Junie's room. I had Pallmeister take the trooper off this morning."

"Will do," he said. "Get here as soon as you can."

*

I was on my way to the Burleigh farm, but I wasn't in any mood to be a solicitous chauffeur, that was for damn sure. I'd stopped in at Robert Patton's office and had dropped off Tomas' laptop, and Patton had literally rubbed his hands together with glee. I lied, and told him that Tomas had left it in my car so that he'd have a clean evidence trail. We discussed what to do about my sister and Rodney Quesnel, but he had already put out the alert, and there wasn't much I could do now except wait. The more I thought about the whole thing the more I wanted to throttle Brooks Burleigh until he led me to Tomas and I shot them both. That's not exactly the attitude you want in a driver.

Yuliana was wearing her pilot's outfit under a fluffy white parka that set off her long, dark hair. I suddenly wanted to split into two, like a paramecium in biology class. One paramecium would go back to Florida and be a loving husband and Super-dad. The other would just stay here with her and swim around in the petri dish.

"Everything OK, Vince?" Brooks asked as I helped him load his luggage in the back of the Escalade.

"No," I said. "Not even close."

"What is it?"

"My sister is missing now," I said. "I thought I had her safely stashed."

"This will all be resolved in a few days," he said.

"Sorry, but that doesn't help."

"What will help?" he said. "I'm trying to undo a lot of damage here."

"Where would Tomas go, if he was running?"

"There's a place just over the border," he said.

"I just came from there," I said.

Brooks frowned. "He can melt away. That's his talent."

"I'm going to find him and kill him," I said.

"That would save a lot of time and money," Brooks said. "But be careful. I'm sorry I ever got involved with him. He brought out my worst instincts."

"Jesus, Brooks," I said. "I can't stay mad at you, you're such a fucking nice guy sometimes."

"I'm going to pay my debt, Vince," he said. "And then I hope that we are going to be friends."

I caught Yuliana's smile in the rearview mirror as I drove. "Get a room, you guys," she said, and reluctantly, I laughed.

We were halfway to the village when the Escalade's motor died, and I was just barely able to coast into the parking lot of a restaurant. I put on the brake, got out and lifted the hood. Nothing looked askew, although a car motor these days is a mass of plastic and computers, and there aren't any plug wires to jiggle or distributor caps to clean. I got back in and tried to start it again, but nothing happened.

"It's done this before," Brooks said. "I should have had it looked at, but it started the next morning."

"Ed's at the airport," Yuliana said. "I'll call him and he can get us. Vince, I'm sorry, we're leaving you with a mess."

"Just not my day," I said.

"Come outside," she said to me.

We stood behind the car, while Brooks made calls from inside. The sun had dropped behind the womanly curves of the Green Mountains, and it was getting dark.

"Please don't hate me," she said.

"Impossible."

"I got you into so much trouble."

"I take responsibility for my actions," I said.

"That's one of the reasons I'm in love with you," she said.

"Yuliana—"

"I'll stop saying that," she said. "I just needed to tell you one more time."

"I wish I was two people," I said.

"You'd just have twice the problems," she said.

"Stop making me laugh," I said. "It makes it harder to let you leave."

"Kiss me and I will shut up."

I took her in my arms and gave her a long kiss. I didn't want to let go, but I did.

"Goodbye, Vince," she said. "And thank you for saving me."

"This isn't goodbye."

"Yes it is," she said. "It has to be."

*

Half an hour later they were gone, and I was waiting for a tow. I had far more important things to do, like find my sister, but I had no choice. I fumed in the cold interior of the big car.

I heard the sound of a text message, but it was not my phone; it came from the back seat. I saw it—Yuliana's purse. She had forgotten it when Ed had come to collect them. She'd be beside herself—for some people, leaving your phone somewhere is like forgetting to wear pants.

On a whim, I tried the key one more time, and the Escalade roared back into life. Fickle bastard. Maybe I could make it to the airport before they left.

*

When I arrived, the Bombardier was on the taxiway with the engines running, moving slowly toward the runway. I flashed the lights of the Escalade, but the cockpit was pointed away from me. I parked, and dashed inside the little building. The attendant was reading a newspaper.

"Can you radio that jet? I have a bag that belongs to the pilot."

"Just gave them clearance to take off," he said. He had rosy cheeks like Rod Quesnel and was about the same age. "Funny, you're the second one with a bag."

"What?"

"Mr. Schultheiss. He stopped by earlier," he said. "He had me load a bag—said it was a surprise for Mr. Burleigh and not to say anything."

Yuliana had taxied the jet out to the lone runway, and I heard the engines whine in the distance as she powered up.

"What?" I felt a rush of panic. "Radio her," I said. "Tell them to abort."

"Why?"

"Just do it. Now."

"I'll try," he said.

Yuliana turned the jet to face south and brought the engines to full power. I remembered that my phone was in the Escalade. I ran out the door, got into the car, and dialed Brooks Burleigh's number. It went to voicemail. I dialed again.

A grey Chrysler minivan pulled into the parking space next to me. There was a single occupant in the front seat, and he held his cell phone in front of him. I watched him dial a number, as I attempted to redial Brooks'. It was Tomas Schultheiss, and he turned to me and smiled as he held the phone in front of him like a TV remote control.

The jet reached the end of the runway and lifted off at a steep angle. It climbed to the height of the surrounding mountains and was illuminated by the dying embers of the sunset as it rose. Then, it exploded. The fragments descended into the dusk, leaving a small cloud of black smoke. It was like a macabre Fourth of July fireworks display, except that someone who I loved was part of the debris that was falling, slowly, to earth. Tomas Schultheiss was smiling in the van next to me.

I reached behind my back for the Glock, but he had already raised a gun, and I felt the sting of shattered glass from the side window against my face. The world became a dazzling, white-hot blur except for the image of my father, Jimmy Tanzi, who was in front of me, reflected in the windshield, beckoning.

"Come with me," he said.

"No, Dad," I said. I could see the blood from my own brain, spattered across the cream-leather interior of the Cadillac. "Not yet."

FEBRUARY

WEDNESDAY

"Maple syrup."

"What? Mr. Tanzi? Did you just say something?" A nurse was washing my face with a washcloth. The room I was in was brightly illuminated like a night baseball game, except that I was inside somewhere, and my head hurt.

"Mmmm," I said.

She ran out of the room, and I fell back to sleep.

*

Barbara was above me, with her mascara smeared. "Mmmm," I said, as I opened my eyes.

"Oh God," she said. "Thank you for answering my prayers."

"You don't go to church," I said, but it came out "Mmmm."

"Vince, I am so, so sorry. I am so goddamn sorry." She bent down and began crying into my bedcovers. I wanted to say something, but I fell asleep again.

*

"Can you hear me?" a woman asked me. I had been awake for a little while and had taken a sip of water from a straw in a cup that a nurse held out. I was surrounded by the nurse, Barbara, my mother, and a slim, dark-haired woman who wore a stethoscope around her neck. She looked like she was the boss, and she was asking the questions.

"Mmmmm," I said.

"Blink once for yes, OK?" she said. "Twice for no."

I blinked, once.

"Good," she said. She turned to the rest of the people in the room. "This is very promising," she said to them.

I was aware of what was going on, including all of the conversation in the room. I just couldn't talk. I wondered what the fuck was happening and how I had ended up here.

My head fell back against the pillow.

*

"Yuliana," I said. It was dark in my room, and somebody was sitting in the lone visitor's chair. It was Robert Patton, and he sprang to his feet.

"You can talk," he said. I looked at him as he peered over me with his broken nose and cockeyed face. All I could think of was the Disney movie where Sleeping Beauty woke up to see the handsome prince poised above her. Not this time.

"Fuck," I said.

"Vince, it's me, Robert," he said.

"I know," I said. My mouth was barely functioning. My teeth felt like little rocks, and my tongue was soft and loose like an undercooked hamburger.

"Jesus fucking Christ am I glad you are alive," he said. "They kept you in a coma for weeks. They said they had to do it because of the swelling."

"Where's…Yuliana?"

"You…what do you remember?"

"Not…don't know," I said. I raised my right arm and felt the side of my head. It was bandaged, and rough around the edges, like razor stubble.

"What happened?" I asked him.

"You were shot," he said. "You made it, somehow."

"Head?"

"Yes," he said. "In the head."

"No vitals," I said.

Patton laughed, and tears filled his eyes. "Yes, your vital organs were spared. The bullet only hit your brain."

"Who…shot?"

"We're going to get the motherfucker," he said. "If it's the last thing I do."

"Sleep," I said, and I checked out again.

THURSDAY

I was awake, but my eyes hadn't opened yet. It took me a while to remember where I was. I had been dreaming about ice—a thick layer of it, and I was trapped underneath it, swimming in a frigid lake. I was running out of air, and I remembered the scene in the Houdini movie where Tony Curtis finds a gap between the top of the water and the bottom of the ice, where there was just enough air to stay alive. He'd found his way out, after escaping from a heavily-chained trunk at the bottom of the river, then being swept downstream from his planned exit by the current, and finally locating the opening in the ice where he'd gone in. I'd later learned that it was all Hollywood bullshit and that Houdini had never done that. Whatever. I could sure use his help finding my way out of a body with a brain that didn't seem to work.

I heard a female voice. "The primary concern is aphasia, which basically means having difficulty speaking. But Mr. Patton told the nurse last night that they had exchanged words. That's huge."

"Really?" It sounded like Barbara.

"Yes," the first voice said. "Frankly, I'm surprised. The bullet was slowed by the window glass, but it still did a lot of damage. I expect he'll need a great deal of therapy, not just for the speaking but also for the motor skills. He appears to be able to move his right side, but not his left."

"Oh," Barbara said.

"It can improve with therapy. Remember, he's very lucky to be here at all."

"I know."

It grew quiet in the room, but I wasn't alone. Someone was stroking the hair on my arm, standing next to the bed. I made a huge effort and opened my eyelids. Everything was a struggle.

"Barbara?" She stood over me, and she looked a lot better than Patton had. She wore a yellow sleeveless tank top that showed off her smooth, round shoulders and her tan.

"Vince, you can talk," she said as she squeezed my arm.

"Sort of," I said, slurring the words.

"I moved in with your mother," she said. "I'm here for the duration."

"School?"

"I quit," she said. "I'll start up again when you're better."

"Roberto. Hat," I said.

"Your mother finished it and sent it to him. He wears it all day, even to bed."

"S'too hot."

"He doesn't care. I called his parents last night to tell them you had come out of the coma. They send their love."

"Carla?"

"She's safe. That one's a long story."

"Who shot?"

"Who shot you?"

"Yes," I said. It was a major effort to get a single syllable out.

"The German. You don't remember?"

"No."

"He was the one who blew up the plane," she said. "The attendant at the airport saw it all."

"Plane?"

I saw her face change. "The one that…you really don't remember?"

"No." But something was trickling back into my consciousness, and Barbara noticed.

"She…she's dead, Vince."

I couldn't get my mouth to form her name, and Barbara saw me struggling.

"Yuliana," she said. "I'm so sorry."

She didn't look sorry, but I wasn't going to point that out. I had done enough talking.

*

They were working a kind of rotation: my mother, Barbara, Mrs. Tomaselli, Patton, and even Carla. They took shifts sitting in the visitor chair, watching me. Carla smiled a lot and looked slightly stoned. I didn't have the energy to ask her what had happened to her, and she didn't volunteer anything. From what I'd overheard I had been asleep for weeks, and I wondered how much I'd missed.

The days before my "incident", as the nurses called it, were scrambled in my mind like one of my mother's breakfasts. I remembered going to Canada, looking for Tomas. I remembered that Carla was missing, but here she was. I'd rented some kind of van. I'd had a long conversation with my father. Barbara and I had had a fight, a bad one.

And then I remembered—she was pregnant. My brain felt like that old video game where rectangles drop from above and you turn them around, as they descend, to make them fit together at the bottom. It was a Russian game, and all the kids played it, years ago. Bits of information were falling out of the sky, and my mind suddenly played back the image of a fireball, and a cloud of black smoke. Some things were simple to remember, and others were still unclear—hidden from me, probably for a reason.

FRIDAY

"Tetris" was the name of that game. I finally remembered. I'd woken up feeling better by several degrees, and Patton was on the early shift. I had a question.

"Computer?"

"You mean the laptop?" he said.

I nodded.

"I've been saving you the articles. What a shitstorm. Two federal judges resigned, and three members of Congress are under investigation. Dulles Stanton checked himself into rehab so he doesn't have to face the music. Talk about a bombshell."

"Ha," I managed.

"That's just the beginning," he said. "This thing is going to take a lot of people down. They're lining up press conferences, saying shit like how sorry they are to have disappointed everybody, while the wife stands there like a prop and gets weepy. What a bunch of dickheads."

"Anyone," I said.

"What?"

"Any…one," I repeated.

"You mean it could happen to anyone?"

"Yes."

"I suppose you're right. They've rounded up all the girls. And guess what?"

"Mmm," I said. I was running out of energy.

"Talk about pros. Tomas trained them in Moldova. They can shoot, fight, and fuck. All incredible lookers."

"Mmm," I said again.

"He forged all the identities, and even got them vetted with whatever they needed to get them placed. References, visas, all bogus. My guess is they brought them in on the submarine, finished the training at your sister's place, and found them a job. And it wasn't just blackmail. They were spies. Tomas had all kinds of shit on his computer.

We had to get the CIA in to break the encryption. One of the girls was fucking the deputy director, so he wasn't too helpful. He's gone now."

"Spies?"

"They passed information on to Tomas. He sold it, to whoever he thought would pay. The CIA had told me he was small-time, but either they were way wrong or he'd put the squeeze on the deputy director."

"Where?"

"Where's Tomas? I don't know. I fucking wish I did. We've got his description out in every country the U.S. has treaties with. Nothing."

"Oh," I said. A nurse came in and shooed away Patton while she took my pulse.

"We're going to remove your catheter," she said. "And then you and I are going to walk to the john."

"Goody," I said, and she smiled.

*

Going to and from the bathroom was like climbing up Mount Mansfield drunk, with a sixty-pound backpack and two frat brothers holding me up by the arms. The nurse took my good side and Patton pretty much carried me on the left side. I could feel his grip on my arm and under my shoulder, but I couldn't make my damn leg move.

It felt good to pee. I was going to get myself out of here, get back to Florida, and pee in my driveway under the cover of nightfall, which is every man's God-given right. And when I'd peed outside enough times, and I had my left side working again, and I could speak in full sentences, and I could put my arms around Barbara and maybe even hold my little baby, I was going to find Tomas Schultheiss and take his life, slowly and painfully. I hated to admit it, but the thought of doing that was a powerful motivator to get well. Bring on the physical therapy and the long, hard journeys to the bathroom. I needed to get my strength back if I was going to kill someone.

SATURDAY

It had been several years since the three Tanzi siblings had all been in the same room. Carla was on her rotation, and Junie wandered in, his arms in a double-sling that was suspended from his neck. Carla got up and hugged him gently, and I met his smile with one of my own.

"We kids sure know how to fuck up," he said. "I guess the apple doesn't fall far, like they say."

"Dad was really trying to not fuck up," Carla said. "At least before he died."

"Yeah," Junie said, "and just look at us. He got us into this, and two out of three of us ended up in the hospital."

"We chose to get into it," Carla said.

"What's this about you and Rod Quesnel?" Junie asked.

"We're getting married," she said. She blushed slightly, under her long gray hair.

"No shit," Junie said. "I thought you…"

"You were right," she said. "But Rod doesn't care."

"Crazy fucking world," he said.

"Congratulations," I said, which was the biggest word I'd tackled so far.

"I know you were looking for me, Vin," she said. "I'm sorry. Rod and I got kinda freaked out and decided to drive out west. We should have told you."

"No worry," I said.

"I taught Rod how to smoke," she said. "He's so sweet when he's high."

"That's a real great fuckin' life skill," Junie said to her. "Maybe you should be a teacher. Teach all the elementary school kids how to get wasted."

"Chill, bro," I said.

"Sorry," he said. "My hands ache all day and night, but all I'm doin' is Advil."

"Proud of you," I said.

"Shit," he said. "Get well, you dumb motherfucker."

"I will," I said, and he left.

*

Mrs. Tomaselli was on duty, and she was rubbing baby oil into my feet and humming softly as I picked at my lunch. Besides needing to find Tomas, my other compelling motivation to get well was to have something to eat that didn't taste like a regurgitated worm from a mother robin. I was starting to have dreams about a grouper sandwich, with hand-cut fries and a cold sixteen-ounce beer. Make that a twenty-two-ounce beer. Aw hell, just bring the pitcher.

Mrs. T. took my right side and a big, burly male nurse named Todd took my left. Half way to the bathroom I said, "Let me go." They did. I couldn't walk, but I could stand. I felt like cracking a bottle of champagne, and I couldn't wait to tell Barbara.

I was going to get better.

MARCH

SATURDAY

Three weeks had passed since I'd taken my first step, and they were now ready to kick me out. I could board a plane and even carry a small bag with my left hand. I could speak in full sentences, although lots of little bits of information were misplaced or missing. I had pretty much pieced together the last few days before I'd been shot, although I couldn't remember the plane going down, or even the ride to the airport in the Escalade. I had a bullet hole in my head that was healing over, but I had done nothing about the hole in my heart, and Barbara and I had tacitly agreed not to discuss it. That was in the past.

Robert Patton and John Pallmeister sat in the front seat of the lieutenant's cruiser with Barbara and me in the back. I'd had a big send-off at the hospital with both my siblings, my mother, a teary Mrs. Tomaselli, and various nurses and doctors who I'd grown fond of. Nobody could believe how quickly I had progressed. Revenge is a powerful motivator, although I kept that to myself. I had a long row to hoe in Florida, but Barbara was going to stay home and would take me to the Indian River Medical Center every morning for therapy. All in all I was either very lucky, or if there was a God, She wasn't finished with me yet.

Patton took our bags into the Burlington terminal and bossed people around until he got a wheelchair. "When you're ready to start drinking, I'm buying," he said.

"Come to Florida, and I'll buy you a whole case," I said.

"Heal fast, Vince," John Pallmeister said. People were looking at us, probably wondering if they were going to have to sit next to a cop and some kind of notorious criminal. I'd seen myself in the mirror, and the half-shaved-head thing didn't do much for my looks. Maybe I could borrow Roberto's homie hat—or knit one for myself, once my left hand got better.

Barbara had booked us in first class so that I'd be comfortable. It wasn't Brooks' jet, but it was nice. In three hours I'd be in West Palm, and we would pay off the small mortgage on my BMW, which had been in the parking garage for eight weeks. Assuming the car started, we'd be home two hours after that. I would spend the night in my own bed.

I looked out across Lake Champlain as we gained altitude. It had thawed early—"ice out", as they called it—after a particularly warm February and March, but the water still looked cold, and I could see whitecaps on the waves. I remembered the time I'd been up in the cockpit of the Bombardier with Yuliana Burleigh, and she'd surprised me with a kiss. I wasn't about to bring any of that up with Barbara—I'd been forgiven, and Yuliana's name would never come up again. If you live long enough, you carry some things inside that you will never let out; that's just part of the deal. Some of them are dark secrets that can eat at you like a cancer. Some of them are special, unique treasures that just shouldn't be shared. Some are a little of both.

AUGUST

SATURDAY

"Barbara," I called into the bathroom. "They're waiting outside and it's hot."

"Ready in a sec," she answered. I could hear her grunting as she tried to get the dress zipped around her middle. She was nine months pregnant, minus a week, and her belly looked like a dangerously overinflated balloon that could explode at any minute. I wore a tie, which felt like a hangman's noose except that I was happy. Gustavo, Lilian, Roberto and a female justice of the peace with close-cropped gray hair sweltered out on the back lawn while my wife-to-be finished dressing. She finally emerged, looking beautiful in her cream-colored wedding dress with a turquoise necklace that my mother had expressed down for the occasion, as it was something borrowed and something blue.

I took her by the arm and led her out to the back patio of my house. The August sun bore down on us, and I wondered why weren't inside in the AC like normal, sane Floridians, but Barbara had insisted that we tie the knot outdoors. All the arrangements had been some-what hasty; she had only recently decided that our forthcoming baby needed parents who were married and that I should propose, which I dutifully did. It was going to be a race as to which happened first: the wedding or the birth.

It was a tie. Barbara's water broke shortly after the J.P. started, and she dashed off to the bathroom. She came back out fifteen minutes later in a new, loose-fitting floral print dress, looking flushed.

"Finish it," she said to the J.P., who had found a seat in the shade and was fanning herself with her papers. "The contractions are ten minutes apart. We're running out of time."

"Are you sure?" I said.

"Yes," she said, and she gave me a smile. "Then we're going to the hospital, and you're going to be a daddy."

"Vince, do you take Barbara to be your lawfully wedded wife?" the J.P. asked.

"Whatever," I said.

Barbara looked at me, and smiled. "Ohhh, you're going to pay for that one," she said.

"I know," I said, smiling back.

"Get the car," she said, and I did exactly what she told me. I was married less than a minute, and I was already a natural.

NOVEMBER

THURSDAY

Some people's favorite holiday is Christmas, or the Fourth of July, or even Halloween. Mine is Thanksgiving, especially in Vermont, where the trees are bare and the wind sings songs of desolation as it blows the last few leaves off the red oaks. Late November is deer season, so you don't take your dog for a walk in the woods without wearing some blaze orange clothing or you could be mistaken for Bambi's mother. I had already been shot in the head once this year; that was quite enough, thank you.

I got a luggage cart at the Burlington airport and leaned on it while Barbara and I waited for the bags. There had been a time when I would fly in for Thanksgiving, solo, and could just carry on a small bag and skip the wait at the carousel. Not anymore. I had joined the ranks of the Sherpa-dads, and I wondered if one luggage cart would be enough for all our gear. I piled on our three suitcases, a car seat, a collapsible stroller, a diaper bag, a folding basinet/crib combo, Barbara's huge purse, and a beach bag full of stuffed animals and other soft things for Royal. He would be three months old in a couple days, and already the kid had more possessions than I did. He'd slept through the whole flight, strapped to Barbara's chest in a Snugli, with his little head peeking out of the top, covered in a soft wool cap that I'd made for him. I couldn't vouch for the quality of the knitting, and it had taken me ages, but I'd done it with the help of my physical therapist who had given me all kinds of exercises and encouragement to regain my dexterity.

I shuffled behind the fully-laden cart toward the rental car desk. I wasn't supposed to drive, but I'd ignored that, and Barbara didn't argue—she had her hands full. My left side was coming back, slowly, except for the foot-dragging, which Barbara called the Vinny Shuffle. I could walk and drive, but I wasn't about to start dance lessons.

"Are we still picking up Junie?" Barbara asked, in her don't-wake-the-baby whisper. Royal had a healthy set of lungs on him and could make his presence known when he was hungry, tired, or just plain cranky. His great-grandfather Basilio Tanzi had been a singer and had entertained the other stonecutters at the Old Labor Hall in Barre on Saturday nights, long before I was born. Everybody had called my grandfather Royal, which was the translation of Basilio, and his little namesake could belt out an ear-splitting aria when he wanted the breast.

"He texted," I said. "He's riding with Carla and Rod. They're not getting there until later."

"Who else is coming?"

"Just Mrs. Tomaselli," I said.

"Your girlfriend," she said.

"She's harmless," I said. "I'm a married man now."

"That won't stop her," she said, and we laughed. I was initialing boxes on the rental form, declining all the add-ons. I'd rented a mommy-van, and when we collected the car and threw all our stuff in it, I finally understood why people bought vans after they had babies. Either you got one or you kept your old car and put on a trailer hitch for a U-Haul.

It hadn't snowed yet, or at least nothing had accumulated on the fields and hills along the interstate. The afternoon sky was clear, and you could see Mount Mansfield from the road. There was a smear of white frosting across the top, and on the cold nights they'd be making snow for the ski trails below at the resort. Part of me wanted to drive up to Stowe and just look around: Tomas' aerie, Brooks' hilltop farm, the shops, the restaurants—and the airport. I had a morbid urge to revisit what had happened ten months ago—to confirm that it had been real. Perhaps when you die it's better to be buried six feet down, under a Rock of Ages memorial, rather than to be cremated. It would allow your loved ones to look at the cold slab, read the inscription, and say, "Yes, he's dead." Scattering an urn full of ashes might be more eco-friendly, but vaporizing like that can leave people wondering. Right now I was wondering if Yuliana Burleigh had ever existed, and why I still couldn't remember what had happened on the day she died. The Tetris puzzle that had started when I'd awakened in a hospital was still missing some pieces.

*

The interstate was busy with people coming north, but traffic was light going south toward Barre, and the town itself was deserted. Everyone was with their families, cooking, eating, watching football, and drinking malt beverages. I stopped at a store and picked up a six-pack of Pilsner Urquell. I could drink again, although not like I used to. Any more than a couple beers and my wires got crossed. But I needed to get something, because I figured that my mother would be offering the same three-liter bottle of Carlo Rossi Paisano that I'd opened last January, and by this time it would only be good for embalming someone.

Mrs. Tomaselli met us at the door and took me into her arms. She gave me a full kiss on the lips, and Barbara guffawed while I turned bright red. She turned to Barbara. "Don't shut him off now, dearie," she said. "Men need sex, even if you don't feel like it."

"Mrs. T—" I began to protest.

"When the baby comes in the door, the love life goes out the window," she said. "Don't deny him, or he'll stray."

"I'm not a dog," I said.

"You're slurring your words, Vinny."

"A little," I said. "I'm a lot better than the last time you saw me."

My mother came up from behind her. "Out of the way, Donna," she said. "Let me see my boy."

I prepared for a hug, but she unzipped the Snugli on Barbara's chest and extruded our little bundle, who woke up and began to howl. He looked his grandmother in the face and abruptly stopped as she held him to her chest. "Let's go inside and get acquainted," she told him. "Vinny, get the bags," she said, and I went back into Sherpa-mode.

∗

I had one of the Pilsner Urquells open and was slumped in my father's old chair in front of the television watching the Patriots win. Royal was dozing in his car seat, next to me. I would have explained some of the finer points of the Pats' pass-rushing strategy, but he showed no interest. A slight odor rose from his basket, and I prepared myself for the diaper changing ritual once he woke up. After only three months of fatherhood I could change him one-handed, blindfolded, chained up, whatever. Harry Houdini had nothing on me.

The last time I had seen my father, not counting the time he lay in his casket, he had been slumped in this very chair, drinking a beer in front of the TV while my mother lay on the floor of the bathroom, screaming from fear and pain. I had learned a lot about him over the past year, some of it bad, and some of it surprising. Being a father myself now, I realize how much stress it brings, and how kids can wear you out. It's an absolute joy, but it's also a challenge, and there is no operating manual. You can buy books that describe a child's development in month one, month two, and so on, but they don't explain how radically different life is going to be. For me, the change was welcome. It was a gift that I felt I barely deserved, and looking after Royal was actually helping my own recovery. But for some people it could be a breaking point, and Jimmy Tanzi might have been one of those people. Three kids running around may have pushed him into drinking, harder than usual, as an escape from the pandemonium. I took a sip of my beer and reflected on the irony—here I was, sitting in his chair, making excuses for his violence and abuse. Maybe that was part of forgiving him, or at least understanding him.

The kitchen was abuzz with activity. Barbara, Mrs. Tomaselli, and my mother were old friends now, after the weeks they'd spent doing shifts at the neurology unit. They were laughing and talking girl-talk while I had my little testosterone-fest out here with the boy. Junie, Carla, and Rod arrived right after half-time, and Carla set the table while Rod and I hung out in the living room, and Junie showed me his trombone. He played it with a slide, which didn't take a great deal of finger dexterity to handle. He was amazingly good at it, and had already sat in with the Vermont Jazz Ensemble. He put it to his lips and played a soft melody, which woke up Royal, and I got up to get the changing pad and baby wipes from the pile of equipment in our old bedroom. I changed my son on the couch while Rod carved the turkey, Junie played trombone, and the girls brought out bowls and platters that held all the trimmings. No wonder Thanksgiving was my favorite—you can't buy it, wrap it, or put it under a tree, and even the greeting card companies can't seem to make a buck off of it. It's just a meal, with people who you love and who love you back, no matter what.

*

Everyone in the house was asleep except for me. I was looking in a side pocket of my suitcase for the charging cord that went to my phone when I noticed something else in there that I had forgotten about—two letters to my mother, from my father. I'd stashed them there in January, and they had lain hidden until now.

I had long ago decided not to read them, as they were obviously personal. But the envelopes were not sealed, and I was curious. I suddenly wanted to know more about my father, even at the expense of my mother's privacy.

The first one was definitely private, and it was oddly encouraging to know that a seventy-four year old man could still have the hots for a seventy-four year old woman. I put that one back and re-sealed the envelope so that it would look like I hadn't read it.

The second letter was more of a chatty account of my father's life as a driver for Brooks Burleigh; the trips he'd made and people he'd met. It went on for three pages, and I read the second-to-last paragraph twice.

And then we went up to the house and I helped Eunice and Kermit with the party. There were people from Montpelier and Washington, D.C. too, and everybody was dressed real nice. You would have liked the ladie's dresses. I sure did. Ha ha, don't get jealis! Miss Burleigh took some of the men down cellar, where they have a shooting gallery and they made a lot a noise. I cleaned up with Kermit but I had to get the car and take Mr. Rudy up to Quebec because he said his car was in the shop. He's a quiet one. Anything ever happens to me Miss Betty Boop, you call Vince and tell him to talk to Mr. Rudy, and not to go alone.

I had no idea who he was talking about, but I was going to find out. I wondered how Patton and Pallmeister would react if I called their cell phones at a quarter to midnight on Thanksgiving.

FRIDAY

My mother never collected the million dollars from the insurance policy, because it was determined that the money was dirty, and the insurance company wriggled off the hook. The investigation after Brooks' death had turned up all kinds of complex schemes to avoid taxes and launder money, and my father's policy was one of them. They did let me keep the twenty grand Brooks had paid me, and I used some of it to buy her a queen bed for the room where Junie's and my bunks had been. Barbara was sleeping in it with Royal asleep at her breast, and I got up to get some coffee going.

Junie was in the kitchen. He'd already made a pot and poured me a cup.

"So your hands are working?" I said.

"A little," he said. "They ache like hell most of the time."

"Sorry," I said.

"Not your fault," he said. "You're getting around OK too, huh? Except that you sound kinda retarded."

"Thanks for pointing that out."

"That's what brothers are for," he said, smiling.

"Did you ever hear from Melissa?"

His smile melted away. "Yeah, I heard from her. She's a celebrity back in Moldova, like the rest of the girls."

"Yes, I read about that," I said. "Anything still going between you?"

"Not really," he said. "I'm a fucking cripple now anyway."

"I doubt that would matter to her," I said.

"She said she wants to fly me there. She made some money posing nude for some magazine."

"I read about that, too, but Barbara found it under the bed."

Junie laughed hard this time. "Fucking Vinny."

"Don't get her pregnant," I said. "Unless you want to be ankle deep in baby poop."

176

"Don't worry," he said.

"Are you going to go see her?"

"I'm thinking about it."

"Junie…did you ever know someone named Rudy? Someone who Brooks Burleigh might have known?"

"I don't want to talk about that guy," he said.

"Rudy?"

"No, Brooks," he said. "It's his fault that I'm like this. And no, I don't know anyone called Rudy."

*

I started with Pallmeister. "Remember those letters my father left in his apartment? Addressed to my mother?"

"Vaguely," he said. "You took them, right?"

"Yes," I said. "Did you read them?"

"Someone on the team did, but they were love letters if I remember. We left them there, and I think I told you about them."

"You did, and I stashed them and forgot about them. I just opened them up. Let me read you something." I read the paragraph from the second letter over the phone.

"He says Mr. Rudy, not Rudy. Is it a first or last name?"

"It could be either," I said.

"Obviously it was someone who Burleigh knew," Pallmeister said. "Well enough to lend him his driver."

"Right. And my father was afraid of him."

"Schultheiss? An alias?"

"I lay awake half the night thinking about that," I said. "I don't get it."

"I've only got a few people in today, but I'll get on it," he said. "Any ideas?"

"You do the name search. See what you can find in motor vehicles or your own records. I'm going to do some field work."

"Where?"

"I'm going to Stowe," I said. "I'm going to visit Kermit and Eunice and see if they have any leftover turkey."

*

I took the Subaru and left the van for Barbara in case she needed to go out. I told her I wanted to drive around for a few hours and get some air. There was no need to worry her.

Stowe was quiet like most of the rest of the state, except for the malls near Burlington where the Black Friday elite-competition shoppers would be scooping up deals if they hadn't already been trampled when the doors opened. What was that I said about Thanksgiving not being commercial?

Kermit and Eunice lived off the Morrisville Road, a few miles outside of Stowe. Their double-wide trailer was tucked behind an abandoned farmhouse that stood empty, with the windows and doors gone, and not a speck of paint remaining on the rotting clapboards. Sooner or later the old building would collapse from the weight of a big snowfall. Smoke curled from the trailer's metal chimney and spread the welcome smell of burning wood.

They greeted me with big smiles and hugs. Kermit had a pot of turkey soup simmering on the stove, and they insisted I stay for a bowl, which was fine as I was already hungry at ten in the morning. When you have someone in your family who feeds every two hours, your own eating schedule goes completely haywire.

"This is delicious," I said, spooning in some of the soup.

"I deep-fried the bird," Kermit said. "Only way to go."

"What else is in it?" I asked.

"Whatever we had in the fridge," he said. "It don't much matter what you put in, it all cooks down real nice."

"Kermit, who was Mr. Rudy? I saw the name in a letter my father wrote."

He looked at his wife, and she didn't say anything. He turned back to me. "You remember that Mr. Tomas?"

"Yes."

"Same feller. When your father took him to Canada, sometimes he was Mr. Tomas and sometimes he was Mr. Rudy. Nobody knew about it, but your father saw the passport."

"I had a feeling that was what you'd say."

"Never liked him much," he said. "Neither did Jimmy. We called him Mr. Rude behind his back."

"Did the police ask you about him?"

"Yep. They quizzed us something awful, after the plane crash. But I'd forgot about the other name he used."

"Any ideas about where he'd be?"

"Nope," he said.

"Did you know his last name?"

"Your father might have," he said. "But we don't. Wish we could help ya."

*

I didn't have the heart to go up the hill to Brooks Burleigh's farm. I figured that the house had been thoroughly picked over by the various federal and state agencies who had a dog in that race. Nor could I face going to Tomas' mountaintop schloss—that place gave me the creeps, and the Feds had no doubt sanitized it as well. I thought about my father's letters. The authorities had missed perhaps the best piece of information you could possibly find, right there in a letter on his desk. He had practically named his killer. What a bunch of boobs. On the other hand, I had taken that critical information, stashed it in a suitcase, and only stumbled on it almost a year later because I was looking for a power cord. Any more mistakes like that and I'd be asked to send back my Dick Tracy decoder ring.

I drove through Stowe and went up the Mountain Road as far as the ski area, thinking. The hill was busy with early-season skiers enjoying the man-made snow. On the way back down I checked in with Patton and Pallmeister separately, but neither of them had turned up anything that looked like a fit. I told them that the Rudy we were looking for was definitely Tomas Schultheiss, according to Kermit and Eunice. He had used an alias, apparently several times, and Pallmeister had nothing to say, but Patton was a different story. He was angry with himself.

"I can't believe I missed this," he said. "You have to present a passport these days, either the regular kind or the card."

"To get into Canada? Yes, I know."

"We keep records. Your father went to and from all the time, we tracked him as part of the investigation. If he drove Mr. Rudy in, I'll have a record. With his whole name."

"I bet I can beat you to it," I said. "Dinner at Leunig's."

"How are you going to do that?"

"I'm not quite sure yet," I said. But as I was driving past a gas station on the Mountain Road, one of the Tetris pieces fell into place. I pulled the Subaru into the lot and parked next to a small building with a sign out front that said LaBounty Car Rental.

*

A rusty truck was parked outside the hut, and a young man waved me in when I knocked at the door. He had a kerosene heater going, but it was still cold inside.

"You work here all winter?" I said.

"We got a woodstove, but my dad took it to his deer camp. Meanwhile I'm sittin' here freezing."

"I have kind of a strange question," I said. "Did I ever rent a van from you?"

"When?" he said. "You look a little familiar."

"Last winter," I said. "The end of January."

"Let me look," he said. "You can't remember?"

"I had an accident," I said. "It kind of jumbled things around."

"What's your name?"

"Vince Tanzi," I said.

He opened his computer and looked for a while. "Nope. You're not a customer."

"You sure?"

"Yes. No Vince Tanzi. You ain't in the database."

I was puzzled. I remembered renting a van that day. I went to Canada, I saw Patton, and I rented some kind of van, and when I'd passed this place it rang a distinct bell. That was all I could remember, however hard I tried.

"Shit," I said. "Dead end."

"You a cop?"

"I used to be," I said. "I'm a private investigator now."

"What are you looking for?"

"A guy named Rudy," I said. "I thought I remembered renting a van from you. I was thinking that might lead me to him."

"You mean Rudolf Meijer," he said. "Now I remember you. You were supposed to meet him here, and I told you where he was. He's the one who rented the van, not you."

"Rudolf Meijer," I said. Bingo. "Do you know where he is?"

"Never saw him after that," he said.

"He's the one who blew up the plane," I said. "Morrisville airport."

"Fuckin' A," he said.

"The police are going to want to interview you. They'll want to look over your records. Don't worry about it, OK? Just cooperate."

"Jeez," he said. "We do a lot of business under the table. Cash."

"I said the police, not the IRS. Help them anyway you can. Rudy Meijer is a killer."

"OK," he said, and I left. It was time to call Patton and tell him I'd won the bet.

*

"You're a father now," Robert Patton said. "You can't risk another Leunig's poutine." He'd driven down from Burlington, and we were getting a coffee at the Red Hen Bakery in Middlesex. Patton had dismissed it as another hippie joint, but he came around after he tried one of their coconut macaroons.

"Sore loser," I said.

"So now what do we do?"

"I'm not running this show."

"You wouldn't know that," he said. "So far you've turned up everything important in this case."

"You're running a whole department," I said. "I'm just a hack who's had eight months to obsess about this."

"If I didn't have to spend the whole day doing paperwork, I might be able to solve something," he said.

"You should be a P.I. The only paperwork I do is when I send the bill to the client."

"I actually like my job," he said.

"And I actually envy you," I said. "I miss being a cop."

"My offer still stands."

"I can barely walk," I said. "Let alone bust people."

"I admire the shit out of you, Tanzi. You're no hack."

"Thanks," I said. "I like you too. But let's not get a room."

He laughed, and I suddenly remembered Yuliana saying that. I was telling Brooks Burleigh that although I ought to detest him, I couldn't help liking him, and he'd said something nice back. We'd been on the way to the airport. In the Escalade. Two more Tetris pieces had fallen into place.

"Do me a favor," I said to Patton. "Play it back for me. That day."

"You still don't remember?"

"No," I said. "Just a few things, and I'm not sure I even have them right. I thought I'd rented a van, but it was Tomas."

"OK," he said. "You went to Canada after him, and then you called me. I got you and your Glock waved through at the border. He was gone when you got there."

"I sort of remember that."

"Then you called me again, and I told you your sister was missing. You drove to my office and gave me the laptop."

"Whose laptop?"

"Tomas'. It had all the sex tapes on it, and tons of other stuff. You said Tomas left it in your car. Without that we would never have broken the case."

Down came another rectangle, and I manipulated it into place. I remembered stealing Tomas' laptop out of his house. Roberto had hacked into it, and led me to the LaBounty car rental place. I'd told Patton that Tomas had left the computer in my car so that he'd have a clean trail, with no illegal searches that would disqualify the evidence.

"You were on your way to Burleigh's after you left my office. You said you'd agreed to drive them to the airport in Morrisville, and you were in a wicked hurry."

"Did I tell you about the Rudy Meijer alias? I think I figured it out from the laptop."

"No, and we apparently never put that together. The guy had everything protected, and the techs said somebody had tried to remote in and clean up. They never said anything about another identity, so either they missed it or it was wiped. They found the sex tapes though."

"The videos might have been something of a distraction," I said.

He laughed, and continued. "According to the airport attendant, Burleigh and the girl were going to D.C., and the guy said Schultheiss had placed a bag on the plane before they got there. The attendant was the one who found you in the parking lot after you'd been shot. We assumed it was Schultheiss who shot you, but you don't remember, right?"

I closed my eyes. Sometimes the right side of my head, where the bullet had entered, would throb like hell and things would go eerily bright, as if I was still under the operating room lights. The Tetris puzzle was almost complete.

I remembered Yuliana's kiss. I remembered the explosion and the plane falling out of the sky. And I remembered seeing a bullet headed for me, rotating in slow motion, coming out of the barrel of Tomas Schultheiss' gun.

*

My mother was sitting in her chair, with Royal on her lap. He was silent and was looking straight at her with his brown eyes wide open and a little string of drool hanging from his chin.

"They've been like that for the past hour," Barbara said as I went into the kitchen. "She has him mesmerized. I wish I could get him to do that."

"Let's take her back to Vero," I said.

"Would she go?"

"Probably not," I said. "All her friends are in Barre."

"OK, then we'll just move here," she said.

"Not a chance," I said. "I want Royal to grow up with access to cultural activities."

"In Florida? Like what?"

"Like gator wrestling," I said.

"He and I are staying here," she said. "You can go back and gator wrestle."

I poured a late cup of coffee, my third and final one for the day. It was after lunchtime, but I'd filled up on soup at Kermit's and a croissant at the Red Hen. "I have to work on the computer for a while," I said.

"What are you doing?" she asked.

"Just catching up on some old business," I said. "I remembered some things I'd forgotten."

*

"We found Meijer's passport record. It's Canadian, and it had a bogus address in Montreal," Robert Patton said. I'd taken the call in the bathroom. I didn't want to alert the whole family to the fact that I was after Tomas Schultheiss.

"Anything else?"

"Two documented crossings with your father. Both at Rouses Point."

"He was probably going to the place where the submarine was kept."

"Yeah."

"But we don't have a good address for Rudy Meijer," I said.

"I'm working on it," he said, "and I've put it out on Interpol, in case he turns up somewhere overseas."

"Good idea," I said.

"He looks different," he said. "The passport was renewed this summer. We compared it to an earlier one. He has longer hair, thicker eyebrows, and so on. We think he got some surgery, and maybe some hair implants."

"Can you email it to me?"

"Sure. You mean, just in case you run into him?"

"Something like that," I said. "It's deer season you know."

There was a silence at the other end of the line. "Vince, are you in any shape for that kind of thing?"

"Not really," I said.

"Be patient. We'll find him," he said. "You lay low."

*

My mother was napping after a hearty sliced turkey sandwich. The food and the bustle of having family around had completely worn her out. I had been on the computer for a good part of the afternoon, searching. I'd learned from Roberto how to use keywords and their variations, and it had easily doubled my efficiency. Barbara had gone out for a walk and Royal lay across my lap, bundled up in a blue fleece outfit that was part pajamas and part sleeping bag. I loved holding him, talking to him, and I even—sort of—enjoyed changing his diaper. It was part of being a dad, and it made me feel like I had a place in the world.

Royal was sound asleep, so I lowered him into his crib-basinet thing and covered him up. It was quiet in the house, and I went to the front hall and pulled down a folding ladder from a door in the ceiling. There was a small, unfinished attic above the house, and I wondered if my father's old guns were still up there.

*

Mrs. Tomaselli caught me red-handed. She was coming in the door with some groceries, and I was hurriedly cleaning my father's old Remington 700 deer rifle. It was in decent shape and had a scope, but it badly needed oiling and cleaning, and I held it between my legs and wiped it with gun oil. An over-under Beretta 20 gauge shotgun was leaning up against a cabinet—that was my father's bird gun, and it also had some corrosion, but I figured I'd at least test it when I got out into the woods. But Mrs. T. had spoiled my little gunsmithing session.

"Are you going to start a war?"

"Sorry," I said. "Just cleaning my dad's old guns."

She picked up the Beretta and sighted it. "I had one just like this, forty years ago. I used to go out for partridge with my nephews."

"If you want it, it's yours," I said.

"Really?"

"Sure," I said. "You may want to have it checked out first though. It's in rough shape."

"This would keep the squirrels off the feeders," she said.

"There wouldn't be any squirrel left if you hit one," I said. "You can have it, but be careful."

"I'll take it out to my car," she said. "There's a baby in the house."

"Take this box of shells too," I said. "They might be too old."

"You better hurry up and finish that before your wife gets home."

"I'm hurrying," I said.

She took the shotgun outside, and then came in and began unpacking groceries, humming while she worked, in a sweet warble like the older women I used to sit next to at Mass. I did what I could to resuscitate the rifle, then I put it back in its leather case and took it out to the Subaru. When I came back into the kitchen, she was seated at the Formica table and she motioned for me to sit down.

"We need to have a little talk," she said.

"OK." I took a chair across from her.

"You're a father now."

"I know that."

"Everything is different, Vinny. You need to put your wife and child first, before anything. And I mean anything."

"Just going out to see if I can get a deer."

"Nonsense," she said. "Like my mother used to say, you can't shit an old-timer."

"Your mother used to say that?"

"Horrors, no," she said, smiling. "My mother was a proper lady. Not me."

I smiled back. "You're a lady, Mrs. T."

Her expression turned serious. "She's in the Hope Cemetery. Go get it out of your system."

"Your mother?"

"No, not my mother," she said. "Your friend. With the cute accent."

"Yuliana? Is in the Hope Cemetery?"

"She and her boss. What's left of them. They didn't find much after the plane crashed. His family buried the remains there, next to each other."

"Oh," I said. My head began to throb, and I began to see the familiar operating-room light.

"Vinny? Are you all right?"

"Yes," I said, but my insides were churning. I took a deep breath and returned to the conversation.

"Are you and Barbara getting along?"

"I guess so," I said.

"I guess so isn't good enough," she said. "You listen to me. You have to worship her. Spoil her. Make her laugh. Especially now, with your baby in the picture."

"You're right," I said. And she was. Some people can just cut to the chase. I needed to step up my husband game, and my dad game, if I really loved them. They needed me.

"The graves are in the Woodside section, way in the back by the trees."

"You've been there?"

"I put some flowers out for you, last spring," she said. "Go. Say goodbye and move on."

*

Barbara came back half an hour after Royal had woken up. I'd been putting on the miles, walking him around the house and trying to calm him. I sang him little songs while I held him, but I wondered if my off-key baritone croaking might be making it worse.

"Here you go," I said to her as soon as she'd put her bags down. "I think he wants something I don't have." I handed him off to her with a move that any NFL quarterback would have admired.

"When we get home, I'm going to buy a breast pump," she said. "Then you won't be able to get out of it so easily."

"Vince Tanzi, Stay-At-Home Private Eye," I said.

"I'll have that stenciled on the glass of your office window," she said. She smiled, her cheeks flush from the cold. The temperature was dropping, and the weather called for a frigid night with the possibility of snow. Deer hunters like fresh snow—it makes it easier to track their quarry. But I was going to put all that out of my mind for now, and have an evening at home with my family.

*

Barbara put Royal back in his little bed and climbed into ours. "You awake?"

"Yeah," I said.

"What are you thinking about?"

"You," I said. "Mrs. Tomaselli was right."

"You mean I have to service you, or you'll stray?"

I laughed. "No, that's not what I meant. You weren't here when she and I were talking."

"What did she say?"

"She said I needed to worship you."

"Damn right," Barbara said. "That woman has a fine head on her shoulders."

"I do, you know," I said. "Worship you."

"Prove it," she said.

"Right here in my mother's house?"

"I guess not," Barbara said. "But as soon as we get home you'd better start worshipping, brother."

"Hallelujah and amen," I said.

SATURDAY

I got up before dawn and dressed. I didn't have any blaze orange clothing, but I figured I could stop on the way and at least get a hat. It wasn't that I was worried so much that a hunter would shoot me, it was more that I didn't want to be seen walking around with my rifle and scope looking like a hit man. I also needed to pick up some ammo.

The drive to Enosburg Falls is one of those you-can't-get-there-from-here journeys that drive GPS units to digital distraction. The shortest route is right through Stowe and then over the Smuggler's Notch road, but the pass is closed from November to May. It's just too narrow and twisty to plow when the snow gets deep. Instead, you have to wind all over God's country to reach it, but the journey was cold and beautiful, and it gave me time to collect my thoughts and firm my resolve. I don't take killing someone lightly.

I had left a note for Barbara saying I was going out for a few hours, and since she and Royal liked to sleep in, I might make it back not long after they awoke. The whole trip could be a wild goose chase anyway—I had dug up the flimsiest of evidence on Google, even after searching for most of the afternoon when I wasn't tending to the baby. But there it was, an environmental permit hearing in St. Albans for a 3,000-acre property that somebody wanted to put windmills on. It dated from seven years ago, and the only news articles I could find about the hearing itself said that it was a hotly contested issue. No one wanted big, ugly windmills spoiling the pristine ridgeline, but on the other hand it was the cleanest, most renewable source of power you could find. It would be easy to be both for it and against it.

The permit applicant was referred to as Cebotari Wind Energy, LLC. I'd cross-referenced "Cebotari" on Wikipedia and found that Maria Cebotari was a spectacularly beautiful soprano who died in 1949. She called herself a Romanian, but she was from Moldova. That was part of what made me decide that it was worth a trip to Enosburg

Falls, way up in northern Vermont, on a frigid morning, when the smartest deer would be deep in the woods.

The other part was that one of the signers on the permit application for Cebotari Wind Energy LLC was a Mr. R. Meijer of Montreal, Quebec.

*

I stopped at the Bakersfield Store, a few miles south of Enosburg. They had a blaze orange hat, ammunition for my rifle, and just about everything else a person could want. Vermont country stores operate by the maxim that if they don't have it, you don't need it. That isn't a bad philosophy to live by, unless you really enjoy lining up in front of Best Buy the day after Thanksgiving for some must-have device that will be hopelessly obsolete in six months.

"You goin' deer huntin' in them sneakers?" the guy behind the counter asked, as I put my items down.

"Nope," I said. "I'm a hit man."

"Ha," he said. "Hope you got a license."

"Whatever happened to that windmill farm?" I said.

"You mean up to Enosburg?"

"Yep," I said. I can speak Vermont when prompted.

"It never got built," he said. "There's a house on it, instead. Some folks are glad, but I'd just as soon see my power bill go down. Wind's just a crop, and this is farm country. Don't know what all the fuss was about."

"Does the owner allow hunting?"

"Naw, it's posted," he said. "Some big deer in there though."

"You ever met the guy?"

"You sure ask a lot of questions, mister."

"Sorry," I said.

"It's OK."

"Anyone know his name?"

"Everybody knows everybody up here. That's Jules Broadbent. English feller. He keeps to himself."

"Thanks," I said. Fuck. Jules Broadbent? I was probably wasting my time.

I was less than ten miles from the property, and it was still early. I decided I could at least swing up to the "Broadbent" place and sniff around. If it was a dead end, I'd drive back to my mother's and keep on Googling.

*

I was four miles out Lost District Road, and the narrow gravel roadway kept getting narrower. With each mile there were more potholes, rocks, and runoff ditches dug diagonally to keep the hard rains from carving impassable trenches into the gravel. I was climbing, and the leafless trees afforded a nice view of farmland to the west. The fresh layer of snow was less than two inches deep, and my Subaru made the only tracks. Nobody had been in or out.

The GPS stopped me at a driveway on the right hand side that climbed another hill through a stand of white birches. It had been well maintained, and the driveway surface appeared smoother than the road that served it. There was no mailbox, no house number, nothing to identify it, except for some faded yellow *No Hunting* signs that had "Cebotari LLC" written in permanent marker along the bottom. But there was a security camera, hidden high in the birches, that would give a clear view of anyone who entered. I took that for a good sign.

I drove a hundred yards past the driveway to a pull-off, and parked. I got out of the car, shouldered my rifle, put a few rounds in my pocket, and trekked through the woods uphill, avoiding the security camera and the driveway itself. Leaving tracks on it would be like begging to be discovered, and although I might want to draw Tomas, or Rudy, or Jules Broadbent out, I wasn't ready to announce my presence yet.

*

Doing the Vinny Shuffle uphill, in sneakers, through puckerbrush, birch leaves, and two inches of snow was a mistake. I couldn't believe how long the climb was, or how slow my progress. I had to stop every five minutes and let my pulse get back to where it didn't feel like the conga beat in a salsa band. It was possible that I might get a shot off at Tomas Schultheiss, but it was also possible that I might die of a heart attack in the effort.

The sun was now high enough to light up the dirty white bark of the birches, and the woods glowed with its reflection off of the carpeting of snow. There is something about a November landscape that chills the bones and warms the soul simultaneously, and even though my toes had frozen, I felt marvelously, miraculously alive. Hikers stay out of the woods at this time of year; they leave them to the hunters for their annual ritual. My father had taken me out to hunt a few times, when I was old enough to carry a gun and not complain. I never got a deer, but I understand the attraction—when you are out hunting, it could be a thousand years ago or it could be today. You spot your prey, line up the crosshairs, and time stops. I just hoped I'd get a clean shot, and then all this would be over.

I heard a noise just before I reached a clearing at the top of the hill. The morning was calm, with no breeze. You could hear for miles, and the sound was a car coming slowly up the driveway. I crouched to the ground and went still. I hoped I was far enough back from the driveway that the driver wouldn't see me. Right as I dropped, a big buck dashed out of his hiding place not twenty yards away, and his fluffy white tail flashed as he ran. I counted eight points on the horns, and found myself glad he wasn't my target; he pranced so beautifully through the brush it would be like shooting a ballerina. The car—a big SUV—passed us, unaware and not slowing. When it was beyond me and out of sight, I stood up and continued my slow shuffle until I came to a split rail fence that bordered an open field, with a new-looking house and outbuildings beyond. Mr. Schultheiss, or Meijer, or Broadbent had built himself a very nice spread, with a view that extended for miles in every direction. It would have been a perfect spot for a windmill, except that there wasn't a breath of wind.

I took a position where I could see the house and kneeled, steadying the rifle in front of me on the fence rail. The scope wasn't the best, but I could clearly see the doors, windows, and house details. The driver had just parked the SUV in a garage and was lowering the bay door. He turned, and I got a close-up look at his face through the scope. He was a middle-aged man with longish, dark hair and bushy eyebrows, and he paused to light a cigarette. There was something in the stiff way he held himself that gave him away, no matter how much he'd spent on surgery.

It was Tomas.

I chambered a bullet in the rifle and quietly closed the bolt. I wished I'd had time to check the sight, but my father always kept his gear in good shape and I trusted it. My finger tightened around the trigger, and I thought—this is for you, Dad. And for Yuliana, and Junie, and even Ginny, and Brooks and the people I'd never met, good, bad or indifferent. No doubt Tomas had a lot of blood on his hands. This would be like shooting a varmint—a garden pest—and no one would ever know.

I watched him through the scope as he walked toward the house, keeping the crosshairs on his temple. Hold your breath. Squeeze. Even pressure, like my father taught me. Squeeze, you dumb bastard, I told myself as my eyes watered in the cold. Pull the fucking trigger.

I lowered the rifle. I couldn't do it. I couldn't shoot Günter Schramm then, and I couldn't kill Tomas Schultheiss now, no matter how evil they were and how much they deserved it.

He disappeared inside.

*

Robert Patton said he had a Special Ops team and that he would mobilize them within minutes. He'd already done some research. Broadbent was a recluse, and had been stopped a few months back at a State Police sobriety check roadblock outside of Enosburg. He blew a point-seven, just under the limit. They decided to detain him anyway, because he was in the company of a sixteen-year-old girl who was not a relation, at two AM. He woke up his attorney, who convinced the cops that the young woman was his au pair, and they let him go, but one of the cops made a note in the log. I gave Patton careful directions and told him that his team needed to watch out.

"You don't have to remind me," he said.

"I know," I said. "I just want him to be caught."

"Can I ask you something?"

"OK," I said.

"How come you didn't shoot him?"

I thought about that before answering. "I think my shooting days are over," I said.

"Because of the baby?"

"Could be," I said. "I've been doing this a long time."

"That's why cops get a pension," he said. "A lot of guys are done by the time they're fifty."

"I might be one of those guys," I said.

*

I had decided to take the longer but easier route back, via the interstate. My phone buzzed as I was passing through St. Albans. I'd missed a call from Carla. The cell coverage was spotty, so I pulled over and dialed her back.

"What's up?"

"Rod said I should call you."

"Why?"

"I got kind of a strange call," she said. "Where are you?"

"Saint A," I said.

"Can you stop here? I'm at the house."

"Sure," I said. "I'm on the way."

*

"Where's Rod?" I asked as she let me in and gave me a peck on the cheek. The inside of the house smelled like weed.

"He works on Saturday mornings," she said. "They're closed, but he catches up on paperwork."

"How's it going with him?" I said. I hadn't had much time with her at my mother's; everyone had been obsessing over Royal.

"OK, I guess," she said.

"Meaning what?"

"You don't want to be gay, Vin," she said.

"It has to be rough sometimes."

"You're not kidding. People are so cruel."

"What happened?"

"Nothing, really. It's just—I get so tired of, you know, being who I am. It's such a struggle. Hanging out with Rod seemed so attractive, like I could finally play mom and dad, and be in a straight relationship, and I wouldn't take any more shit."

"But it's not working out."

"Right," she said. "He really wants the sex. And I just can't do it, even though I love him."

"What are you going to do?"

"I don't know," she said. "I'm so bad at decisions."

"Have you talked to him about this?"

"No. I'm afraid to."

"You need to."

"I know," she said.

"Carla…"

"Yes?" she said.

"When was the last time you didn't smoke dope?"

"About thirty years ago. I quit for a week when I had bronchitis."

"Our family has a problem with those things," I said. "Booze, pot, pills."

"I know," she said.

"It's not any easier to make decisions when you're clean," I said. "But you can make them. If you stay high, you just keep putting them off."

"I'll think about it," she said.

"Is that why you called?"

"No," she said. "It was the guy who called, before I called you. It sounded funny. I called Rod, and he said to call you."

"What did the guy say?"

"He said he had a delivery for me, and I needed to be here, this afternoon, to sign for it. I haven't ordered anything. It just kind of gave me the creeps."

"Did he have an accent?"

"Maybe. I couldn't really tell."

"Pack a bag," I said. "We'll pick up Rod on the way."

*

Junie had received the same call, but in typical Junie fashion he had told the guy to go fuck himself. He said it sounded like a scam. I stashed the three of them at the Marriott and said I would call as soon as I got the all-clear from Patton. Tomas Schultheiss was back, and he was going after my family.

I called Barbara. "Where were you?" she said.

"Carla's," I said. "Giving her love advice."

"I hope she didn't listen to you."

"Barbara, I need you to pack up everything and go to Mrs. Tomaselli's. Mom too."

"Vin, what's going on?"

"I think I might have stirred up a snake."

"That guy?"

"Yes," I said.

"How can you do this? You have a son. You're not even well yet."

"Please, just go," I said. "We'll discuss it later."

She hung up, and I knew she was angry, but that was not what I was concerned about right now.

*

Robert Patton looked tense in his office chair. "He was gone when they got there," he said. "They saw the tracks leading out. The tread pattern was the kind of Michelins they use on the new GMCs."

"It was dark gray. I told you that already, right?"

"Yes. Pallmeister has an unmarked cruiser sitting near your mother's house. He said he's going to take a shift himself. We want to get this guy, real bad."

"I'm heading there next."

"Stay away from the house," he said.

"How did he know it was me?" I said. "I didn't think he saw me."

"The Special Ops guys think he saw your car tracks and followed them to the pull-off, before he went up the driveway and you saw him. They found boot tracks, coming and going, inside your Subaru's tracks. So he must have seen your car, and maybe he ran a plate check somehow."

"He might have remembered the car," I said. "I thought I'd parked it well out of sight."

"He's a careful bastard," Patton said. "But he'll make a mistake soon."

"We hope," I said.

"Vince," he said, "there's something I need to show you."

"OK," I said.

He opened the top drawer of his desk and took out a cellphone with a pink protective cover. I remembered it. It was Yuliana's.

"It was in the Escalade. You don't remember?"

"No."

He turned it on and navigated with his stubby fingers. "I got it released from evidence."

Patton pushed at the screen and handed the phone to me. It was playing a video, shot at the Hôtel Le St-James; I recognized the fleur-de-lis wallpaper. I also recognized Yuliana Burleigh's naked body, straddling mine and moving furiously up and down. I turned the video off and tried to hand the phone back to him.

"Keep it," he said, waving it off.

"Who else has seen this?"

"Nobody who's going to say anything."

"Why are you giving it to me?"

"I debated that with myself for a long time," he said. "I decided if it was me, I'd want to know."

"Thanks," I said, but my insides were churning. Yuliana had filmed us making love, with me looking like a dumb-ass john. That was ancient history now, but it still hurt like I'd been punched.

*

I got a cool reception at Mrs. Tomaselli's. The girls were all sitting at a card table, and my mother and Mrs. Tomaselli were teaching Barbara how to play Canasta. Royal was asleep in his car seat at Barbara's feet. I looked at her cards from behind. Two of them were jokers, which was an excellent hand and she wore a broad smile. Barbara didn't have much of a poker face, or a Canasta face for that matter. No one had acknowledged me.

"I'm back," I said.

"This is like being in prison," my mother said.

"There's a police car down the street, between here and your house," I said. "You'll be safe. They'll get the guy."

"I don't know how you could do this, Vincent," my mother said. "Putting your family in danger."

"Mom—" I began, but it was no use. She was right. My head began to throb. "I'm going to lie down for a while."

*

I'm not a nap-taker, even on the occasions when Royal has completely worn me out and I really need one. I was in Mrs. Tomaselli's spare bedroom, lying on top of an old-fashioned full bed with my feet extending over the end. My mind was on two things: how I had stupidly put my family at risk all over again by stirring up Tomas Schultheiss, and how I'd been conned by a beautiful woman. I had somehow believed that Yuliana was attracted to me, but she had been working. She was still a honey trap. Brooks had no doubt assigned her to me, and I'd fallen for it. The guy liked to hedge his bets, all right.

She'd left the lights on at the hotel in Montreal and had captured us in flagrante delicto with her smartphone. The video must have been Brooks' insurance policy against me misbehaving. Granted, she'd softened later, on the night she was drunk, in my mother's house. She had confessed that she was supposed to be keeping an eye on me, and in the same confession she'd said that she wasn't supposed to be "feeling like this". Like what? Maybe she really had loved me. Or maybe she was just one of Brooks Burleigh's very convincing high-class hookers. Either way, she was dead.

I got a beer from Mrs. Tomaselli's refrigerator and popped it open. It was a Bud Light—not what I'd usually choose, but I wanted a beer, or perhaps several. I thought of how I'd lectured Carla about smoking pot, and winced. The girls were still at the card table, and were still pretending I wasn't there.

"I'm going out for some air," I told them. I downed the whole can of beer, tossed it in the trash and put on my jacket. Maybe I'd hit the bars and stagger home after dark like Jimmy Tanzi used to.

*

The Hope Cemetery is about a quarter mile out of Barre on the East Montpelier Road. The layout is the product of careful planning, and unlike other cemeteries, every stone is fashioned from Barre Gray granite, giving the place a sense of uniformity. The sameness ends there, as it has a wild variety of headstones displaying the pinnacle of the stonecutter's art. Some of them represented the deceased's hobby: a racing car, a soccer ball, even a life-sized easy chair. One was a bizarre double bed with profiles of the husband and wife in relief, rising from the bedcovers in their pajamas. I had parked near the road and passed Giuseppe Donati's stone as I walked in, which was an eerie relief carving of a soldier smoking a cigarette, with the face of his wife floating in the smoke. It was nearly dark, and I was alone, although there were several sets of tire tracks in the snow from earlier visitors. The holiday weekend was a good opportunity for relatives from out of town to come visit their loved ones' graves.

I found them, all the way in the back where the newer stones were. Theirs were plain, old-fashioned tablets; just two simple granite slabs, side-by-side like twin dominoes. Brooks' was to the right, and Yuliana's was to the left. They were set close to each other as if they had been married, and Yuliana's said "Burleigh" instead of her unpronounceable last name. I took off my hat. I could feel the sting of the November chill, especially on the side of my head where the bullet wound had now scarred over.

I was here to say goodbye. But I didn't know how to say it. The beer had calmed me down, and despite what I'd seen on her phone, I realized that Yuliana had loved me in her way, and I had loved her back in my way. She may have been doing her job, but it had changed somewhere along the line, and it had felt real. It wasn't a love like Barbara's or Glory's—we had hardly known each other—but it had been much more than a fling. Possibly, to be brutally honest with myself, it had seemed like more because I was getting old, and she was young and beautiful—and I'd let myself get sucked into a classic midlife crisis just like all the philandering spouses I had followed around Florida as a P.I. Reaching my fiftieth year seemed to herald the beginning of my disintegration. Little pieces of me were falling off—at the dentist's, or the dermatologist's, or on the operating room floor— and people were dying, or were fading out of my life. I could barely talk, or walk, or shoot. I examined the cold granite slabs and imagined myself lying underneath one of my own, in the not-so-distant future.

"Goodbye," I said to the faceless gray stone.

"Goodbye," a voice said, behind me.

I turned around. Tomas Schultheiss stood facing me in his long black overcoat and leather gloves. His arm was outstretched, and in his hand was a matte-black Smith and Wesson automatic, pointed at my head.

"Mr. Broadbent," I said.

"He's no longer viable, thanks to you," he said. "You've cost me far too much. I never should have let you live. I thought the last shot had rendered you harmless."

His dark, bushy eyebrows almost looked comic, like a Groucho disguise. "You should get your money back from whoever did the plastic surgery."

"Very funny," he said.

"How did you find me?"

He held up a small black box. I recognized it. It was the tracker that I'd put on his Audi, ten months ago. He must have attached it to my Subaru before he'd gone up his driveway this morning in Enosburg Falls.

"When I'm done with you, I'm going to kill your family," he said. "Just so you know."

I lunged at him, but he sidestepped me and hit me on the head with his pistol. The blow landed on the same side where the bullet had, and everything went white. I fell onto my back, next to Yuliana's stone, struggling to stay conscious. I saw him approach and hold the gun out. He was going to shoot me where I lay.

A shot rang out in the cold, and the sound echoed and groaned among the mausoleums and gravestones like the cracking of ice on a frozen lake. The back of Tomas Schultheiss' head turned red and he fell over on top of me, his chest against mine in a grisly embrace, soaking me in his blood.

It took all my strength to push his lifeless body off of me and sit up in the snow. A woman stood twenty feet away, and was slowly lowering my father's old shotgun.

"It works," she said. She was dressed in a black leather coat that contrasted with her short blonde hair. She had had surgery too, but the effect was much nicer than Tomas'.

"You knew I was here?"

"Mrs. Tomaselli. She lent me the gun."

"And you knew that Tomas—"

"Jenny told me. He dumped her for a younger one. She still lived with him, but she hated him."

"Quite the network," I said.

"Yes," she said. "I don't exist anymore, but I still have contacts."

I rose to my feet, trying to shake off the effect of the blow to the head. I was dizzy, and the white light was still clouding my vision. Yuliana Burleigh was standing in front of me. Or not. She was dead—as dead as my father—but she was alive.

"So…how—" I started.

"I never got on the plane," she said. "Ed told me to take his car. I was going to disappear. I did, until Jenny called me today and told me that Tomas was going to kill you. I found out where you were from your girlfriend."

"Barbara?"

"Mrs. Tomaselli," she said. "We were in touch when you were in the hospital. She was my inside source. She's the type that can keep a secret."

"Mrs. Tomaselli sent me out here. She said I needed to say good-bye."

"She's right."

"Yuliana, I…" I desperately wanted to take her in my arms. But she was standing just out of my reach.

"We can't," she said.

"I know."

She handed me the shotgun. "Cover my tracks, Vince," she said. "You saved me, and now I saved you."

"Please," I said, but I didn't know what to say next.

"Just say goodbye," she said, and she turned away. Away from me, and from her own gravestone.

SUNDAY

Royal had howled the whole ride to the Burlington airport, and Barbara's and my nerves were on edge. It's a primitive way of telling your parents that you need something—a fresh diaper, sleep, breast milk, the toy you dropped—and it works. We should all communicate so effectively, but we'd probably all kill each other first.

We had our second airport send-off of the year, and once again my mother, Mrs. Tomaselli, Carla, Rod, Junie, and both Pallmeister and Patton were there. It was good to have some help with the bags and gear, though I would still have to heft most of it myself through security and take it on the plane.

Everybody promised to visit us in Florida, and we promised to be back. Barbara had fallen in love with Vermont and, on the ride to the airport in the rare moments that Royal wasn't crying, had been lobbying me to move us north permanently. It had been less than twenty-four hours since Tomas Schultheiss had nearly killed me in the cemetery, and I told her we would discuss it, but I was in no shape to make any life decisions. I wanted to be sitting in a lawn chair in my back yard in Vero, drinking something cold, shooting the breeze with Roberto, and bouncing my little guy on my lap. One thing I did tell her was that we would return, and we wouldn't wait a whole year until the next Thanksgiving. I had grown closer to my brother and sister, and I felt like I had a true friend and a kindred spirit in Robert Patton.

He had commandeered a wheelchair again, but I refused. The Vinny Shuffle had gotten worse after I'd taken a hit on the head from Schultheiss' gun, but I didn't want to see any more wheelchairs until I was at least ninety.

"You sure?" he said.

"I'm sure," I said. "It starts with the wheelchair, then the shuffle-board, and then you take sixteen different pills every morning before bingo, and you're in bed by six."

"Jeez," he said. "I was going to retire to Florida someday, but I'm suddenly having second thoughts."

"You'd like it," I said. "I'll take you dike-jumping."

"I'm not even going to ask what that is," he said.

"I'm retired, by the way," I said.

"Seriously?"

"Yes. I promised Barbara, last night. I can't put them at risk anymore."

"All of us think about that," he said. "Good for you."

I shook his hand, and Pallmeister's, and then hugged Junie, my sister, Rod, my mother, and last of all, Mrs. Tomaselli. "Thanks," I said, as we embraced. "Not just for saving my life. I think you might have saved my marriage, too."

"For the time being," she said. "You'll need to keep on saving it. Things come up."

"Love you, Mrs. T," I said.

"Oh! My Vinny, you said it!" she said. "I've died and gone to heaven!" She fanned her face with a magazine.

I led my family to the security line, where we undressed, were irradiated, and then dressed again. Nobody offered to check Royal's diaper for explosives. Thirty minutes later we were above Lake Champlain with Royal asleep on the cushion between us—we had miraculously scored an unoccupied seat.

Barbara was reading a magazine, and she put it down. "What are you thinking about, Vince?"

I had been looking out the window at the lake below. I was not thinking about Yuliana Burleigh. The gray stone slab had told the world that she was dead. I knew she was alive, but more to the point, my family was alive. We had survived.

"Nursery school," I said. "There's a good one in Vero, but we'd better sign up now."

Barbara laughed and went back to her magazine, and I watched my son's tiny nostrils move in and out as he slept.

Acknowledgements

Thanks to Joni Cole and Deb Heimann for their superb editorial skills, also to Andrew Kerth, Bob Recupero, Heidi Recupero, Meleta Kardos, Isabel Dennis, Sara Dennis, Dr. Betsy Jaffe, and Lt. Terry Lewis of the Vermont State Police for their valuable advice, encouragement and reality checks.

About the Author

C.I. Dennis lives in Vermont and New Hampshire with his family and a whole lot of dogs.

Also by C.I. Dennis:

Tanzi's Heat
Tanzi's Game
Tanzi's Luck

As Zig Davidson:

Unglued

Cover artwork and concept by Alexander Dennis
Additional cover design and production by Morgan Kinney Designs
Author photo by Peter Lange
Formatting by ebooklaunch.com

www.cidennis.com

Made in the USA
Coppell, TX
03 November 2019

10921452R00122